A Drowned Maiden's Hair

A
DROWNED
MAIDEN'S
HAIR

A Melodrama

LAURA AMY SCHLITZ

CANDLEWICK PRESS
CAMBRIDGE, MASSACHUSETTS

Copyright © 2006 by Laura Amy Schlitz

First edition 2006

Library of Congress Cataloging-in-Publication Data is available.

Library of Congress Catalog Card Number pending

ISBN-13: 978-0-7636-2930-4
ISBN-10: 0-7636-2930-8

2 4 6 8 10 9 7 5 3 1

Printed in the United States of America

This book was typeset in Sabon.

Candlewick Press
2067 Massachusetts Avenue
Cambridge, Massachusetts 02140

visit us at www.candlewick.com

For my writers' group, magicians and midwives: Anna, Anne, Christine, Greg, Howard, Kevin, Kirk, Peter, and later, Tina

and for Louise, who made the writers' group possible,

and for Eva Ibbotson, who said this sounded like a bloody good story and I ought to write it down

The Sands of Dee
by Charles Kingsley

"O Mary, go and call the cattle home,
*   And call the cattle home,*
*   And call the cattle home,*
*   Across the sands of Dee."*
The western wind was wild and dank with foam,
*   And all alone went she.*

The western tide crept up along the sand,
*   And o'er and o'er the sand,*
*   And round and round the sand,*
*   As far as eye could see.*
The rolling mist came down and hid the land:
*   And never home came she.*

"O is it weed, or fish, or floating hair—
  A tress of golden hair,
  A drownèd maiden's hair
  Above the nets at sea?"
Was never salmon yet that shone so fair
  Among the stakes of Dee.

They row'd her in across the rolling foam,
  The cruel crawling foam,
  The cruel hungry foam,
  To her grave beside the sea.
But still the boatmen hear her call the cattle home,
  Across the sands of Dee.

PART ONE

THE
SECRET
CHILD

Spring 1909

CHAPTER ONE

On the morning of the best day of her life, Maud Flynn was locked in the outhouse, singing "The Battle Hymn of the Republic."

She was locked in because she was being punished. The Barbary Asylum for Female Orphans was overcrowded; every room in the wide brick building was in use. There were few places where one could imprison a child who had misbehaved. The outhouse was one such place, and very suitable for the purpose, because the children hated it. Though the janitor scrubbed it clean every day, it stank; the single window was high and narrow and let in just enough light to show that there were spiders. Maud boasted that she was not afraid of spiders, but she was no happier than anyone else when she sat on the high bench, feet dangling, and wondered whether any of the itches she felt were spiders creeping over her skin.

She finished the first verse of the song and began on the chorus. The outhouse was chilly, and singing warmed her blood. It also served to advertise—to anyone who might be passing by—that the spirit of Maud Flynn had not been broken. Maud had a hazy idea that the Battle Hymn had something to do with war and slavery. She felt that by singing it she was defying authority and striking a blow against the general awfulness of the day.

Two maiden ladies, the Misses Hawthorne, were coming to the Barbary Asylum to adopt a little girl of eight or nine years: Maud was eleven and therefore ineligible. The three girls who might be chosen— Polly, Millicent, and Irma—had been given what Maud considered unfair privileges. They had taken hot baths the night before, though it was neither Wednesday nor Saturday, and their hair had been put up in rags for curls. The newest of the blue houndstooth uniforms had been washed, mended, and starched, so that they might appear to advantage. As a result, the three little girls were as curly, clean, and splendid as the Asylum's scant means could make them, and they put on airs—Maud told them so—that were perfectly sickening. Maud's hair was thin and wispy; under no circumstances would it curl.

So Maud began the day in a frenzy of jealousy, and the proximity of the three candidates only served to inflame her further. Maud was small for her age, so small that she shared the third-grade desks with Polly, Millicent, and Irma: she had tweaked Millicent's curls and kicked Polly when Miss Clarke was reading the morning prayer. Irma was out of reach, but Maud made herself as disagreeable as she could, glaring across the aisle and snorting when the younger girl made a mistake in arithmetic. During the history lesson, Maud disrupted the class by swinging her feet back and forth, so that the toes of her boots scraped against the floor. It was not a loud noise, but it was irritating. When Miss Clarke told her to stop, Maud gazed at the teacher with half-shut eyes and went on swinging her feet.

That had been too much. Miss Clarke was neither cruel nor even very strict, but she could not allow a child to defy her before the whole class. She swooped down the aisle and seized Maud by the forearm. Maud's heart pounded. She knew she had gone too far, and punishment was bound to follow. She hoped she would not cry before the others.

When Miss Clarke took the key to the outhouse off the nail, Maud almost laughed with relief. She did not like being locked up in a dark smelly place, but she had been locked up before; she knew she could bear it. She also knew that her imprisonment would be brief. Sooner or later, some child would need to use the outhouse, and Maud would be set free. She braced herself against the yanking of Miss Clarke's arm and raised her chin defiantly. One of the schoolroom windows looked out toward the yard. If any of the girls were watching her, they would see her go down fighting.

All that had happened an hour ago. Maud shifted on the wooden bench and hugged her arms. Outside, it was windy; inside, it was drafty and very damp. When Maud stopped singing, she began to shiver. She wondered if the Misses Hawthorne had arrived yet and which of the girls they would choose. Probably they would take Polly; Millicent was prettier, but her father had been a drunkard; Irma, mysteriously, had never had a father at all. Maud did not understand this, but she knew that the girls' fathers

would be held against them. No doubt Polly
Andrews would be chosen: Polly, it was said, came
from a good family; Polly was a dutiful little girl,
conscientious about her chores, and the best speller
in the Asylum. Maud ground her teeth. She detested
Polly. She opened her mouth and started the chorus
again, letting her voice ring out like a trumpet.
"Glory, glory, hallelujah—!"

"Little girl!" chimed a voice from the other side
of the outhouse door. "Little girl, why are you
singing in there?"

Maud froze. The voice was unfamiliar. The idea
that a stranger was listening was somehow frightening. She stared at the crack of light that framed the
door. She did not breathe.

"Little girl," coaxed the voice, "don't stop! Go
on with your song!"

Maud considered the voice. It was high without
being shrill, with a queer lilt of music in it. Maud,
who had heard very few beautiful voices in her life,
had no hesitation in judging it beautiful. After a moment, she ventured, "Who are you?"

"I'm Hyacinth," answered the voice, clear as a
bell. "Who are you?"

Hyacinth. Maud had an idea that a hyacinth was

a flower—not a common flower like a daisy or a rose, for which anyone might be named, but something more exotic. She analyzed the voice again and decided it sounded young, but grown-up. Inside her mind a picture of a young lady took shape, her hair just up: rosy cheeks and a white lacy dress and a pink parasol with fringe around the edges.

"Who are you?" repeated the voice. "Why were you singing?"

"I'm locked in," said Maud.

"But why are you locked in?"

Maud ran through a number of possible answers and discarded them all. "It's cold," she stated, "and singing warms me up. That's why I was singing."

She listened for an answer and heard, instead, the sound of the key in the lock. The crack of light widened, the door opened, and Maud tumbled out, blinking like an owl in the spring sunshine.

She saw, with disappointment, that the stranger was not young at all. In fact, she was old: her hair was white, and her skin was lined. At second glance, Maud's disappointment was less acute. The stranger was erect and dainty, like an elderly fairy. She wore a plum-colored suit made of some lustrous fabric that had a pinkish bloom to it; her waist was snow white and frothy with lace. At the collar, there was a gold brooch studded with amethysts and moonstones. Maud had an instinct for finery: the lace, the jewels, and the purplish cloth were all things to be coveted. She felt a surge of fury. She had no such things, and no chance of getting them.

"Who locked you in?" asked the stranger. "Was it some hateful big girl?"

Maud grimaced. She could tell from the phrase "big girl" that the stranger had made a common error. "I'm a big girl myself," she informed the stranger. "I'm eleven."

"Eleven!" The lady named Hyacinth clasped her hands. "You aren't, really!"

Maud clenched her teeth. "I am," she asserted, rather coldly. "I'm small for my age, that's all."

The lady had stopped listening. She was staring at Maud almost fiercely, as if something had just occurred to her. "Eleven," she repeated.

"I am," argued Maud. "Ask Miss Kitteridge."

The lady drummed one set of gloved forefingers against the back of her other hand. "And what is your name?"

"Maud Mary Flynn," said Maud, baffled by the way the lady flew from subject to subject.

"And you're eleven years old?"

"I told you I was," flashed back Maud.

The lady startled her by laughing. Her laughter had the same musical quality as her voice. Halfway through the laugh, one gloved hand pinched Maud's chin, tilting her face upward. Maud flinched, though the touch was soft. She caught a whiff of violets.

"You sing very prettily, Maud Mary Flynn."

"Thank you," said Maud, with dignity. She had always suspected that her voice was good, though no one had told her so. She glanced over her shoulder at the schoolroom window. If Miss Clarke looked out and saw her, she would be in trouble.

"Poor child!" The strange lady had changed again; now her voice was tender, with only a faint hint of mockery. "Locked up in that nasty cold place without any coat! You ought to tell the teacher that the others locked you in."

"She already knows," said Maud. Once the words were out, she wished she could take them back.

"She knows and she didn't stop them?"

Maud fished for a lie but was unable, on such short notice, to find one. "She was the one who locked me in."

"Do you mean" — Hyacinth sounded indignant —

"do you mean she locked you in there, with no coat, on purpose?"

Maud nodded.

"For what reason?"

Maud stole a glance at the lady's face. "I was swinging my legs during class. My boots made a noise against the floor."

"Is that all?" Hyacinth asked in disbelief. "How unjust! You poor little thing!"

Maud felt her eyes fill with tears. She knew that her bad behavior had not been limited to swinging her feet. She knew that she had all but forced Miss Clarke to punish her. And yet—under Hyacinth's pitying eyes—she did feel like a poor little thing. It was an intensely pleasurable feeling—close to embarrassment, and yet agreeable. Speechless with surprise, she raised her face to the Hyacinth-lady, who reached out and stroked the salt water from her eyes. The gray gloves were soft as the skin of a peach.

"Maud Flynn!" Hyacinth bent down as if she were about to tell a secret. Her voice lowered to a thrilling whisper. "Maud Flynn, what if I were to take you away from this horrid place? What if you were to come home with me and my sister Judith and be our little girl?"

Maud's eyes widened. "You're Miss Hawthorne," she exclaimed in a whisper. "You're the ones—" She remembered in the nick of time that the Misses Hawthorne wanted a child of eight or nine years of age, and shut her mouth.

"Yes, I am Hyacinth Hawthorne," agreed the stranger. "Would you like to come home with me? I promise Judith and I won't shut you in the necessary-house. We haven't one. Our house has all the modern improvements."

Maud could not speak. She clutched the hand that was offered her and followed Hyacinth Hawthorne away from the outhouse.

CHAPTER TWO

The office of Miss Kitteridge, Superintendent of the Asylum, was a cramped room at the front of the brick building. Maud had been sent there whenever her behavior went beyond what Miss Clarke could tolerate, and she hated every inch of the room. She also hated Miss Kitteridge, who sat beneath an engraving of Jesus blessing the children of Judea. Under the picture was a woolen sampler, with the words "Suffer the Little Children to Come Unto Me" cross-stitched in red and black. When Maud was a little younger, she had thought that the caption referred to

Miss Kitteridge: any child who came unto Miss Kitteridge, Maud figured, was bound to suffer.

Miss Kitteridge was a tall woman with a yellow pompadour and a deceptive air of fragility. Maud's eyes darted over her and settled on the other woman in the room. The other Miss Hawthorne—her sister Judith, Maud supposed—appeared twenty years older than her sister. Her face was stern and her costume sober: a rich, red-brown silk—a good dress, Maud judged, but plain.

Miss Kitteridge sighed. Her sentences often began and ended with a sigh; she always spoke as if she were not quite strong enough to finish a whole thought. Maud was not misled by this. She knew Miss Kitteridge was not too weak to be cruel.

"A most respectable family," said Miss Kitteridge, as if it were a complaint. She was speaking, then, of Polly Andrews. "I think you will find—"

"Judith," interrupted Hyacinth, "I've found our little girl."

She spoke serenely, as if she had no idea that she was breaking into the conversation. Maud felt the same peculiar weakness in her stomach that she felt when Hyacinth called her a poor little thing. She fitted one knee behind the other and curtsied to Judith Hawthorne. She knew her dress was wrinkled and her stockings were sagging. She wished she had thought to pull them up.

Judith Hawthorne turned to her sister. "Miss Kitteridge has been telling me that there are several little girls the right age for us—" she began, but Hyacinth interrupted a second time.

"But there is no need to see any of them," she parried sweetly. "This is Maud, and she will do splendidly."

Miss Kitteridge cleared her throat. "Maud is too old," she said, fixing Maud with a baleful blue eye. "Maud is eleven. You specifically requested a child of eight."

"Maud is perfect," contradicted Hyacinth. "Look how tiny she is, Judith. And she has a lovely singing voice."

Maud glanced anxiously at Judith. The older woman's face was disapproving, though her disapproval was directed at Hyacinth rather than Maud. "Miss Kitteridge has gone to a considerable amount of trouble to prepare three other children—"

This time it was Miss Kitteridge who interrupted. "The other little girls are the right age," she said plaintively. "You wanted a younger child."

"That was before I met Maud," countered Hyacinth.

"Of course, if you've taken one of your fancies to Maud, there is nothing more to be said," stated Judith, who sounded, nevertheless, as if she thought a good deal more might be said.

Miss Kitteridge looked baffled. Maud could read her thoughts: it was beyond her wildest imaginings that anyone might take a fancy to Maud Flynn. Maud was not pretty; her manners were pert and displeasing; even her posture suggested what Miss Clarke called "sauce." Maud almost sympathized with Miss Kitteridge: she was baffled herself.

"Maud Flynn is not suitable," Miss Kitteridge said. Her nostrils twitched as if she were smelling something nasty. "Even if you wanted an older child, I would not recommend her."

"Why not?" demanded Hyacinth.

Maud's heart sank.

Miss Kitteridge did not answer at once. She straightened the papers that lay before her. Then she glanced at Maud, and the corners of her lips tightened maliciously. "Maud Flynn is a troublemaker," she said. "She has no respect for her elders. She is conceited and untruthful." She tapped the edges of the paper together. "She makes up boastful stories and tells them to the other girls. She shirks her share of the chores. I would like"—her voice changed from disapproving to mournful—"to state that every child in the Barbary Asylum is a credit to the institution, but I cannot speak well of Maud Flynn."

Maud clenched her teeth and lifted her head. She had never hated Miss Kitteridge more. She stared at the sampler, willing herself not to cry. The black crosses turned to blots.

"You seem very certain." It was Judith Hawthorne who spoke, and her voice was dry. Maud pricked up her ears. Something in the way those four words were spoken gave her hope. Judith Hawthorne did not like Miss Kitteridge telling her what to do.

"Poor Maud!" said Hyacinth. She sounded amused, as if none of what Miss Kitteridge said was of any importance. "Are you really such a wicked little thing?"

Maud looked at her bleakly. All at once she found her tongue. "If you took me," she said desperately, "I wouldn't be. I'd be different. I'd do anything you told me. I'd be grateful."

Judith Hawthorne made an odd noise. Her hand went out as if to brush aside Maud's promise.

"Did you hear that, Miss Kitteridge?" said Hyacinth. "Maud has promised to be a good girl. I believe her, don't you, Judith?"

"Hyacinth," said Judith warningly.

"We'll take her," announced Hyacinth. "Won't we, Judith?"

The elder Miss Hawthorne turned to Miss Kitteridge. "Draw up the papers," she commanded. "We appreciate your advice, but we prefer to be guided by our own judgment."

"What a dreadful woman!" exclaimed Hyacinth as the carriage from the livery stable drew away from the Asylum.

Maud was so startled that she burst out laughing. Her laughter sounded overloud, and she clapped her hands over her mouth. Her heart was singing. She was going away. She was going home. And Hyacinth Hawthorne was taking her: Hyacinth, who was unlike anyone Maud had ever met. What other grownup would criticize the Superintendent in front of a child? One of the most detestable things about grown-ups, Maud felt, was the way they took up for one another. Even the nicer ones did it—as if a child, any child, required a whole army of grown-ups to subdue it.

"Hyacinth," said Judith repressively.

"But she is," insisted Hyacinth. Her voice was

still tremulous with laughter. "All that tatty crocheted lace."

Greatly to Maud's amazement, Judith nodded.

"A tiresome woman," she conceded, "but all the same—" She jerked her head toward Maud.

Maud picked up the cue. "I ought to respect her." She fished in her memory for a moral sentiment and found one. "The Asylum gave me a roof over my head and clothes to wear." The words had been drummed into her so many times that she could parrot them exactly.

"But such frightful clothes!" Hyacinth shook her head at Maud's houndstooth check. "I never saw such an ugly dress in my life. She simply must have new ones, Judith."

"We'll stop in town and buy her ready-made ones," said Judith, "and perhaps stop at a tearoom. It's past noon. No doubt the child is hungry."

"She'd like an ice-cream soda, I imagine," suggested Hyacinth.

Maud felt a surge of rapture. An ice-cream soda. Ready-made dresses. A home with modern improvements. She saw herself as a new person: a blissful, pampered, graceful little girl, the sort of child whom adults petted and adored. She would be good. She would be very good; she would say yes ma'am and no ma'am, and while she was being good, she would wear pink and white dresses and drink ice-cream sodas. She was so happy she wanted to jump up and down and drum her heels against the floor of the carriage. She contented herself with sitting up very straight, linking her fingers, and turning her hands inside out. It was the best day of her life. The carriage was taking her away. And all at once, as it turned from the drive to the road, Maud felt an unwelcome and wholly genuine pang of sorrow for Polly, Millicent, and Irma.

Chapter Three

Two hours later, Maud stood before the mirror of a department store.

She could scarcely believe her good fortune. On the counter beside her was a mounting pile of clothes: new stockings and petticoats and drawers and nightgowns. A saleslady in a starched shirtwaist was wrapping them up in tissue paper so that they could be sent to Maud's new home. Ladies like the Hawthorne sisters did not walk through the streets carrying armfuls of packages.

"That green suits her," pronounced Hyacinth. "Then the rosebud print and perhaps the yellow stripe?"

"She ought to have something warmer," argued the elder Miss Hawthorne. "It's drafty on the third floor, and it'll be chilly for some weeks yet."

Maud gazed into the mirror. Her reflection startled her. The bright glass reflected the splendid carnival of goods around her: the transparent countertops, the dazzling lights, the cabinets full of linens and cottons and silks. The green sailor suit, with its sharp pleats and crisp tie, belonged to that fascinating world. Only Maud looked out of place. Her bootlaces had been knotted together in three places, and her red flannel petticoat sagged on one side. Even her face was wrong. Maud had made up her mind that this was the best day of her life, but the girl in the mirror had a queer strained look on her face: a look divided between a grin and the grimace that comes before tears.

"Something red might be cheerful," Hyacinth suggested. "She ought to wear bright colors. She needs color." She reached out and drew a strand of Maud's dirty hair between her fingers. "Perhaps if her hair were cut shorter—"

Maud objected. "I want to grow it long," she

said. "It used to be longer, but—" She stopped. Better not mention the time when half the girls at the Barbary Asylum were plagued by head lice. "I want it to grow long so I can have ringlets."

"It won't do for ringlets," Hyacinth said. "It's too thin and it won't curl. It must be cut here—just below the jaw." She ran a finger across Maud's throat and turned back to the saleslady. "We won't take the yellow, then. Let's see that red plaid there—is that wool?"

"Red shows at a distance," Judith pointed out. She sounded as if this were a disadvantage.

"She'll have a coat," argued Hyacinth.

Maud said nothing. She held up her arms while the saleswoman removed the green dress and brought forth the red. From time to time she injected a "thank you" into the conversation, but her voice sounded breathy and unreal.

"And then a white dress . . . for best." Hyacinth turned back to Maud. "You've no choice about this, Maud; it must be white. Something with lace," she told the saleswoman.

"She can choose the sash, if she likes," suggested Judith.

Maud chose a scarlet sash with long fringe.

"What about toys?" asked Hyacinth, after the

saleswoman had taken her money and given her change. "What would you like, Maud?"

"There's Victoria's dollhouse—" began Judith.

"If Victoria will let her use it," said Hyacinth.

"Who's Victoria?" asked Maud.

The Misses Hawthorne exchanged glances. "Victoria is our sister," explained Judith. "I am the eldest, and Hyacinth is the youngest. Victoria is in the middle. She has an old dollhouse—a very beautiful one, which I imagine she'll share with you."

"Once she gets over the shock," qualified Hyacinth.

"Hyacinth," said Judith warningly.

"What about books?" asked Hyacinth briskly. "Are you fond of reading, Maud?"

Maud's head came up sharply. She had read her way through the single shelf of the books at the Asylum. They were an ill-assorted lot: mostly moral tales with broken spines and missing pages. As if in a dream, she nodded.

The bookstore was even more imposing than the department store. Inside were row upon row of volumes, bound in jewel-toned covers ornamented with gold. The air smelled of leather and enchantment. Maud felt almost as if she were about to be sick. She squeezed her hands together to keep from grabbing the books off the shelf.

"Why don't you look about?" suggested Hyacinth. "Find whatever you like, and we'll buy it."

Maud cast a searching glance at Judith Hawthorne.

"Judith's buying your schoolbooks," Hyacinth explained. "History and arithmetic and tedious things like that. You won't go to school—not at first—so you'll need to study at home. But you may have storybooks as well."

Maud's hand crept toward a copy of *David Copperfield*. There was a copy of *David Copperfield* at the Barbary Asylum, but it had only the first hundred pages. Maud had never been able to find out if Davy escaped from the cruel Murdstones.

"Not that," Hyacinth said carelessly. "We have a set of Dickens at home. And Scott, of course. Choose something else—whatever you like."

Whatever you like. Maud trembled. It could not be true. Perhaps it was a trap, a test to see how greedy she was. She drew her hands back together, interlaced her fingers, and squeezed hard. Judith Hawthorne caught the look on her face. She spoke directly to Maud.

"You may have two books," she said firmly. "Two of the ones marked a dollar and a half, or a dollar and a quarter."

Maud let out her breath in a sigh of bliss. Unconsciously, she fitted one knee behind the other and curtsied. "Thank you, ma'am."

It was not until the Misses Hawthorne boarded the train that Maud was able to open her book. She had ridden in a train once before, when she left St. Anne's Children's Home for the Barbary Asylum, and she was glad of it, because it allowed her to assume the nonchalance of a world traveler. She sat down primly, back straight.

"You mustn't read in the train," said Judith Hawthorne. "You'll be sick."

Maud was sure she would not be sick. She opened her mouth to argue and then remembered that she had made up her mind to be perfectly good. She shut her book, folded her hands on top of it, and answered, "No, ma'am."

"Miss Hyacinth has something to say to you," continued Judith, and Maud, getting the hang of it, piped up, "Yes, ma'am."

The two sisters looked at each other. After a moment, Hyacinth gave a little laugh. "Maudy, do you remember what you said earlier today—about how you would do whatever we asked of you?"

Maud had once slapped a little girl who tried to nickname her Maudy. She replied, "Yes, ma'am. I remember. I meant it, too," she added generously.

"Good." Hyacinth hesitated for a moment. "Do you like secrets, Maud?"

Maud thought about it. "I like to *know* secrets," she said at last, "but I don't like secrets that aren't mine."

Apparently this was not the answer Hyacinth had expected. She changed the subject. "Do you remember what I told you in the bookstore? That you wouldn't be going to school right away?"

"Yes, ma'am."

"Are you sorry for that? Do you mind very much?"

"No, ma'am."

"That's good." Hyacinth lowered her voice mysteriously. "You see, Maud, Judith and I have a secret. If you were to go to school, that secret might come out. In a little while, once we are sure of you, we will tell you everything, but first we have to make sure we can trust you. Later on, we'll ask you to help us with our work."

Maud wrinkled her nose at that word *work*. Then she rallied. After all, even if she had to empty chamber pots, or peel potatoes, there would be fewer chamber pots and fewer potatoes than were required for sixty-three little girls. "I'll help you," she promised. "At the Asylum . . . well, sometimes I didn't do exactly what I was supposed to, but that was because Miss Kitteridge was so mean."

Hyacinth seemed to follow her thoughts. "I don't mean that kind of work. You won't have many chores to do, because we have a hired girl. Our work is different. It isn't hard, but it's secret. And—just at first—you, too, must be a secret. You're going to be our secret child."

Maud's forehead puckered with bewilderment.

"Our secret child," repeated Hyacinth. "Doesn't it sound nice? During the first few weeks of being our little girl, no one's going to know about you. You won't go to school. You won't lack for exercise, because we have a lovely garden, with a high wall round it—but when callers come to the house, you'll go upstairs, to the third floor and stay hidden. It will be like a game of hide-and-seek. Do you understand?"

Maud cast a sidelong glance at Judith, whose face was serious, almost grim. "I understand the part about hiding," she ventured. "I mean, I can stay hidden from other people, if you want me to. But I don't understand why."

"No, of course you don't," Hyacinth said tenderly. "All this must seem terribly mysterious to you—and so sudden." She put an arm around Maud's shoulders and drew her close. Her voice grew even softer, as if she were talking to a very little child. "Is it very hard, not knowing? Are you frightened? I can't bear to think that you should be afraid."

For a moment, Maud could not think what to do. One part of her wanted to bury her face in Hyacinth's violet-scented coat. Another part of her understood that she had it in her power to confer a favor. She gave herself a little shake. "No," she said stoutly. "No, ma'am, I'm not frightened."

Hyacinth squeezed her again. "You really are a darling girl," said Hyacinth Hawthorne. "Isn't she, Judith?"

Judith didn't answer. The elder Miss Hawthorne had turned to face the window. Her profile was hawklike, with its sharp eyes and Roman nose. Maud had a feeling that Judith didn't talk about "darlings" very much. A little daunted, she glanced back at Hyacinth.

Hyacinth was smiling faintly. Maud relaxed. It was Hyacinth who mattered, after all—and Hyacinth thought she was a darling girl.

CHAPTER FOUR

Maud dreamed. All at once Hyacinth was shaking her, calling her name. The dream broke into fragments and melted away. The train had stopped.

"We get out here," Judith told her. "Quickly, gather your things."

Maud fumbled for her books and the brown paper parcel that contained the remnants of her past life: a calico nightgown from the Barbary Asylum, a toothbrush, a comb, and a framed photograph of her mother when her brother was still a baby. She ran her tongue over her dry mouth, tasted the foulness of long sleep, and got to her feet. The Misses Hawthorne led her down the aisle of the train and out onto the platform.

The cold night roused her fully. She was in the country. Overhead, the moon was rising, and the stars were sharp and white. The railroad depot stood at the edge of an empty field, with a grove of trees beyond it. The ground was hard with frost.

"This way," Hyacinth directed her. "We have a short walk."

Maud followed her. Never, as long as she remembered, had she been outside by night. With one quick leap, she reached Hyacinth's side and caught hold of her hand, but Hyacinth's hand, so caressing before, had grown stiff and cold, like the hand of a doll. Maud's mind flitted back to the events of the day: the Asylum, the department store, the bookshop, the train ride. She could not think of anything she had done wrong.

"Here." They had come to the edge of the field and stood before the wood. "Here's where we go in."

"Here" was a tangle of black branches and shadowy brush. Maud clutched her new books to her breast. She stepped forward into the greater darkness, raising her face to the moon.

"You're not afraid of the dark, are you?" asked Hyacinth.

"No," Maud lied quickly. "That's for babies."

"I love the woods at night." Hyacinth bent over a mound of bushes. She appeared to be searching for something. At last she retrieved it: a lantern. Maud watched as she struck a match and kindled the light. As the flame grew in height, it elongated Hyacinth's long jaw and the hollows below her cheekbones. For a moment, she looked less like a fairy than a witch.

"It's three miles to Hawthorne Grove," Judith said in a low voice. "Come along."

Maud stepped forward. She kept her eyes fixed downward, lest a snake curl around her ankle or a toad leap out from the underbrush. She wondered if there were large animals in the woods—bobcats or bears. She considered catching hold of the edge of Judith's coat but thought better of it. Her eyes followed the light as it bobbed along ahead. Hyacinth held the lantern high, stepping briskly. She did not move like an old woman at all.

Maud tagged after her. Her stomach growled: the ice-cream soda had been delicious but not filling. She tucked her fingers in the crooks of her elbows, hugging her books to her chest. She wished she had gloves.

"Come, Maudy!" hissed Hyacinth. "Don't be slow! I don't mind crawling along for Judith's sake—she's an old woman—but you're a child; you ought to be able to keep up with me!"

Maud hesitated. Then she plunged forward, careless of the shadows before her. She caught Hyacinth's mood, and all at once the night was magic. She felt a wildness in her blood. She drank in the sounds of the wood: the brittle underbrush snapping, the small scuffling of her feet against the earth. Her cheeks tingled with the cold. The great dark trees loomed like ogres, but she would be swift and nimble, like a child in a fairy tale; she would dart past them before they could snatch her. Hunger and nightmare forgotten, she danced over the silver grass.

Maud awakened at dawn. Her eyes went from wall to wall, seeking the mustard-colored paint of her old dormitory. It took her a moment to realize that she was in a new room: her room. She sat up in bed and examined it, first with curiosity and then with approval. Wallpaper. It was pale gray, with bunches of pale pink roses and cornflowers—faded, but still pretty. The bed was made of dark wood, with acorns carved on the end of the bedposts. The sheets were clean, the blankets thick. There was a grate but no fire, a washstand, a small table, a straight chair, and a chest for clothing. Nothing was ugly. The only ugly things in sight were her Asylum clothes, lying on the floor.

Maud scrambled out of bed and gathered them up. If she was going to be perfectly good, she would have to take care not to leave her clothes lying about. She folded each item, even her stockings, and laid them on the chair. Then she looked under the bed.

There was no chamber pot. Maud shifted uneasily. She tried to sort out the events of the night before. The wonders of the moonlit wood had not sustained her throughout the walk. It was past midnight when Hyacinth led her out of the woods and through the sleeping town. Maud had meant to look over her new home carefully, but by the time they climbed the stairs of the wide porch, she was staggering with tiredness, longing only for a flat place where she could lie down.

She remembered passing through rooms that seemed to be stocked with treasure: heavy draperies, glass-fronted bookcases, thick carpets, little shelves crowded with china ornaments. She remembered climbing dozens of stairs to her new bedroom. She had a vague memory of visiting the room with the Modern Improvement, and she wondered if she could locate it again. It seemed impolite to use it a second time without asking permission. Still, her need was urgent, and it was possible that she might be able to creep in and out without anyone knowing.

Maud tiptoed to the door. She put her hand on the knob, which turned noiselessly. The carpet under her bare feet muffled her footsteps. She found the staircase and descended to the second floor.

The corridor was dim. It was hung with a wallpaper so dark that Maud couldn't tell if it was purple or brown. One of the doors along the corridor was closed. Maud halted, pressing her thighs together. She was almost certain that it was the door she wanted, but she was afraid to touch the doorknob. It would be horrible if someone—Judith or the unknown Victoria—was inside and she opened the door while the older woman was using the Improvement.

As she stood nerving herself, she heard a voice from below. It was a female voice, unfamiliar and raised in anger.

"I never thought you would go through with it! If I had dreamed you were in earnest—"

Maud had an impulse to run back to her bedroom and hide. She cast a look of longing at the door to the water closet.

"Don't be such a hypocrite! You knew perfectly well—"

The voices quieted, almost as if the speakers sensed she might be listening. Maud could not catch the words. Then one of the voices rose again. This time she recognized it: Judith's low-pitched, somewhat raspy voice was distinctive.

"What is the point, if we don't do it properly?"

"The point is that we shouldn't do it at all."

"You forget that this is not a question of what we should like or not like—"

"I believe it is." The response came back quickly. "For Hyacinth, I really think it is. She thinks of it as a sport."

Hyacinth's voice, quick and girlish, cut in. "It was you who began it—"

"And I repent of it—"

The voices lowered again. Maud could not sort them out. At last she heard, "a child of that age—!" They were talking about her. She stepped close to the balustrade, leaning toward the sound.

"—can't believe you would subject a child—"

"For heaven's sake, Victoria!" It was Judith's voice again. "Children are working in coal mines, blacking boots in the street! For that matter, the Asylum where the child was living—"

"Where she ought to be living still—"

"She doesn't think so." Hyacinth's voice was sharp, the consonants very crisp. "Ask her. She'd rather be here, I promise you."

"You'd have taken her, too," Judith argued. "I admit I was of two minds, Victoria, but the child did everything but get down on her knees to us. Of course, she's under Hyacinth's spell, but even so—*I* couldn't have refused her, and you're a deal more tenderhearted than I ever was. And you must admit that Hyacinth has an instinct. If she thinks the child—"

Once again the voices fell. Maud strained to hear. She had all but forgotten her discomfort. She wondered confusedly if Victoria meant to have her thrown out in the streets or sent to work in the coal mines. If Hyacinth and Judith adopted her, could their sister throw her out?

Victoria spoke again. "If you take her to the Cape, I will not go with you. I will not continue with this—"

Hyacinth interrupted. She was evidently furious; her voice was lowered to a hiss. Maud could not decipher her words. A door slammed. Maud jumped. Before she knew it, she had turned the door handle and was inside the water closet. No one was there. Quickly, soundlessly, she closed the door, grateful for a place to hide.

CHAPTER FIVE

Later that morning, Maud spent a good ten minutes making her bed. She stroked the sheets and swatted the pillows. She dressed carefully, rolling the waistband of her petticoat so that it wouldn't hang crookedly. She was stalling, giving the Hawthorne sisters time to make peace before she saw them again. While she was combing her hair a second time, the door opened, and a woman came in.

Maud supposed the woman must be Victoria. She was, Maud judged, the plainest of the Hawthorne sisters. She was dumpy, though her corsets trussed her fat into tidy mounds. She wore spectacles, which made her eyes appear misty and overlarge. It was clear that her hair had once been red, and the reddish streaks amidst the gray looked peculiar. Maud made up her mind that if she ever had to be an old woman, she would have snow-white hair, like Hyacinth's.

"Good morning, Maud," said the woman. She sounded surprisingly cordial. "How neatly you've made your bed!"

Maud, remembering the words she had overheard, eyed her skeptically. This was the sister who thought she belonged back at the Asylum. Then she reminded herself that she was being perfectly good. She lowered her eyes modestly. "Thank you, ma'am."

"I am Victoria Hawthorne. You may call me Aunt Victoria. I was wondering"—Victoria's voice was a little uncertain—"if you'd like a bath before breakfast."

Maud felt suddenly dirty. Her eyes strayed to the mirror, where she saw a face as plain as Victoria's own: wide bony forehead, deep-set eyes, a crooked mouth with frown shadows at the corners. She wondered if she smelled bad. She had noticed a sour reek when she pulled her dress over her head, but she hoped it was only the dress.

"I drew the water for you. Hyacinth said you weren't used to modern conveniences, and the boiler is a little dangerous, so I thought you might like some help—"

"Yes, ma'am. Thank you, ma'am." Maud trailed behind Victoria to the second floor, where she beheld the second Improvement in the Hawthorne home: the bathroom.

It was resplendent. In fact, it was so fine, so luxurious, that Maud forgot her grievance against Victoria and her hunger for breakfast. There was a huge white tub, with lion's paws at the corners. The water for the bath poured out of a rust-stained lion's mouth. Victoria tipped a handful of sweet-smelling granules into the palm of her hand. "Bath salts," she explained, and sprinkled them over the water. "Of course, it's wrong for a child to use scent, but I thought for your first day . . . They're only lavender."

Maud inhaled appreciatively. The gift of bath salts confirmed her worse suspicion—she must smell bad—but she was grateful for the treat. She waited until Victoria was gone before she stripped off her clothes, threw them on the floor, and squatted down to bathe. The water was warm, and no one had bathed in it before her. There was no one else's scrubbed-off skin making a scum on the top of the water. Maud picked up the big sponge and squeezed water down her chest. The soap was translucent, golden as honey, and smoky sweet. Maud scrubbed until even her armpits smelled good. She emerged from the bath cleaner than she'd ever been in her life.

Pulling on her dirty clothes was a shock. Maud shuddered like a cat in the rain, trying to touch her dress with nothing but the tips of her fingers.

Victoria was waiting at the bottom of the stairs. "Come to breakfast," she said, and seemed pleased when Maud said, "Yes ma'am." At breakfast, Maud realized, she would see Hyacinth. At the thought, her pace quickened, and she tripped down the stairs so rapidly Victoria took a step backward.

The breakfast room was nearly empty. Judith Hawthorne sat before a crumb-spotted plate, drinking a cup of tea. Beside her was a place setting of clean china. "Where's Hyacinth?" demanded Maud.

"Hyacinth has a sick headache," Victoria answered.

"Hyacinth generally has a sick headache when she hasn't had her own way," Judith said dryly.

Maud looked at her uncertainly.

Victoria pulled out a chair, indicating Maud's place at table. "I'm afraid we weren't quite sure what you would like for breakfast," she said apologetically. "What did you have at the Asylum?"

"Oatmeal," said Maud, airing a long-held grudge.

"Oh, dear." Victoria surveyed the breakfast table as if it worried her. "None of us are very fond of oatmeal, I'm afraid. We generally have toast and bacon and marmalade—or jam. In the future, we could manage oatmeal, but for this morning, do you think you could eat a little toast and bacon?"

Maud had no doubt about it. Now that food was within reach, she realized that she was ravenous. She accepted the toast with fingers that trembled with hunger and sawed at her bacon with such force that the knife squeaked against the plate. "I *hate* oatmeal," she said around a mouthful of toast. "At the Asylum, half the time the milk was sour, and there were always lumps. We used to pick them out—the oatmeal lumps, I mean—and line them up on the table to see who had the most. I remember one time—" She recalled the beautiful day she had collected the hard, spitty lumps and hidden them in Miss Kitteridge's muff. It occurred to her, midsentence, that this was not a good story to share with grown-ups.

"Maud," Judith said sternly, "don't talk with your mouth full."

Maud nodded hard and resumed eating. Luckily neither of the Misses Hawthorne seemed eager for her to finish the story. She spread a second piece of toast with marmalade, which she had never tasted before and which she found very good. After devouring the toast, she dragged the bacon dish across the tablecloth, only to discover that it was empty. The Hawthorne ladies were staring at her, appalled by her table manners. Maud shrank back against her chair. "I'm sorry," she said in a small voice.

"You appear to be rather hungry," remarked Judith.

"It is more—usual," Victoria said, "to ask to be served. We don't, as a rule, drag the plates across the table. It wrinkles the cloth. There isn't any more bacon, I'm afraid, but Muffet—oh, here she is! I asked Muffet to make more toast!"

Maud's head turned quickly. A swarthy, middle-aged woman had come into the room. She wore an apron and a printed housedress that was so short that it showed the tops of her boots. Her dark hair had been cut short like a man's, and she had a shadowy line above her lips: a mustache. Maud stared at her, repelled.

The woman continued to limp toward the table. A queer sound came from her closed mouth. The sound was wholly unlike anything Maud had ever heard and seemed to be connected, in some way, to the woman's left foot. Every time the foot touched the floor, the woman uttered a cry. The noises ranged from creaking to guttural, with no two sounds alike.

Judith took the saucer of toast and placed a slice on Maud's plate. Victoria said, "Thank you, Muffet," and jerked her head toward the door. The woman turned with a cry like a foghorn and stalked away.

"What's wrong with her?" whispered Maud, after the bulky shape had vanished from the doorway. "Why does she make those noises?"

"She's deaf," Judith explained. "She can't hear. And she can't speak."

Victoria moved the marmalade to one side. "Once the knife has been used to cut the bacon, dear, it mustn't go back in the marmalade—let me give you a little with the jam spoon. . . . I don't know why Muffet makes those noises, but it isn't her fault. She isn't aware that she makes those sounds."

"She makes all that noise and she doesn't know it?"

"No, how would she? She can't hear."

Maud shook her head in confusion. "Is there something the matter with her foot?"

"I don't know." Victoria looked a little sad. "She's always limped, ever since I've known her. There's no way of asking her what the trouble is."

"If she works for you, how do you talk to her?"

"We don't," answered Judith. "Muffet knows her duties. If we have to give an order, Victoria acts it out or draws a picture."

"I thought a deaf person would be quiet."

"Perhaps some are. Muffet isn't. Come to think of it, her name isn't Muffet. That's just one of Hyacinth's foolish nicknames." Judith's lips were tight with disapproval.

Maud remembered how Hyacinth had dubbed her Maudy. "Why does Hyacinth call her Muffet?"

"She's very much afraid of spiders," replied Victoria. "Her real name—" She stopped in midsentence. "Gracious, how dreadful of Hyacinth! It's been so long since we called her anything but Muffet, I can't remember her real name."

Maud wasn't listening. Her memory had reached back in time, bringing to mind a green book with shiny pages. She saw herself, very small, curled up against her mother, while an Irish voice lilted, *Along came a spider, and sat down beside her—and fright-*

ened Miss Muffet away! She had forgotten that book of nursery rhymes. Now she remembered the cow on the front, a fawn-colored cow that flew over the moon with all its hooves stuck out. One corner of the book cover had been sucked into a curve instead of a point. Samm'l had done that. Maud's brow knotted. She didn't want to think about Samm'l. Automatically she reached for the last piece of toast.

"'May I have more toast, please,'" Victoria prompted her.

"May I have more toast, please, ma'am," Maud echoed, in a voice that Miss Kitteridge would not have recognized.

"Certainly." Victoria put a little more marmalade onto her plate. Maud chewed in silence until the last crumb was gone. Then: "If Hyacinth has a headache, does that mean I can't see her?"

"Not *cannot, may not*," corrected Victoria.

"Does that mean—" began Maud again. Victoria and Judith were looking at her with something like pity. "I wouldn't be noisy," Maud promised. "I'd just say how sorry I was."

"She wouldn't like that," answered Victoria. "I'm sorry if you're disappointed, dear, but there are times when it's best to leave Hyacinth to herself."

*   *   *

It was not so very difficult, Maud found, to be perfectly good. During the next two days, she practiced taking small bites at the table and doing meekly what she was told. She said "yes ma'am" and "no ma'am," and folded her clothes when she took them off. Judith showed her over the house, paying special attention to the passages that led to the back staircase. "If you hear the doorbell or any voice that isn't familiar, you must tiptoe, quick as you can, to the back stairs. Then sit down, take off your shoes, and carry them with you. Go upstairs in your stocking feet."

Maud agreed to do this. With a straight face, she demonstrated how stealthy she could be. She did not ask questions. Later Victoria showed her through the third-floor rooms, most of which were empty. One large room, which had been the nursery, contained Victoria's old dollhouse, an elaborate building almost as tall as Maud herself. To Maud's surprise, Victoria seemed quite willing to share her dollhouse with Maud. The old woman became quite animated as she took out tiny chairs and tables and wiped them clean with her handkerchief. The dolls, Victoria explained, had all been lost, but Maud might rearrange the furniture as much as she liked. Maud thanked her dutifully. Just in time she realized it would not be tactful to say that she saw no point in moving around little bits of furniture.

The hardest thing about Maud's first week in her new home was that Hyacinth remained in her room. Judith and Victoria were adamant: Hyacinth was unwell, and she wished to be left alone. Maud could not see her. Maud said, "Yes, ma'am," but her obedience was flawed. More than once, she tiptoed to the door of Hyacinth's room and listened for sounds from within. There were none. The silence made her uneasy, as if a Hyacinth that could remain so still were somehow a different Hyacinth.

On the third day, the boxes arrived from the department store. Maud stripped off her asylum clothes with glee. Once clad in her red wool dress, she made up her mind: Hyacinth must see her new finery. She would slip up the back stairs when she was supposed to be walking in the garden. There were three stunted daffodils by the brick wall; she would steal them and smuggle them up to Hyacinth.

Her plan worked perfectly. She plucked the flowers, slipped indoors without anyone seeing her, and tiptoed upstairs. Without knocking, she turned the doorknob and stepped inside Hyacinth's room.

It was white and shining, like a palace. There

were lace curtains at the windows and a lace canopy over the bed. The crystal chandelier was lit, though the day was only slightly overcast. Four mirrors, surrounded by gold cupids and rosettes, tossed the light back and forth, reflecting one another's reflections. Hyacinth, in a pale blue bed jacket, rested against the pillows. Her finger against the satin counterpane looked faintly pale and tapering as icicles. The mirrors multiplied her fingers: ten, twenty, eighty— all still.

"Maud!" Hyacinth's eyes flew open. She sat up and leaned forward, hands held out. "Maud, you darling child! You came to see me!"

Maud was flooded with happiness. Judith and Victoria had been wrong. Hyacinth did want to see her. "I brung you these," she said, losing her grammar in her eagerness. Shyly she held out the daffodils, with their mud-splashed trumpets.

"Have you been out in the garden, then?" demanded Hyacinth, as if the garden held some incomparable treasure. "Do you like it?"

"Yes," lied Maud. "I've been missing you, though."

"Have you?" Hyacinth took the flowers and held them two inches from her nose. "I've missed you, too, but I do have such dreadful headaches—and

Victoria gets cross with me because I don't eat anything." She waved her hand toward the untouched tray beside her bed. "I hope you don't miss me too terribly badly."

"I do," vowed Maud.

Hyacinth laughed, and then sighed. "That's a pity, really. I shall have to go away soon. I have a friend in Cape Calypso who is very low-spirited. She expects me to come for a visit. But never mind. You'll soon grow fond of Judith and Victoria."

Maud wrinkled her nose. "I like them," she conceded, "but they aren't *you*. Can't you take me with you?"

"Certainly not," reproved Hyacinth. "For one thing, you haven't been invited, and for another, you ought to settle down here. Besides, Mrs. Lambert . . ." She broke off as if she had just lost interest in Mrs. Lambert. Her smile shone out, bright as a diamond. "What about your bedroom—do you like it? Do you like having your own room, or are you lonely, sleeping all by yourself?"

"I like it," Maud asserted. "I never had wallpaper before."

"And Muffet." Hyacinth's eyes danced. "What do you think about Muffet?"

Maud decided to take a risk. "She has a

mustache," she said cautiously, and was rewarded with a ripple of laughter from Hyacinth.

"Yes, hasn't she? She looks like a blacksmith in petticoats. She really is a terrible-looking old thing— but such a good cook, and so devoted to Victoria." Hyacinth fetched an exaggerated sigh. "And our modern improvements—do you like using them? Do you like pulling the chain in the water closet?"

Maud giggled uncontrollably. Imagine a grown-up who knew that water closets were funny and admitted it. "I love pulling the chain," she said. "And the bathtub with the lion's mouth."

"I knew you would be happy here," Hyacinth said triumphantly. "Come and sit on the bed and let me look at you. Gracious, how pretty you look! We were quite right to choose that dress."

Maud sat down sidesaddle. "It's good, isn't it?" she said earnestly. "And look at my boots." She pointed her toes. "They're shiny."

"Lovely," agreed Hyacinth. "You have dear little feet. Only you must have your hair cut. Are Judith and Victoria taking good care of you?"

"Yes, ma'am," responded Maud. "They've been teaching me the secret things—like going upstairs when the doorbell rings. And Victoria changed the curtains in my room for thicker ones; they're called brocade and they're pinkish red." She paused for a moment. "I guess if the curtains were too thin, people might be able to see someone moving around inside . . . or if I lit a candle. Judith warned me about that. She says I can have all the blankets I want, but no fire."

She waited for Hyacinth to answer. Perhaps Hyacinth would drop some hint as to why it would be so bad if light shone from the third-floor window.

"Maud!" Hyacinth squeezed her hand. "Have you ever seen my jewel box?"

"No," replied Maud. "How would I have seen your jewel box? I've only known you five days."

Hyacinth pinched her so that she yelped. "It's over there on the chest of drawers—the red Chinese box. Go and get it, and we'll dress ourselves up in every jewel in the box. We'll play at being queens."

Maud giggled with happiness. She ran to the chest of drawers and scooped up the jewel box, eager to be a queen.

CHAPTER SIX

Dear Hyacinth Hawthorne,
Aunt Victoria said since I was missing you
so much, I ought to write you a letter.
When I say Aunt Victoria, I mean your
sister. She said from now on I should say
Aunt Victoria and Aunt Judith—

Maud leaned her chin on her fist and thought about her two new aunts. In the past two weeks, she had learned that Aunt Judith was the sort of adult who wanted to be left alone and that Aunt Victoria was inclined to preach. Aunt Victoria seemed to feel that Maud ought to be improved. She didn't scold, but she nagged. Maud had yes ma'amed her way through a number of gentle little talks about ladylike manners, tidy habits, and doing her duty. Her resolve to be perfectly good was beginning to fray at the edges.

> *—but she said I shouldn't call you Aunt*
> *Hyacinth because you mightn't like it. She*
> *said she was tired of me calling her*
> *"ma'am" all the time.*

Maud dipped her pen in ink. She thought it ungrateful of Victoria to tire of "ma'am" when she was working so hard to be polite. On the other hand, she was tired of it, too.

> *I miss you very much.*

Maud searched the ceiling for something else to write. She thought of writing *I wish you hadn't gone* or *Why do you have to stay with Mrs. Lambert instead of me?* but she didn't dare.

*Thank you for the book you sent me
about Little Lord Fauntleroy. I read it
twice. His mother, that he called Dearest,
reminded me of you, because her voice
sounded like little silver bells.*

There, that was good. Hyacinth would be flattered by the comparison.

*I liked how Fauntleroy rode that pony
even though he never rode before.*

Maud paused, considering the perfection of Lord Fauntleroy. The storybook hero was so perfect that the adults around him spent every spare minute comparing notes on just how perfect he was. Lord Fauntleroy had golden curls and lace collars. If he had been an orphan, he would have been adopted immediately. Maud sighed with envy.

*I have a lot of time for reading since I
don't go to school. At first I read all the
time but then Aunt Victoria said I should
have a timetable. So now I dust the first
floor every morning before anyone would
come to the house and then I read and do*

arithmetic and help Muffet set the table.
And then I have to sew, which I hate
because it's boring—

Maud stopped and crossed out the second half of the sentence, cross-hatching the lines so that it was no longer legible. Ladies, Aunt Victoria informed her, were sparing with the word *hate*. Victoria had also complained that Maud was too fond of the words *boring, stupid,* and *horrid.* Maud was puzzled as to how Victoria knew this, since she took care to guard her tongue in Victoria's presence. Maud felt, in fact, that she was growing downright mealymouthed. ·

—which is tedious except it will be a
summer dress with stripes. Of course I like
the dresses you bought me better. I let Aunt
Victoria cut my hair the way you wanted.
Anyway, I have to sew and then read
history or geography and walk in the
garden. The plants are all dead.

Maud reread the last sentence, which was not complimentary. But what did Hyacinth expect? She had told Maud that the garden was large and lovely, but it wasn't lovely at all. It was full of stickers, and the tall hemlocks cast so much shade that there was still snow on the ground. The hour that Maud spent outdoors was the dullest hour of the day. Victoria, however, insisted. Children needed fresh air and exercise.

Maud changed the period at the end of her sentence to a comma and continued on.

> *—but I suppose something might bloom if the weather ever gets warm. Thursday we had sleet. Aunt Victoria says it's too cold for April.*

Maud scratched her nose with the end of her pen. She wondered if Hyacinth Hawthorne had any idea how cold it was in her third-floor bedroom. There were no stoves, and Maud was not allowed a fire in the grate. During the recent cold snap, the only way to get warm was to climb into bed. Sometimes it took her a long time to stop shivering, even under the blankets.

> *I've started reading* Oliver Twist. *It's so creepy, because that undertaker made the boy sleep among the coffins. Even Miss*

*Kitteridge never made us sleep among
coffins, though that might have been
because she didn't have any. That day when
you said Miss Kitteridge was dreadful and
took me away from the Barbary Asylum
was the best day of my life, because before
that—*

Maud stopped short. There was no point in writing about, or even thinking about, the worst day of her life.

before that—

Maud stared at the unfinished sentence. She recalled Hyacinth saying *poor little thing!* in that sweet, piteous voice. Tears welled up in Maud's eyes. She concentrated on hearing the echo of Hyacinth's voice, reliving that moment of sympathy.

*because before that, I never met you. You
are like my fairy godmother.*

The rest of the empty page yawned before Maud. She eyed the clock, wishing it were time for supper. She knew there would be scalloped potatoes; she had helped Muffet peel and slice them. She dipped her pen in ink, determined to finish the letter.

Aunt Victoria says I do a good job dusting and that my table manners are improving. I do not wolf my food as bad as I did. Yesterday when I was getting the silverware for dinner, I heard Muffet. She was backing up so fast she banged the table. There was a great big spider on the floor. With its legs it was as big as a tablespoon, the round part I mean, not the handle. Muffet was so frightened she was crying. I never saw a grown-up person as scared as that. I felt sorry for her so I stamped on it hard and it was horrid because it made a disgusting smear on the floor. But Muffet stopped crying and she ran to me and put her hands on my arms. I thought she was going to shake me but she didn't. I think what she meant was she was glad I killed it. Then last night we had Floating Island and that is my favorite pudding. I didn't think she would know what I like to eat because she can't hear, but I guess Aunt Victoria is right and being deaf doesn't mean she's stupid.

My hand is tired now. Please come home soon. Or if you can't, please, please, please write me a letter.

Your loving—

Maud paused. Should she write *daughter*?

Your loving girl,
Maud Mary Flynn

Maud had never liked Sundays. At the Barbary Asylum, Sunday was a day of the utmost tedium, with church all morning and enforced silence in the afternoon. Maud was pained to discover that Sundays with the Hawthorne sisters followed a similar pattern. In the morning, Victoria read aloud from the New Testament and selected a psalm for Maud to memorize. In the afternoon, the sisters received callers, which meant that Maud was confined to the third floor.

On the Sunday five weeks after her arrival, it rained so hard that no one was likely to call. Maud was allowed to learn her psalm in the back parlor. The sisters sat by the fire. Judith read the newspaper while Victoria refurbished an ancient bonnet.

Maud eyed the bonnet speculatively. It was horribly out of fashion, and she wondered if Victoria could be dissuaded from wearing it. Victoria was not elegant like Hyacinth or distinguished-looking like Judith, but Maud saw no reason why she should look as dowdy as she did.

"Aunt Victoria," Maud began coaxingly, "wouldn't it be easier to buy a new hat than to trim that old bonnet?"

Victoria pushed her spectacles higher on her nose, as if by doing so she could come to grips with Maud.

"If you wore a hat instead of a bonnet, you could do your hair in a pompadour," persisted Maud. "Pompadours are stylish. And a pompadour would make your face look taller."

Judith snapped the newspaper against her lap. "Maud Flynn! Weren't you given a psalm to memorize?"

"Yes, ma'am," Maud said, "but I'm almost finished.

I'm up to the part where God breaks the teeth of the ungodly."

Judith sniffed. The doorbell chimed. The two sisters looked at each other in surprise. Maud sprang up and set the Bible on the parlor table.

"I wonder who's calling in this rain." Victoria stuffed the bonnet into her sewing basket. "I'll get it, Judith." She caught Maud's eye and jerked her head toward the back staircase.

Maud darted out on tiptoe. She could hear Victoria speaking and a man's voice answering. She was halfway up to the third floor when she heard Victoria call her name in a whisper.

"Maud! Come downstairs!"

Maud scurried back down the steps. She found Victoria and Judith arguing in the second-floor corridor.

"—in the front parlor—" Victoria whispered.

"Left him!" Judith sounded furious. "Have you lost your mind, Victoria? Why didn't you tell him she doesn't live here?"

"I did. He didn't believe me," hissed back Victoria. "I was afraid he'd ask the neighbors—" She kept her finger on her lips, warning Maud to keep silent. Judith took Maud's arm and pulled her into the nearest bedroom. Victoria followed, shutting the door.

Judith's fingers dug into Maud's arm. "Maud Flynn, have you been writing letters?"

"Yes," gasped Maud. She saw Judith's eyebrows draw together in a deeper frown. She added hastily, "To Hyacinth. Aunt Victoria said—"

"Not to Hyacinth," Judith said sternly. "To your brother. Have you got a brother?"

Maud gaped at her. She felt as if the wind had been knocked out of her. Judith gave her a little shake, and she gasped, "Yes."

Judith threw up her hands. "Now what shall we do? After all this, to have the child's brother on our doorstep! It shows the folly of trusting a child—"

"It isn't her fault," Victoria said, defending Maud. "We should never have taken her in the first place—"

Maud uttered a cry of anguish. Judith hissed, "Be quiet!" and Victoria asked, "What is it, Maud?"

"I didn't write," Maud said urgently. "My brother can't be here. He's in Pennsylvania."

"Pennsylvania?" echoed Judith.

"With the Vines," Maud said. "He was adopted."

"Why didn't you tell us you had a brother?" demanded Judith.

"I didn't *not* tell you," parried Maud. "You never asked. Samm'l's in the picture—the photograph in my bedroom." She appealed to Victoria. "You saw it. He's the baby on Mother's lap."

Victoria said, "I thought that was you."

Maud shook her head. Sometimes she liked to pretend that the lace-clad infant was herself, but she knew better. "No. That's Samm'l." She pronounced the name as she had when she was little, so that it rhymed with *camel*.

"Have you any other family members we ought to know about?" Judith's voice was crisp with sarcasm. Maud flinched.

"There's Kit," she said reluctantly. "My little sister."

"Kit?" Victoria repeated. "Maud, I don't understand. What—"

Maud leaped ahead, forestalling the next question. "She lives with Samm'l. With the Vines."

"Maud, forgive me—" Maud didn't know what she was supposed to forgive. She gazed alertly at Victoria. "Maud, are you telling me that both your sister and your brother were adopted by the same family? And you weren't?"

Maud set her teeth. "Yes."

"But that's barbaric." Victoria spoke almost passionately. "Separating a child from her family! It's like something from the days of slavery. How could they?"

Maud shrugged.

"Don't shrug your shoulders when Victoria asks you questions," barked Judith. "It's rude."

Maud felt cornered. She cast a nervous glance around the room. Her eyes darted over the pattern in the wallpaper, the faded watercolors on either side of the bed, the swirled plasterwork at the edge of the ceiling. She couldn't remember what question she had been asked.

"Out with it," commanded Judith. "The whole story, please. Don't leave out any more long-lost brothers. And be quick. While we chatter up here, your brother's waiting. We must think what to do."

Maud gripped the back of her neck with both hands. She wanted to twist herself into some other shape. "There were three of us," she began shakily. "Father was a farmer. He died just before Kit was born. Then, when Kit was two, Mama died, so we went to St. Anne's. That's the orphanage in Baltimore. I was five and Samm'l was eleven. That's when the Vines came. They had a farm, and they wanted a boy to help out. People always want boys that are strong enough to do farmwork."

She stopped.

"Go on." Judith's voice had softened.

Maud clamped her arms behind her back, bracing herself. "So—the Vines wanted Samm'l. The nuns took Kit and me to say good-bye. Kit was a baby, she didn't understand, but Kit"—Maud was breathing hard—"she was real pretty. She had yellow curls, and Mrs. Vine liked her, and she made up her mind she'd adopt Kit, too. But they didn't want three children. So they left me." Maud swallowed. "I stayed at St. Anne's two more years. Then the nuns closed it down and sent me to the Barbary Asylum."

Judith looked thoughtful. She pressed her thumbnail against her lower lip. "I suppose your brother traced you here. Miss Kitteridge must have told him where you were—"

"Judith, what are we to do?" Victoria laid her hand on her sister's arm. "If Maud's brother came all this way—"

"What are we to do?" echoed Judith. "You can't mean we ought to let her see him!"

"We must." Color rose in Victoria's cheeks. "When I told him she wasn't here, he didn't believe me. That's why—"

"You invited him in," snapped Judith. "Well done, Victoria!"

The two women faced each other. Victoria was flushed and trembling. Judith had raised her voice. It was up to Maud to keep her head.

"It's all right," she said. They turned startled faces toward her, as if they had forgotten she was there. "I don't have to see him."

"Of course you'll see him," Victoria said. "Really, Maud! Have you no family feeling?" She faced her sister. "He already suspects she's here. If we deny it now, he'll ask the neighbors. You know he will, Judith."

Judith was silent, disconcerted.

"Once he sees Maud, he'll go back to Pennsylvania." Victoria sounded as if she were trying to convince herself as well as Judith. "He doesn't know anyone in Hawthorne Grove. He may not tell. It's the best we can hope for, Judith."

Maud risked a look at Judith's face. "Very well," Judith conceded. "You may see him."

Maud felt that Judith expected to be thanked, but the words would not come. Before she could speak, Victoria seized her hand and led her out of the room.

Maud followed in a daze. On the stair landing, she caught sight of herself in the mirror. She stopped, staring at herself. Her face was white, and the tie on her sailor suit hung crooked. Maud reached up to straighten it.

"Maud," Victoria said gently, "this is no time to primp."

Maud finished straightening the tie and gave her hand back to Victoria. She hoped that Victoria would go with her into the parlor. But Victoria opened the parlor door and stood aside. There was nothing to do but to walk past her.

The first thing Maud noticed was that the man who stood waiting—for somehow her brother had become a man—was ill at ease. Samm'l's hands were in his pockets and the cloth over them was taut, as if his fists were clenched. Maud tried to recognize him, but all she could think of was the photograph of Samm'l as a baby.

"Maud?" he asked her. His voice had a funny creak in it.

"Yes," she croaked back, "it's me."

They gazed at each other with an alertness, even a skepticism, that a spectator might have thought funny. "I wasn't sure you were really here," Samm'l said warily. He added, "You look well."

"I am well," answered Maud, raising her chin.

She knew he was not speaking of her health. She was suddenly conscious of the shine on her new boots, the crispness of her petticoats, the dainty cleanliness of her whole person. She inspected him in turn. His clothes were drenched with rainwater and looked too wide for him. He was tall and lanky, and his sandy hair had darkened to mouse color.

"I'm glad you're well," he said awkwardly.

"So'm I," said Maud. She looked away from him. Her eyes passed over the furniture she dusted every day, the gold-framed pictures and wax flowers under glass. Samm'l was out of place in this parlor. He knew it, too.

"Won't you sit down?" asked Maud, as stately as Judith herself.

"No." He dug his hands deeper into his pockets. "That is, yes. Maybe I will." He looked at the needlepoint chairs with their spindly legs and the rococo settee. "I'm kind of wet. You're sure it's all right?"

"Yes, of course."

He lowered himself to the settee and took his hands out of his pockets. He held them between his knees and stared down at the carpet. *Hold your head up, Samm'l!* Maud almost jumped; her mother's voice was so clear in her mind. *Throw your shoulders back! It's the cheapest way to tell the world you're somebody!*

"Maud," Samm'l said hesitantly, "I wanted to see you—well, I wanted to see you before I said good-bye."

Maud felt as if he had punched her in the stomach. For a moment she could not breathe. Then she spoke. "We already said good-bye," she reminded him.

"I know." Samm'l's face was pale. "That day—at St. Anne's. That's part of what I wanted to say—how sorry I am about that day." He looked up again. His eyes were like hers—blue-gray, but so deep set that they looked darker. "I've been sorry for six years."

"Then why are you going away again?" argued Maud.

Samm'l flushed, tweaking Maud's memory a second time. As a child he had reddened easily: with anger, with embarrassment, with laughter. "It's not my fault," he said. "The Vines are going west. The last few years, the harvest hasn't been good, and they can get cheap land out there." He seemed to sense that he was getting nowhere, and began again. "I asked Mr. Vine if we could take you with us, seeing as how we're starting out fresh, but there isn't much money. But I'll be grown-up soon." He leaned forward. Something kindled in his eyes. "I'll get my own farm, and when I do, I'll send for you and give you a home."

Maud broke in. "I have a home," she said tightly. She waved a hand, directing his attention to the parlor. "This is my home."

He had not expected that. Once again, she saw his face change and his color rise. She felt a flash of pity for him.

"Look here, Maud, are you still angry with me?"

"For what?"

"For taking a home with the Vines." He opened his hands, palms up. "Look here. Are you going to stand up the whole time? Because if you are, I'll stand up, too."

Maud flopped down in the nearest chair. The words *look here* unlocked a roomful of memories. A boy with a serious freckled face . . . *Look here, Maud, if you want to make a fist, you've got to keep your thumb on top of the other fingers.* And *Look here, Maud, you can't bathe the cat!* She remembered how impressed she had been by his knowledge of the world. Her face softened, and she almost smiled.

"I'm sitting," she informed her brother.

"I see you are." He risked a brief grin before going back to what he came to say. "That day—when the Vines came and Kit and I left you behind—I've always felt bad about it. I must have seemed old to you, being eleven and all, but I guess I still felt young to me. I thought I had to do what everyone told me."

Maud considered. She was eleven. "Maybe you did."

"What do you mean, I did?" His face twisted in pain. "There you were, five years old, and I was your big brother. I ought to have stayed behind to look after you—I ought to have told them—"

Maud interrupted him. "Don't be stupid," she said crossly. "They wouldn't have let you. Grown-ups always get their own way."

Samm'l's face was filled with hope. "Do you really believe that?" he asked. "I mean, do you forgive me?"

Maud shook her head in confusion. "I don't know," she said. "I don't ever think about that day. It was the worst day of my life." She saw him wince and felt sorry for him again. "I guess when Mama died, that was really the worst, but I don't remember that. Anyway"—she swallowed—"I was pretty bad that day."

"You weren't bad," Samm'l said gently.

"Yes, I was," Maud contradicted him. "I kicked that old Mr. Vine and I screamed. It's no wonder they didn't want me."

"That's not what happened," Samm'l said firmly. "Don't you remember? That was what you did *after* they said they were taking me and Kit. That was when you threw a fit."

Maud shook her head. "No."

"Yes, it was," insisted Sam. "When you understood we were leaving you behind—that was when you threw a tantrum." His mouth twisted into a grin. "It was a pretty good tantrum, too. You left teeth marks in my hand."

Maud had forgotten that. She glanced guiltily at his hand, as if the marks might be there still. "Are you sure?"

"I'm sure." Samm'l looked at her intently. "By God and all the saints, I swear it."

Maud's voice was a thread. "Then why didn't they like me?"

"Well," gulped Samm'l, "I don't rightly know— but it wasn't anything bad you *did*. The thing was, they wanted me for farmwork, and then, Mrs. Vine, she just fell in love with Kit. Kit's always been as pretty as a picture—still is, in fact—and you'd been making mud pies." He looked at her, shame-faced. "I don't know what to tell you, Maud. They took a fancy to Kit, and they needed me, and I guess that's about it."

Maud nodded dumbly.

"I wish it had been different."

"I don't," Maud said, between clenched teeth. "Because if those Vines had adopted me, I'd never have come here." Her gesture took in the faded splendor of the parlor. "This is a better home for me. And Hyacinth Hawthorne—she's the one who chose me—she *wanted* me." She threw the word at him as if it could knock him flat. "She liked me the minute she set eyes on me. And she's rich," she finished stoutly.

"I can see she is." Samm'l inclined his head. "That's right, Maud! You look at the bright side. Mother used to say, 'Maud'll fall on her feet no matter what.' That's what she used to say."

"I have four dresses and books of my own," Maud shot back, "and we never have oatmeal, and there's a servant."

"Good!" Samm'l said heartily. "That's great, Maud! I couldn't be happier."

There was a sudden silence.

"Though it's funny," said Samm'l.

Maud had lost track of the conversation. "What's funny?"

"The way the old lady acted," answered Samm'l. "When I asked her if you lived here, she said you didn't. And then I said you must, and she told me to go away. I said I *had* to see you, because I was your brother, and that's when she got red in the face and started stammering. First she said I couldn't, and then she told me to come inside and wait."

"Oh."

Samm'l waited for her to explain.

Maud linked her fingers together and turned them inside out. "I'm kind of a secret."

"A secret?" Samm'l's brows drew together. "What kind of secret?"

Maud took a few moments before she answered. "I don't know," she said blankly. "They haven't told me yet. All I know is, no one's supposed to know I live here. The neighbors don't know, and they mustn't. You can't tell, either."

Samm'l leaned forward, peering into his sister's eyes. "I think you're telling a lie," he said.

"I'm not," Maud said earnestly. "Honest. That's how it is."

"It doesn't make sense," Samm'l argued. "Why

would anybody adopt a little girl and keep her secret? It sounds to me as if they're up to something that isn't right."

"What, then?" Maud threw out her hands. "What could it be?"

Samm'l's brow knotted.

Maud's voice sank to a whisper. "I can't figure it out, either."

"Are they good to you?"

Maud nodded vehemently. "They give me everything I want," she said. "Beautiful dresses and books and the food is so good—bacon at breakfast and meat every night—and dessert. They let me eat s'much as I want. And there's a bathtub and a water closet, and I don't have to do any chores except lessons and setting the table and dusting. And Hyacinth Hawthorne, she says I'm clever, and she likes the way I sing. And nobody's hit me—ever—or even slapped me."

"There aren't any men around, are there?" inquired Samm'l. "Coming to the house at night, after dark?"

"No," Maud said firmly. "They're old maids. And they're *ladies*," she added, as if that clinched it. Maud's ideas of social class were as vague as they were snobbish, but she knew that ladies did not do wicked things.

"Do they go to church?"

"Judith does," Maud answered. "Victoria doesn't. But she's always reading the Bible, and she makes me learn a psalm every Sunday."

Samm'l shook his head again. Then he gave a little leap, as if he had just remembered something. "I almost forgot." He dug into his pockets and brought out a necklace of coral beads. "I wanted you to have it. 'Twas Mother's."

Maud's hand went out. The beads were warm from the heat of her brother's body. A silver crucifix hung from one end of the necklace. Carefully she spread the string of beads over her fingers, preparing to put it on.

"You don't wear it," Samm'l said critically. "It's a rosary — Mother's coral rosary. Each bead is a prayer. Don't you remember? Mother was Catholic. Kit and I" — he frowned, as if embarrassed — "well, the Vines are Presbyterian, so we've had to be Presbyterians, too, but once I'm a man, I'm going to be Catholic again. You ought to be Catholic, too. It's what Mother would want. You ought to go to Mass every Sunday."

"I can't," Maud said. "I don't go out."

They were back to the secret again. Maud watched her brother's face knot with incomprehension. "I don't like it," he said. "I don't like leaving you in a place where I don't know what's going on."

Maud watched him. A cold wisdom passed through her mind. She knew that he would leave her whether he liked it or not.

"I like it here." She spoke so forcefully that he flinched. "I don't care if I have to be a secret. I want to stay here. Promise me"—she clutched his hand—"promise me you won't tell anyone. If the neighbors find out I live here, I might get sent back to the Asylum." She held out the rosary. "Promise. Swear it on Mama's necklace."

Samm'l took her hand, but he did not promise. Instead, he pulled her into his arms.

Maud hid her face against his sodden jacket. He smelled of wet wool and wood smoke and cows. It was the smell of the home she had lost, and all at once she could remember it. She envisioned the farmhouse kitchen, with her father's boots just inside the door and her mother's geraniums by the window. She remembered the touch of her mother's skirts and the softness of her mother's lap. She gritted her teeth. She had raged and cried when Samm'l left before.

This time she wouldn't shed a tear. She threw back her head and spoke fiercely. "Promise. Promise not to tell."

"I promise," Samm'l said. He drew her close again and she sagged against him, closing her eyes in relief.

CHAPTER EIGHT

After Samm'l's visit, Maud became a spy in her own home.

She knew that curiosity was risky. She wasn't supposed to ferret out the secret that hung over her; she was supposed to wait patiently until the Hawthorne sisters trusted her enough to explain it. That was part of being perfectly good. But Samm'l's doubts were catching. He had seemed convinced that there was something sinister about being a secret child. Maud wanted to prove him wrong.

Accordingly, she began to search. She knew not to ask questions, but she eavesdropped whenever she could. She discovered that one of the empty rooms on the third floor had a broken shutter: if she squatted down eye level to the break, she could look out the window.

She saw nothing that seemed strange to her. The little town of Hawthorne Grove appeared sunny and prosperous. She saw horses and carriages, the ladies with their parasols, the gentlemen returning home in the evening. Enviously, she watched the children: the boys who ran races, the girls who walked arm in arm. It occurred to Maud that she missed being with other children. She had never been popular with girls her own age, but it was odd, living in a world of old ladies.

Maud spied when she dusted the parlor. She pored over the family photograph album, noting that the child Hyacinth had been irresistibly pretty, while her sisters—Judith and Victoria were at least ten years older—were only so-so. She scrutinized the books in the locked bookcases, observing that a depressing number of volumes were devoted to the subject of God and the spiritual life.

There was only one conclusion that Maud was

able to draw from the Hawthorne parlor, and it was an unwelcome one: the Hawthorne sisters were not as rich as she had thought. The parlor, so rich and imposing at first glance, showed signs of age. The heavy curtains were stiff with dry rot, and the upholstery of the chairs was riddled with tiny rents, as if someone had pierced them with a dagger. The garden was overgrown. The Hawthorne ladies kept no carriage and no servant but Muffet. They were sparing with coal.

Maud puzzled over these economies. She wondered why, if the Hawthorne sisters were in need of money, they had chosen to adopt a child. She estimated the price of her dresses and books, and she realized that she had cost the sisters nearly thirty dollars on the very first day. It was a shocking sum of money to waste. Maud remembered what Hyacinth had said: she was going to help them with their work. What kind of work would require the help of a secret child?

Pondering these questions, Maud grew reckless. On an afternoon when the sisters had set off for a concert, she determined to search their bedrooms. As Judith had taught her, she removed her boots and descended the stairs in stocking feet. The room closest to the stairway was Judith's. Maud hesitated only a moment before going in.

Judith's room was large and dim. The curtains were drawn and the wallpaper was olive green. The four-poster bed with its matching dresser was carved walnut, glossy and nearly black. A portrait of a stern-faced gentleman hung over the mantel. Maud knew from the photograph album that it was the Hawthorne sisters' father. Cowed by his disapproving glare, Maud hastened to the next room.

Hyacinth's bedroom was the most beautiful room in the house. It had a freshness that the other chambers lacked: the colors were lighter and the furniture less heavy. The two armchairs before the fireplace were cozily padded, with slender legs that ended in little gold claws. Everything, from the curtains at the window to the canopy over the bed, was dainty and new. Maud took a nostalgic peep into the jewel box and proceeded to open the drawers of the dressing table. Handkerchiefs, gloves, fans . . . There was an ivory powder box with a swansdown puff, a silver lorgnette, and a bottle of scent. Maud stroked the powder puff over her face, eyed the results in the mirror, and rubbed the powder onto her sleeve. It would be agreeable to linger and play with Hyacinth's things, but she had no idea how long the sisters would be gone. She replaced the powder box and tip-toed out of the room.

Victoria's room was the least tidy of the three and held a small bookcase with glass doors. Maud squatted down to look inside. *Jane Eyre, Lady Audley's Secret, Northanger Abbey, Hesper the Home Spirit, The White People, The Woman in White . . . The Woman in White* had a piece of paper sticking out of it—not, Maud saw, a bookmark.

She slid it out and unfolded it, catching the scent of violets. That was Hyacinth's scent; the miniature, curlicue handwriting belonged to Hyacinth. Unfortunately, in an attempt to save paper, Hyacinth had written the beginning of her letter in one direction and then turned the paper sideways, writing the second half of the letter on top of the first, so that the lines crossed at right angles. It was almost impossible to read. Maud turned it, squinting, trying to catch a line here and there.

> *. . . though Mrs. Lambert is a generous hostess, she is unwilling to tell me much about Caroline. Even now, she does not trust me. I feel certain that she is holding*

something back—some circumstance about
Caroline's death that she has told no one—

Maud frowned. She knew that Mrs. Lambert was the friend that kept Hyacinth in Cape Calypso. Maud resented her. She wasn't interested in stupid Mrs. Lambert or the dead Caroline. She skipped several paragraphs.

Of course it is not in keeping with our
agreement that we should entertain
Burckhardt in Hawthorne Grove, but I
assure you there is no risk, since he leaves
the following morning to catch the steamer
from Baltimore. I expect to arrive home on
the twenty-ninth, which should give us time
to get ready—Burckhardt will visit on the
seventh. This is the perfect occasion to try
out Maud, and see how she shapes.

Maud's breath quickened at the sight of her name.

By the by, how is Maud? It's been an
entire week without one of her blotchy

*little letters, and I feel quite neglected. Has
she forgotten me? I rejoice to hear that her
table manners are improving, though, to
judge from her letters, her grammar is not
yet perfect. Never mind, I have great hopes
for Maud. I am convinced she will be our
perfect little angel child—*

Maud glowed. An angel child! She caught a
glimpse of her face in the mirror and saw herself rosy
with happiness. She looked quite pretty. So that was
how Hyacinth saw her—as an angel child! Maud
was as astonished as she was delighted. At the Barbary
Asylum, every child was strictly classified: a girl was
pretty or plain, clever or stupid, good or bad. Maud
knew quite well that she was plain, clever, and bad.
She gave her reflection a disbelieving smile before returning to the letter.

*You might want to examine her and see if
she knows any hymns. "In the Sweet Bye
and Bye," I think, and "Blest Be the Tie
That Binds." We probably won't need them
for Burckhardt, when I shall assume the
role of the depressing Agnes—*

"Maud!"

Maud almost jumped out of her skin. Victoria stood in the doorway, dressed in her shawl and street clothes. Her face was so forbidding that Maud backed up, crumbling the letter behind her back.

"Maud, how could you? Reading my letter! Creeping into my bedroom behind my back!"

"I didn't," said Maud. It was the feeblest lie she had ever told, but her wits were so rattled she could think of nothing better.

"You did." Victoria's eyes were flashing behind her spectacles. "You're holding my letter behind your back—I can see it in the glass."

Maud switched tactics. "Why didn't you tell me Hyacinth was coming home?" she demanded.

For a second, Victoria simply stared. Then she stretched out her hand, palm upward. "Give me my letter."

Meekly, Maud put it into her hand.

"Has no one told you that it is *wrong* to read other people's letters?"

Maud wondered if she could get away with saying no. She opened her eyes wide, trying to look innocent and hurt. "I never got any letters at the Asylum." She had noticed that Victoria often looked sorry for her when she talked about the Asylum. She added, pleadingly, "Ma'am."

Neither the excuse nor the "ma'am" succeeded in softening Victoria's wrath. "It was very wrong of you. To read other people's letters is *vulgar*. Dishonest— and vulgar—and wrong. And what were you doing in my room?"

Maud's eyes darted back and forth, looking for an answer. She caught sight of the bookcase door, which was still ajar. She spoke breathlessly. "Please, Aunt Victoria, I didn't have anything to read."

This was a watertight lie. Both the Hawthorne sisters understood that Maud had a hunger for books that could not be satisfied.

"You ought to have waited and asked me for a book. You had no right to enter my room, and still less right to read my letter."

"Why don't Hyacinth write to me?"

The question surprised them both. Maud had not expected to ask, and Victoria was not prepared to answer. The old woman sidestepped the issue. "*Why doesn't,* not *Why don't.*"

"Why doesn't she, then?" persisted Maud. "I've written her. I've written her three times, and she doesn't write back."

"That is beside the point." Victoria swept aside

Maud's argument with the wave of a hand. "Don't try to distract me, Maud. You have done wrong, and you are going to be punished."

Maud had to choose between looking pleading and looking proud. She calculated the choice. Victoria was too indignant to be softened by pleading. Maud lifted her chin bravely: the child martyr.

"Go upstairs," said Victoria slowly, and Maud realized that Victoria hadn't yet figured out what the punishment ought to be. "Go upstairs and—take out your arithmetic book. You will do problems in long division for the next two hours. I will inspect your work tomorrow, and if you haven't done enough, you will work during playtime."

Privately Maud decided this was not too bad. If she had to do the arithmetic, she would miss her walk in the dreary garden.

"You will not come downstairs for the rest of the day," Victoria continued, "and none of us will speak to you until tomorrow morning. Muffet will bring your supper on a tray."

Cheered to learn there would be supper, Maud started to leave the room.

"Wait!" Victoria's voice was commanding. "Haven't you something to say to me?"

"What?" stammered Maud.

"Don't say *what*!" snapped Victoria. "It's rude! Oughtn't you apologize to me?"

Maud put her hands behind her back. During her years at the Asylum, she had mastered the art of the insincere apology. "I'm sorry I read your letter, ma'am," she said in a tone of voice that was grave and polite but didn't sound sorry in the least.

"I accept your apology," said Victoria. Her forgiveness was as frosty as Maud's apology was false.

When the clock struck six, Muffet brought the supper tray, putting an end to Maud's struggles with long division. Maud was surprised how glad she was to see the hired woman. She was used to being alone on the third floor, but the knowledge that she was being punished made her solitude irksome. She threw down her pencil and shoved her books to the floor, making room for the supper tray.

The plates were generously full: fried pork, corn bread, and apple fritters. Maud had anticipated that there would be no dessert, but there was a large bowl of Muffet's bread pudding, with a thick crust of cinnamon and sugar on top. Maud looked at Muffet's swarthy, unjudging face, and felt an urge to throw her arms around her. She pointed to the bowl and nodded. "Thank you," she said, pronouncing the words very clearly, as if that would enable the deaf woman to hear.

Muffet stepped closer. She took her forefinger and drew a line on Maud's face, starting from the eye and descending down the cheek. Maud pulled back, and then understood. "Oh!" she said. "You think I've been crying!" She imitated Muffet's gesture and shook her head. "Not crying," she said firmly.

Muffet shrugged. It might have meant anything, Maud knew, but it didn't. Muffet's shrug meant that Maud was lying, which she was.

"Well, maybe a little," Maud admitted. It went against the grain to admit that Victoria had made her cry, but Muffet wasn't going to tell anyone.

Muffet continued to gaze at her doubtfully. Maud understood why the hired girl was puzzled. Usually, Maud set the table and helped prepare supper. Tonight, she was confined to her room.

Muffet pressed her fingers against her forehead and assumed a look of anguish. Then she crossed her arms over her belly and doubled over. She straightened up, threw out her palms, and gazed inquiringly at Maud.

Maud giggled and shook her head. "No, I'm not sick." She thought for a moment, picked up a spare sheet of paper, and began to draw.

She drew two stick figures, one half the size of the other. The larger stick figure was Victoria—recognizable by her spectacles and the way she dressed her hair. In the drawing, the stick Victoria stood scowling down at a stick child. "See?" Maud pointed to the drawing. "Victoria's angry with me. I'm being punished."

Muffet reached for the pencil. She corrected Maud's drawing with a few masterful lines. A real Victoria emerged from the stick Victoria—a woman of soft curves and voluminous skirts, with a wide brow and an anxious expression. Maud had never seen a skillful artist draw, and the process fascinated her. She leaned closer. "How do you do that?"

Muffet understood Maud's excitement, if not the words. A gleam of pride came into her eyes.

"Draw me," begged Maud. She pointed to the paper, then to her own face.

Muffet studied her for perhaps ten seconds. Then her pencil began to move. Maud gazed, entranced, as her likeness appeared: a little girl with cropped hair and skeptical eyes. It was not a pretty portrait, but Maud was flattered. The girl in the drawing looked clever and resolute. She even had a certain panache. It struck Maud that Muffet must have observed her very carefully. For the first time, Maud wondered if the hired woman understood her life as a secret child. Did Muffet know the secret that was hidden from Maud?

An idea sprang into Maud's head. She thrust out her hand, palm up, and waggled her fingers imperiously. Muffet surrendered the pencil.

Maud printed her name underneath her portrait. MAUD. She said, "Maud," and tapped the paper. She repeated the name, thumping her breast. "Maud. See? Those letters make my name."

To Maud's delight, Muffet took back the pencil and copied the word. MAUD, she wrote, copying Maud's crooked A, which leaned to the right. The inscription was as exact as a forgery.

Maud nodded vigorously. "That's right, Muffet! See, these letters make a word! If you could learn to write letters—" Her voice died away. It dawned on her that Muffet would never be able to understand letters. She had no sounds with which to connect them. Even if the hired woman knew the secrets of the house, she would never be able to write them to Maud.

Muffet was tapping her breast. Maud realized with a twinge of pity that the woman wanted her own name. She pointed to Muffet and wrote MUFFET on the page.

Muffet shook her head. She took back the pencil and wrote a single word in a child's handwriting. The letters were rounder and softer than Maud's: ANNA.

Anna. At some point—perhaps when she was a little girl—someone had taught Muffet to write her name. Maud raised her eyebrows to signify a question. She pointed to Muffet. "Your name?"

Muffet struck her chest and then the word. ANNA. Then she reached over and struck the bed. She drew the briefest of sketches on the page—a four-poster like Maud's own. She extended the paper to Maud.

Maud wrote BED and passed it back.

Muffet moved around the room. She drew the chair, the table, the washstand. After each sketch, she passed the paper to Maud, who wrote CHAIR. TABLE. WASHSTAND. WINDOW. CURTAIN. COMB. BOOK.

Muffet copied each word. When there were a dozen words on the sheet of paper, she folded it and slipped it under the bib of her apron. Then she tapped her fingers against Maud's supper tray. Maud understood the gesture. She was being told to eat her supper while it was still hot.

Chapter Nine

On the day when Hyacinth was due to return, Maud waited on the third floor, eyes glued to the hole in the shutter.

She saw the hired carriage approach. Hyacinth descended, and the cabby lifted her trunks from the back of the carriage. Hyacinth's face was hidden by the brim of her hat. Maud wanted to rush headlong down the stairs and fling herself into Hyacinth's arms. Instead she waited, listening in vain for voices two floors below.

A bell jangled. The bells in the Hawthorne house, once used to summon the servants, had fallen into disuse when Muffet became the hired girl. Now the sisters rang to summon Maud.

Maud dashed from the room and clattered down the back steps. She flew to the parlor and hurled herself at Hyacinth, who put out her hands to catch her, holding her at arm's length.

"Maudy!" Hyacinth's face was so radiant that Maud scarcely felt the sting of the lost embrace. "My darling girl! Let me look at you!"

Maud lifted her chin, holding herself so straight that she quivered.

"I've brought you presents!" Hyacinth gestured toward the trunk and valises on the floor. "A string of green beads—Venetian glass, such trumpery, but so pretty! And a box of White Rose soap and a whole pound of saltwater taffy—there's another box for Judith and Victoria, so you don't have to share."

Maud beamed. Once again, Hyacinth had understood. At the Asylum, every treat that fell to an orphan's lot had to be shared. A box of peppermints or a bucket of ice cream was divided into microscopic parts and served with a reminder to be grateful. Maud always felt that her portion was particularly small. She was sick of sharing.

Victoria warned her sister, "You're encouraging her to be selfish," but Hyacinth only laughed.

"Oh hush, Victoria, you don't want Maud's salt-water taffy. Last time I brought it home, you complained it made your jaw sore." Hyacinth cupped her fingers around Maud's chin. "Your hair is much better cropped, do you know that? Not so ramshackle. Really, you are quite respectable." She turned to her sisters. "Shall we tell her?" she asked gaily. "Shall we tell her?"

Maud felt her fears dissolve. All at once, she knew that the secret that Hyacinth was going to tell was a delightful thing. She had been foolish to feel anxious about it, and still more foolish to try to puzzle it out for herself.

"Perhaps later," Judith answered. "Let the child settle. She's off her head with excitement."

"She missed you." Victoria's voice was reproachful. Maud understood that Victoria was speaking on her behalf, but she disapproved. She felt that she would have died before reproaching Hyacinth. "Let her get used to you being home—"

"Burckhardt is coming next week," Hyacinth pointed out.

"Very well," conceded Judith. "Tonight. After supper."

It was a glorious day. Maud helped Hyacinth unpack her trunk, putting away clean garments and relaying soiled ones downstairs to Muffet. To Maud's dismay, Muffet tried to waylay her whenever she appeared in the kitchen, brandishing a pencil and paper. Maud knew what she wanted; Muffet had developed a passion for nouns. Since the day of Maud's punishment, she had learned over a hundred, committing to memory the exact shape and order of Maud's letters. Maud was impressed by her quickness, but she had no time to waste. Hyacinth needed her. She dodged the hired woman, dropped Hyacinth's laundry in the basket beside the sink, and galloped upstairs to Hyacinth's bedroom.

In her absence, Hyacinth had unearthed more presents: a child-sized fan painted with poppies, a handful of hair ribbons, and a rock-candy goldfish too pretty to eat. Maud crowed over these and accepted the invitation to try on Hyacinth's new hat.

"It's ess-quisite," breathed Maud as the crown came down over her eyebrows, robbing her of half her vision.

"It's stylish, isn't it?" agreed Hyacinth. "Judith does croak so—and over the tiniest sums of money!—

but it's only economical to buy a good hat. You get so much more wear out of them when they're becoming. How are you doing with *Little Lord Fauntleroy?*"

Maud looked blank.

"I mean," explained Hyacinth, "do you know it well? Did you really read it?"

"I read it twice," Maud said pertly. "Didn't you read my letter?"

Hyacinth clapped her hands together. "Go and get it," she ordered, "and we'll read it together. Like a play. You can be Lord Fauntleroy and I'll be all the other characters."

Maud stopped halfway to the door. "Shouldn't you be Lord Fauntleroy?" she said anxiously. "He's the best part."

"No, you must be Fauntleroy," Hyacinth assured her. "I want to hear you be him."

Maud gave her a look of shining admiration. Not only was Hyacinth willing to play, but Maud was to have the starring role.

"Don't stand there mooning," Hyacinth said merrily. "Run and get it. Don't keep me waiting a second longer, you tiresome girl!"

Maud charged up the stairs.

*   *   *

After so heady and joyful an afternoon, supper was curiously subdued. Victoria and Judith had little to say. As the meal progressed and the evening wore on, the sisters spoke less and less.

Maud was also silent—not because she had nothing to say, but because she had resumed being perfectly good. In fact, she was showing off. Judith had told her that children should not speak at the table unless a grown-up spoke to them. Maud felt that this was as unjust as it was idiotic, but for one night only, she was willing to obey. From time to time, she stole a sideways glance at Hyacinth, checking to see if her good manners were making the proper impression. Hyacinth rewarded her with a smile that made her glow with happiness.

Maud was altogether blissful. For the first time, she was wearing the white muslin dress that was her best, and she was drunk with the glory of so much lace. Hyacinth had tied the bow of her sash and encouraged her to adorn herself with her new glass beads. Maud felt almost too fine to breathe. She sat dagger straight, cut her food into minuscule portions, and ate with impeccable daintiness.

Dessert was blancmange. Maud remembered not

to suck her spoon, or even to turn it upside down against her tongue, though this was a very pleasant thing to do and only the most evil-minded adult would consider it rude. She didn't scrape the bowl; when most of the pudding was gone, she folded her napkin and cupped her hands in her lap. After Muffet had cleared the plates away, Judith turned to Hyacinth. "You wanted to be the one to tell her."

"Yes," agreed Hyacinth. She looked at Maud, who gave a little bounce of excitement.

But it seemed that Hyacinth was not quite sure where to begin. Victoria rose and began to draw the curtains. Maud turned to watch. Afterward, it was that moment her eye remembered: the gathering dark outside the glass, the windows reflecting the candle flames and the four females in the room: Hyacinth in silver, Judith in gray, Victoria in dull green, herself in white. The clock in the hall struck seven.

"Maud," Hyacinth said softly, "what do you think happens when people die?"

This was not what Maud had been expecting, but she answered readily enough. "They go to heaven," she said primly. "Or they don't."

Silence repossessed the room. Hyacinth leaned closer to the candle flames, her eyes searching Maud's.

"Have you ever heard that there are spirits who come back from the grave in order to speak to the people who loved them?"

"You mean ghosts?" Maud's gaze strayed to the shadows of the room, checking the places where a ghost might materialize. "Miss Clarke said there was no such thing as ghosts."

"Not ghosts." Hyacinth's face crinkled with amusement. "We never say 'ghost,' child. Spirits. Good spirits who come back from the dead."

Maud shook her head.

"Jesus of Nazareth," Victoria said unexpectedly. "Jesus Christ rose from the dead."

Maud gave her a skeptical glance. "Jesus was different."

"What Victoria means," Hyacinth explained, "is that part of our Christian faith is the belief that the spirit cannot die. The body dies, but the spirit lives on after death."

"In heaven," Maud stipulated.

"Ye-es . . ." agreed Hyacinth, but she drew the word out, as if she didn't quite agree. "Do you know what spiritualism is, Maud?"

Again, Maud shook her head.

It was Victoria who answered. "Spiritualism is a religion. Spiritualists believe that the spirits of the dead dwell with God. They have been made pure, and they wish to help the living on earth."

"Victoria is a spiritualist," commented Judith.

Maud turned interested eyes on Victoria. "Is that why you never go to church?"

Hyacinth's smile broadened, but Victoria remained serious. "Yes, it is. Spiritualists don't believe that God is kept inside a church. We believe that He is present all around us, and He has no need of priests or ministers. We believe that all men and women—women, too, mind you—are equal in the sight of God. The Lord speaks directly to every one of us."

Maud considered this. "I *think* I'm a Catholic," she said politely, "but spiritualism sounds good, too. I like it that you don't go to church."

Hyacinth giggled. "Oh, Maud, you are the most delicious child!"—but Judith shook her head.

"We seem to be wandering from the point," complained Judith. "She doesn't have to know everything about spiritualism."

"I wanted her to know that there was another side—" began Victoria. Her cheeks were flushed with annoyance. This time it was Hyacinth who interrupted.

"You may tell her as much as you like later on.

Judith is right. We ought to go on. Maud, do you know what a medium is?"

Maud's puzzlement increased. "It's between good and bad," she answered. "Or hot or cold. It's halfway between two things."

"No," Hyacinth said. "Or rather, yes, that's one kind of medium, but there is another. In spiritualism, a medium is one who can call up the spirits of the dead."

"You mean—raise the ghosts?"

"Not ghosts," Hyacinth said irritably. "For heaven's sake, child, take that word out of your vocabulary! No, a medium is a person who stands between the living and the dead. The medium can put the living in touch with the spirits." She paused, waiting for the words to sink in. "And because a great many people miss their loved ones, sometimes they pay a medium a lot of money in order to speak with those who have gone before."

She let the words trail off. Maud gazed into Hyacinth's face. The old woman's eyes were sparkling with mischief and pride. Maud sensed that there was something she was meant to guess. When she realized what it was, her hand shot up, as if she were in school. "I know!" she cried out triumphantly. "You're a medium!"

Hyacinth nodded demurely. She lowered her lashes, her lips curved like the mouth of a cat. "I have that power, yes," she acknowledged. "Not always, but sometimes, the spirits speak through me—"

A thought flashed through Maud's head like a jag of lightning. "Could you find my mother?" she begged. She forgot her manners and knelt up on her chair, straining across the table toward Hyacinth. "Could you make it so I could talk to my mother?"

She was startled by the sound of Victoria's chair scraping against the floor. Victoria was halfway to the door. "I can't bear this," the old woman said in a low, taut voice. "Better to have a millstone around my neck and be cast into the sea—"

"Victoria, be quiet!" Judith commanded. "Come and sit. We have all agreed." She looked back toward Maud. "You have not been plain with her, Hyacinth. She's a sharp child, but she's still a child. You must tell her—truthfully—what we are and what you do."

"It sounds so coarse," protested Hyacinth.

"Very well, then, I will say it." Judith looked directly into Maud's eyes. "We are frauds, shams, tricksters. Hyacinth can no more raise the dead than I can fly to the moon. There is no way that you could use Hyacinth's powers to speak to your dead mother. There are no such powers."

"Judith—"

"Be quiet, Victoria. Let us be plain." Judith held up her hand for silence. "Victoria believes that there are genuine mediums—but I have never met with one. I never expect to meet one. *We* deal in trickery."

"Why?" asked Maud.

"Why?" Judith gave a short laugh. "Because there is money in trickery, and we need the money."

Maud leaned back in her chair. It was true then: the Hawthorne sisters weren't rich after all. Her eyes went from the silver candlesticks to the gold-framed pictures on the walls.

"This house is mortgaged," Judith said. "Victoria owns a cottage in Cape Calypso—we could sell that, except that is where we ply our trade. We seldom hold séances here, in Hawthorne Grove." She sounded scandalized by the very thought. "The Hawthornes have always been respected in Hawthorne Grove."

"What's a séance?" asked Maud.

Hyacinth leaned forward, her face crinkling with amusement and excitement. "A séance is like . . . oh, like a very exciting party game. People who want to talk to the dead sit around the table, with the lights very low—the spirits don't like the light, you see, which is just as well, because we don't like it, either.

It's so much easier to trick people in the dark. At any rate, once the lights are out, we pray or sing hymns, and after a while, the medium—that is, I—fall into a trance. It looks a bit like fainting, but I can still speak. Then the spirits of the dead talk to the living—using my voice, you understand. Or sometimes, the dead appear."

"I thought you said you couldn't do that," protested Maud.

"We can't *really* do it," Hyacinth explained, "but we can manage a very pretty little show. A mask at the end of a fishing pole, for example, is very effective. Remember, it's quite dark. People see a white face floating in midair, and they're sure it's dear old Cousin Lucy. Add a beard and it's Uncle Matthew."

"Do people really believe that?" Maud was incredulous.

"My poppet," said Hyacinth, "you would be amazed at what people believe. You must remember that the lights are low, and they came here wanting, longing—oh, *dying* to see Cousin Lucy or Uncle Matthew. And then, we prepare them, with music and darkness and prayers. . . . Your singing voice will be a godsend—so pure, so childish . . . and I brought you a little glockenspiel—I thought you might learn to play it."

"Me?"

"Of course, you," answered Hyacinth. "I knew the minute I saw you that you were just the person to help us. You're so tiny—you can fit into all sorts of places—under the table, in the map cupboard, even in the dumbwaiter, if need be. I'll teach you how to play the tambourine and how to make the chandelier swing in the wind when there isn't any wind—"

Maud's face broke out into a grin of stupefaction.

"And I'll teach you to be Caroline." Hyacinth reached across the table—Maud could have told her that this was bad manners—so that her fingertips brushed the hair by Maud's earlobe. The caress was so light that it made Maud's skin prickle. "We'll need a wig—Caroline had long ringlets. But—"

"Who's Caroline?" Maud knew that she had encountered the name recently, but she couldn't remember when.

"Caroline Lambert. The dead child of my very wealthy friend Mrs. Lambert. The drowned child. That's why I brought you home with me, my darling Maud—so that you could play the part of Caroline Lambert."

CHAPTER TEN

On the following day, Hyacinth took charge of Maud's education. Victoria's timetable was set aside and replaced with lessons in playacting, elocution, and music. The glockenspiel that Maud was to learn to play turned out to be a musical instrument made up of metal bars. Hyacinth showed Maud how to strike the notes with a little mallet so that the chimes rang out sweetly. Maud was enchanted. Never in her life had she tinkered with a musical instrument, and she was charmed to find she could make music. By the end of the first day, she had taught herself to hammer out tunes.

"She has such an ear for music," proclaimed Hyacinth. "I knew it the first day, when I heard her singing. Listen to her! Maud, you are altogether the cleverest child I ever saw."

Maud glowed at the praise. She continued to bang out "Mary Had a Little Lamb" until Judith announced that she had a headache and told Maud to take the glockenspiel up to the third floor.

"Judith is such a wet blanket," Hyacinth whispered as she and Maud tiptoed up the back stairs. "She doesn't *mind* the séances, but she never gets any fun out of them, poor thing. Of course, during the séances, the room will be dark. You'll have to make music without being able to see. You might as well practice that way—with your eyes shut."

"That's impossible," complained Maud, more for the pleasure of arguing than anything else. With Hyacinth's praise ringing in her ears, she felt she could do anything.

Hyacinth laughed softly. "It won't be so very difficult," she coaxed, touching the mallet to the tip of Maud's nose. "An ordinary child couldn't play music in the dark, but it will be nothing for you."

Maud ducked her head, trying to conceal her happiness. When Hyacinth teased and flattered her, she was helpless to resist. Once upstairs, she began to practice with her eyes squeezed shut, using her left hand to measure the space between the notes. It was less difficult than she had expected.

She found the glockenspiel so enthralling that she could hardly tear herself away long enough to eat. She abandoned her studies of history, geography, and arithmetic, and Hyacinth defended her. "It's nearly summer anyway," she told Victoria, "and music is essential to a young lady's education."

On the third day after Hyacinth's return, Maud made an earth-shaking discovery: she could play harmonies. If she struck one note with the mallet and another with the end of a pencil, she could make chords. She was banging her way up and down the scale when she heard heavy footsteps on the staircase. The footsteps were accompanied by a curious droning noise. It was Muffet.

Maud felt a twinge of conscience. It had been days since she provided Muffet with any new words. The hired woman had taken to staring hypnotically at Maud when she waited at table. She wanted more nouns. Maud sighed. She wished she could explain to Muffet just how fascinating the glockenspiel was.

Muffet came into the room. There was a look of wonder and rapture on her face. She held open a tattered book, which Maud recognized as collection of recipes. Muffet held out the book and pointed to the words *sugar, milk,* and *bowl.* These were words that Maud had taught her. All at once, Maud understood. Muffet was reading.

Maud's face lit up. "That's right, Muffet!" she exclaimed. "See, this book has lots of words you know—you might even be able to read a whole recipe!" She thumbed through the pages. "Here's one for apple pie—you know how to make that, and you know most of the words." She pointed them out. "Flour—lard—apples." She mimed washing. *Wash apples.* It was one of the verbs she had succeeded in teaching. "Wash and peel—"

Muffet shook her head. Her finger poked at the word *apple.* Maud had come to understand this gesture as a request for information.

"You know that one, Muffet. Apple." Maud made her hand into a circle and mimed taking a bite. "Apple."

Muffet dismissed the mime with another shake of the head.

Maud pointed to Muffet's pocket. "Give me your tablet," she said impatiently. She dug into Muffet's apron and took out the notebook that had become Muffet's dictionary. She leafed through the pages, looking for the drawings she had made. "Here. I taught you." She thumped the page, where she had drawn a circle with a stem. APPLE. She pointed at the word.

Obstinately, Muffet shook her head. She took a pencil from her pocket and copied the word from the book: *apple*. Then she thumped the page.

"I taught you that. See, it's right here—" Maud began. Then she groaned, seeing the problem. She had written the words for Muffet's dictionary in both capital and small letters, depending on her mood at the time. Muffet had learned the words exactly as written. To Muffet, the "apple" in the book had nothing to do with the APPLE Maud had taught her. Maud could have kicked herself. How would she ever explain to Muffet that capital letters were the same as small ones? She gazed at Muffet with such despair that the woman reached out to pat her cheek, as if begging pardon for causing trouble. Maud felt even guiltier.

A light footstep, a rustle of silk, and Hyacinth stood in the hall. "Gracious, what's this?" she asked.

Muffet moved quickly. With the swiftness of a conjuror, she pocketed the writing tablet. She closed the cookery book and hugged it between her arm and bosom.

Hyacinth cocked her head toward Muffet. "Haven't you got work to do?" She used both hands to mime sweeping the floor and pointed to the floor-boards. "Downstairs?"

Maud shifted uneasily. For a split second, she found herself disliking Hyacinth. It seemed to her that there was no need for Hyacinth to speak so sharply or stab her finger through the air with such energy. She reminded herself that Muffet could not hear; Muffet wouldn't catch the insulting note in Hyacinth's voice.

But Muffet understood. She lurched out of Maud's room, turning her back on Hyacinth with a suddenness that was as rude as Hyacinth's pantomime.

"What on earth was she doing here?" asked Hyacinth. "She ought to be preparing dinner. She wasn't bothering you, was she?"

"No," Maud said shortly. She remembered how she and Hyacinth had laughed at Muffet, likening her to a blacksmith in petticoats. She didn't know whether to be ashamed of Muffet or herself. "She's all right."

Hyacinth shrugged. "Come downstairs to the back parlor. I want to show you what to do for the séance."

"Will I play the glockenspiel?"

"No," Hyacinth answered. "That's for the Lambert séances—this is for Burckhardt. For next week." She saw the confusion in Maud's face. "Heavens, didn't I explain to you? Horace Burckhardt is coming here next week. He wants a séance, and I want you to participate."

"Does he have a dead daughter?"

"No. A dead wife. I'll be the dead wife—you won't have much to do, but Burckhardt's an easy client, and I want you to have a little practice." Hyacinth extended a hand. "Come along!"

Maud descended to the first floor. Evidently Victoria and Judith were out, as the rooms were empty. Hyacinth led her past the dining room. "The night of the séance, we'll have supper at six," she explained, "cheese soufflé, probably—people who want to see spirits shouldn't eat meat, though I can't think why. At any rate, by six o'clock, all of us will be in the dining room with the door shut. You'll be upstairs, with my little china clock. I want you to wait ten minutes before you come down. Then you come down the back steps—as quietly as you can—and

· · · 117 · · ·

creep into the back parlor. Now—when do you come downstairs?"

"Ten after six," Maud answered promptly.

"Good girl. We'll be in the dining room with the door shut, so there should be no danger of you being seen. In the back parlor, one lamp will be lit—the one with the red globe—and there will be light from two or three candles in the chandelier. You'll be barefoot and wearing your nightgown."

"My nightgown?" echoed Maud, shocked. Her education in music and manners might have been spotty, but both the nuns and Miss Kitteridge were in agreement about the shamefulness of being scantily clad. "With a strange man in the house?"

"Your asylum nightgown," repeated Hyacinth, "because it's skimpy. You're going to hide under the table, and the less you're wearing, the better. I don't want a bit of your skirt creeping out from under the tablecloth."

Maud squirmed. "But if he should see me—"

"If he sees you, there's more at stake than your modesty," snapped Hyacinth. Then her lips twitched; impatience had turned to amusement. "But he won't see you. Of course, if you would prefer to wear nothing at all, that would be even better. No danger of cloth showing—"

"I'll wear my nightgown," said Maud quickly. Hyacinth's sharpness had cowed her a little.

"Good. That's settled." Hyacinth went to the round table in the corner of the room and lifted the cloth. "Climb under here and see if there's room for you."

Maud obeyed. The table had been draped with two cloths: a dark green brocade that reached to the floor and an overcloth of creamy lace. Maud crawled underneath and sat with her knees close to her chest. The table was nearly three feet in diameter, with a single pedestal that poked into her behind.

"Can you see me?"

"No—not a bit. What about you? Can you see out?"

Maud squinted. "I can see where it's lighter and dark, but that's—ouch!" She had shifted position and sat on something hard. She pulled up the table-cloth to shed light on what it was. "What's this?"

Hyacinth took the funnel-shaped tube away from her. "It's an ear trumpet. You'll be using it at the end of the séance. If you speak into it, it makes your voice echo." She turned the trumpet so that the wide end was at her lips and half whispered, half sang. "Farewell, my only love! Farewell!"

Maud felt her skin crawl. Hyacinth's voice sounded exactly the way she imagined a ghost would sound.

"You try," ordered Hyacinth. "I'll be doing most of the talking, but I think I'll have you join me for the final farewell. Go ahead."

Maud tried to imitate Hyacinth's singsong. "Farewell, my only—" She giggled, and a cascade of eerie laughter came from the end of the trumpet.

"Maud." Hyacinth's voice was very firm. "You may *not* giggle during the séance."

Maud tried to control herself. She managed to gulp back the giggles, but her mouth twisted in a smirk.

"A little giggle is understandable during rehearsal, but unforgivable—*unforgivable*—during the séance. Do you understand?"

Maud's smirk vanished. "Yes, ma'am."

Hyacinth laughed. "Don't 'ma'am' me! That's for Judith and Victoria." She held the green cloth between her thumb and forefinger. "There's a little slit here, under the lace. Once the lights are out, you put the small end of the trumpet through the hole. The room will be dark, remember."

Maud searched for the open seam. Carefully she tilted the trumpet, guiding the small end through the hole. "Farewell, my love!" she whispered.

"Perfect. Very good. There's something else." Hyacinth lowered herself to sit on the floor. She took

Maud's hand and guided her fingers to the pedestal. "Feel that nail, Maud? And the other one, with the thread wrapped around it?"

Maud was already unwrapping the two threads. She pulled one, which had a wooden bead at the end. She was rewarded with a faint tinkling sound.

"That's the chandelier." Hyacinth pointed to the ceiling. "See, there's a thread that goes up the chain of the chandelier, and across the ceiling to an eye-screw"—she pointed—"where the ceiling meets the wall. Then the thread goes down the wall, through the cloth, and under the table. If you pull both ends of the thread, you can make the chandelier swing back and forth. Burckhardt will think the spirits are moving it."

Maud experimented with the threads, entranced by the movement of the big chandelier. "Won't Mr. Burckhardt see the thread?"

"No. Remember, it'll be dark. Besides—you didn't notice any threads when you came in the room, did you?"

"No, but I wasn't looking."

"Neither will Burckhardt be looking." Hyacinth tapped Maud's left hand. "Let go of the end without the bead."

Maud released the thread. Hyacinth took the other

end, winding the thread around her palm. "There. After you play with the chandelier a little, you let go of one end, pull, wind the thread round your fingers, and tuck it away. If anyone wants to examine the chandelier after the lights come back on, there will be no thread to find."

Maud raised herself to her knees, gazing at the ceiling. A fluttery feeling had come into her stomach. To creep downstairs at the right time, to make the chandelier sway without tangling the threads, to speak into the speaking trumpet . . . What if she could not manage it? She pointed to the eye screw at the edge of the molding. "What if Mr. Burckhardt notices the screw? Won't he wonder why it's there?"

Hyacinth shook her head. "He won't. For one thing, it's small. It's not very noticeable, even if you're looking for it. And the truth of the matter is, he won't be looking." She touched Maud's cheek with the tips of her fingers. "That's the most important thing of all, Maud. Not the tricks—they're simple. A child could find us out. But our clients don't want to find us out. They want to believe."

"But—"

"Take Burckhardt," Hyacinth went on, as if Maud had not spoken. "He's been coming to us for eight years. Never once has he examined the room or questioned any of our tricks. And why not? Because we understand him. We know what he wants and we make sure he gets it."

"And what he wants is to talk to ghosts?"

Hyacinth took Maud's hand and slapped it. "Bad girl! Stop saying 'ghosts'!"

Maud was startled. She had thought that Hyacinth wanted to hold her hand. "I'm sorry," she pleaded. The shock of the slap was greater than the pain.

"That's better." Hyacinth did not seem angry in the least. "I call Burckhardt the Weeping Walrus," she said dreamily. "Victoria says it's cruel, but he's very big and fat, you know, with one of those mustaches that hangs down like tusks. Everything he eats gets caught in it." She gave a little shudder and waited for Maud to laugh. "Gracious, you're not sulking, are you? Over that tiny, baby, little slap?"

Maud blinked. "No," she lied.

"That's good." Hyacinth rose from the floor and sank down into a chair. "Now, what was I saying? Oh, yes, Burckhardt. Burckhardt comes to see us because he wants to talk to Agnes, his dead wife. She's been dead thirty years. She wasn't much to look at—

an insipid, frog-eyed little thing—but he adored her. She died when she was only nineteen, a year after the wedding. Childbirth. It's a cruel world for women, Maudy."

Maud remained silent.

"Burckhardt never remarried. You should hear the airs he puts on about it—" Hyacinth's voice underwent a startling change, turning to a meaty tenor. Her mimicry was so remarkable that Maud jumped. "'When a Burckhardt loves, ma'am, he is true unto death!' That's what he says. Imagine being proud of being a Burckhardt."

"How do you do that?" gasped Maud. "You sound like a man!"

Hyacinth looked pleased. "I've always been clever with voices. I'll teach you, if I can—though not everyone has the knack of it. At any rate, Burckhardt gets lonely, the absurd thing, and he likes to remember being young and handsome—he *was* handsome once, I'll give him that; I saw his wedding photograph. So he comes to speak to Agnes." Hyacinth's voice became faint and girlish. "'Horace! My husband! I shall love you eternally!'" Then her voice deepened. "'Agnes! My angel! I am always true!' . . . He often cries; he's quite maudlin. People shouldn't carry on like that unless they're good-looking."

Maud agreed with Hyacinth. Men who looked like walruses should not weep.

"But now the plot thickens." Hyacinth leaned back luxuriously, violating the rule that no lady's shoulders should ever touch the back of a chair. "At the age of nearly sixty, Burckhardt has found himself a pretty little Englishwoman, a mere baby of forty-nine. After all that talk about being 'true,' he wants to get married again. Not that he's told us, mind you. I read of his engagement in the newspaper. If you mean to be a spiritualist, Maudy, you must always read the society pages. And the obituaries, of course."

Maud nodded.

"Now, here's a question that will show me how clever you are—and how well you've been listening. Imagine one Horace Burckhardt. He plans to marry, the wedding date is set, he's booked a steamer to carry him off to his new bride . . . but before he leaves the country, he wants one last séance. He wants to talk to Agnes. What does he want her to say?"

Maud pondered. She was beginning to be bored by Horace Burckhardt, even though she'd never met him. On the other hand, if this was a question to test her cleverness, she had better put her mind to it.

"Does he want to say good-bye?"

"Not quite. You're close, but not quite. He wants—" Hyacinth's voice bubbled with laughter. "He wants her *permission* to marry again. He wants to marry a new wife without feeling guilty about the old one. In other words, he wants to have his cake and eat it too."

"If I was Agnes, I'd be jealous," said Maud.

"No doubt. But Agnes will know her place. In short, Agnes will behave beautifully. As for Burckhardt, he's the easiest man in the world to fool, and very generous, which is good, as my summer dresses are getting a little shabby."

Maud said slowly, "What if he doesn't give you any money?"

Hyacinth shook her head. "Oh! Maud!" she gurgled. She rose from the chair and swept out of the room without looking back, leaving Maud with the feeling that she had just asked the stupidest question in the world.

CHAPTER ELEVEN

At ten after six on the night of the séance, Maud stole downstairs.

Never had it taken so long to go downstairs. She was in the habit of moving stealthily, but never before had she tried to walk in utter silence, without a single board creaking. Her very bones seemed to snap and bark. Her heart beat so fast that she was reminded of one of Miss Kitteridge's pet complaints: "palpitations." Maud had always thought the Superintendent's "palpitations" a myth, but the tympany below her breastbone hinted that there might be something to it after all.

From the dining room came the sounds of voices: one of them a man's. Maud paused, listening. It had been nearly two months since she heard the voice of an adult male, and the depth and strength of Mr. Burckhardt's voice surprised her. She heard the clink of plates and cutlery, and her stomach growled. She froze, wondering if it could be heard through the door, and then tiptoed away, secure in the knowledge that Muffet would feed her later.

The back parlor was dim but not frightening. The lamp, with its red globe, cast a cozy light. Maud's little white feet crossed the carpet rapidly. She crouched down, lifted the two tablecloths, and crawled under the table. The ear trumpet was in readiness: she made sure of the placement of the open seam in the cloth and the threads that would control the movement of the chandelier. Then she waited.

It was very hot. Maud had chosen to wear her underclothing under her nightgown, and already she regretted it. There seemed to be no air under the table, and in five minutes she was damp with sweat, though her hands were cold and clammy. As the time passed, her heartbeat slowed. Maud had begun to feel almost drowsy when she heard the door of the dining room open.

"Come into the back parlor—there's a table there," Victoria was saying.

The unfamiliar voice of Mr. Burckhardt answered her: "I cannot tell you ladies how grateful I am—how much I appreciate the attempt—"

Judith spoke next. She sounded disapproving, as she so often did with Maud—for a brief moment, Maud experienced a wave of sympathy for the Weeping Walrus. "I hope the attempt will be a brief one, Mr. Burckhardt. You must remember that these attempts take a good deal out of my sister. Hyacinth is not strong. After the last séance, she was seriously unwell. We were forced to have the doctor three times that week."

Mr. Burckhardt spoke again: "I cannot tell you how sorry I am to hear it. Believe me, I wish I need not put you to such trouble. . . . If there is anything I can do—" He seemed flustered. "At least let me be responsible for the expense of the doctor—"

"Always so generous!" It was Hyacinth's voice, but she sounded fluttery and unsure of herself. "Please, Judith, don't scold him! He *must* try—I feel it. You know I have an instinct for such things. I almost feel as if . . ." She paused. "You will think me silly, I'm sure, but I feel as if someone from the other side *wants* me to try."

There was a brief silence. Then Victoria said reluctantly, "It's true that you are sensitive to such things."

"Miss Hawthorne is a true medium," Mr. Burckhardt said reverently.

Maud heard the sound of chairs scraping against carpet. The participants of the séance were seating themselves around the table. Hyacinth said, "Oh no! My gift is a very small one! And it's so hard for me— you cannot guess how difficult it is!" Maud put her fingers over her lips, cautioning herself not to giggle. "If you only knew, dear Horace, how I long to be able to help you—and yet I may fail!"

"Stop fussing," Judith commanded. "Mr. Burckhardt, you must take my sister's hand."

Maud listened intently. She wished she could lift the tablecloth and take a peek.

"Shall we begin with a hymn?" asked Victoria.

They had come to the part of the program that had been rehearsed. Victoria began "In the Sweet Bye and Bye," and the others joined in. Maud was surprised by how good they sounded. She knew that

Victoria had a fine contralto voice, but the beauty of Burckhardt's tenor surprised her. He sang harmony—Maud would have liked to listen, to understand the notes he chose, but she had work to do. After the second verse, Maud began to sing along: *But no words, just "ah"—and softly,* as Hyacinth had cautioned her. *It will suggest the idea of a heavenly choir. If you hear Burckhardt stop singing, you stop, too—you don't want him to ask himself where the voices are coming from.*

Burckhardt did not stop to listen. The tune went to the end, and then Victoria began "Blest Be the Tie That Binds." As they began the final verse, Maud's fingers unwound the two threads. She then began to pull gently, still singing her angelic "ah."

For perhaps five seconds, no one noticed. Then Burckhardt gasped, "The chandelier!" and Maud heard the tinkling of the prisms.

"Be still!" commanded Judith. "Don't move! Hyacinth has fallen into a trance—it is death to startle her now!"

"The spirits are here," Burckhardt whispered hoarsely. "I heard them as we sang. They are close at hand—they are in the room!"

Gleefully, Maud continued to manipulate the

strings. The tinkling was louder now. It was a pity she couldn't watch.

"Look!" Victoria's voice was hushed. "One of the candles has gone out. And there's another!"

This, too, was no surprise. Judith had doctored the candles, cutting the wicks short and digging out the wax around them. As the candles swung back and forth, the molten wax doused the flames.

"Agnes?" queried Burckhardt. Hyacinth had mimicked his intonation with deadly accuracy, but she had failed to convey the anguish in his tones. "Agnes, is it you?"

Maud let go of one thread. Steadily, noiselessly, she wound it around her hand. The tinkling of the prisms was subdued.

"Is there a spirit present?" intoned Judith.

Rap!

Maud felt her skin creep. She had not expected this. She had no idea what was making the rapping noise.

"If there is a spirit present," Judith said doggedly, "rap once for *yes* and twice for *no*."

Rap!

"Agnes!" cried Burckhardt. His voice shook with emotion. "Agnes, is it you?"

There was no response. Maud heard the sound of chairs shifting. Then she heard a voice, low and sweet—Hyacinth's voice, though it had undergone a change. It was breathy and faraway, as if it came from the ends of the earth. "Horace—?"

"Agnes!" bellowed Burckhardt, like a bull in agony. Once again, Maud covered her mouth with her hand. "Oh, Agnes, my angel! My only love!"

"Dear Horace!" There was the faintest hint of laughter in the ghostly voice. "Am I truly your only love? Now?"

There was a pregnant pause; then Maud heard a creak from the table. She wondered if Burckhardt had collapsed. "Oh, Agnes! Do not torment me! In my heart, I have always been true!"

"Dear Horace!" Only Hyacinth's voice could be so bell-like. "I am not angry. I know you have always been faithful."

"The bride of my youth," gasped Mr. Burckhardt. He was sobbing. Maud had never heard a man sob before. Something about the sound made her throat ache. She remembered Hyacinth saying, "People shouldn't carry on like that unless they're good-looking." She swallowed.

"I have never forgotten you, my beloved Agnes!

The way you looked on our wedding day—like a white lily, a lily of the valley—"

"Horace—" Though the voice was still sweet, Mr. Burckhardt's sentiments had been cut off, almost as if Agnes didn't want to hear any more love talk. "Horace, my darling, I must be quick! The medium's power is waning! I have only a few moments left—"

"Speak to me, my love!"

Maud's flash of sympathy flickered and died. She bit her hand to keep from snickering.

"Horace, I am your bride for all time. When you join me in the great beyond, I will be yours eternally. But now—in the world of the living—you have claimed another love. There is another who will be your bride."

Burckhardt gulped. "It is true. Forgive me, my angel! I have been so lonely—but I will cast her aside if you wish it, Agnes! I will love only you!"

"You do not understand," the silvery voice chided. "My darling Horace, you have been faithful too long! The time has come for you to love again! It is your earthly duty!"

There was a pause. Burckhardt was adjusting to his amazement. "Agnes!" he sobbed.

Good heavens, thought Maud.

"God has chosen this woman for you! Love her as best you can!" commanded Agnes/Hyacinth. "Shelter and protect her! When you come to the land of light, we shall both be thine! And now, farewell!" Hyacinth's voice was dying away. "Farewell, my darling, my only love! Horace, farewell!"

Maud picked up the ear trumpet and fumbled for the open seam, inserting the mouth of the instrument through the slit. *After three farewells,* Hyacinth had cautioned her. *Wait for your cue.*

"Agnes, do not leave me!" begged Mr. Burckhardt. "Stay a little longer! Comfort me!"

"Farewell, my only love! I am always your own Agnes," breathed Hyacinth—and Maud joined in, whispering through the ear trumpet. She and Hyacinth had practiced intoning the words in unison. The effect was both haunting and precise. "Darling Horace, farewell!"

The final line was Maud's alone. She knew that Hyacinth had fallen back in her chair so that her face was tilted upward, toward the light. Burckhardt would see that the medium's lips were still, but the ghostly voice would go on speaking. "I will be yours . . . always!"

In the silence that followed, Maud withdrew the

ear trumpet from the slit. She could hear Burckhardt gulping back sobs. Since he was making a good bit of noise, Maud shifted slightly, squirming into a more comfortable position. *Next time,* she thought, *I won't wear so much underwear.*

"The spirit has passed," stated Judith.

"Hyacinth?" said Victoria. Maud heard footsteps, the rustle of skirts, a light slapping sound. "Hyacinth, awake! Oh, heavens—she is so pale—she's in a swoon. Hyacinth, come back!"

"Her pulse is rapid." It was Burckhardt speaking. "Oh, God forgive me—what have I done? Shall I go for a doctor?"

Maud heard a gasping sound from Hyacinth. After a moment, Judith announced, "No. She's better—her eyes are open—"

"Judith?" Hyacinth sounded babyishly meek. "I—I feel so queer. And oh, Mr. Burckhardt, I'm sorry! I—I had no strength. The spirits did not come."

"The spirit came," Burckhardt told her. "How can I thank you enough?"

Judith's voice directed him. "Help me support her—she must go to bed at once—oh, that's better! Can you carry her all the way up the stairs?"

"Easily," gasped Burckhardt valiantly. "She weighs nothing."

The conversation dissolved into murmuring, the voices growing more distant. Maud heard "nervous strain," "all unselfishness," "true medium," and "sea air." Then there was the sound of footsteps receding and footsteps on the stairs. At long last, Maud was alone. She lifted the tablecloth and crawled out. The fresh air was cool against her sweaty face.

CHAPTER TWELVE

Maud," announced Hyacinth at the breakfast table, "was magnificent."

Maud stopped chewing her bacon and tried to look magnificent. It was the morning after the séance, and a lovely one: the sunlight stole through the lace curtains and dappled the tablecloth. Maud was eager to discuss the séance. She felt like an actor after a successful show. She knew she had done well, and she was ready for the others to tell her so. Unfortunately, Judith was scanning the columns of the newspaper; Victoria was removing the crusts from her toast.

"She was," insisted Hyacinth. "I told you she would be."

Judith looked up. "She did well enough," she remarked, to Maud's disgust. Judith felt that lavish praise, like rich food, was bad for children.

"She did a good deal better than well enough," Hyacinth insisted, defending her protégée. "She did everything at exactly the right time, and she never giggled once. And her singing was perfect—neither too loud nor too soft."

"Did we get the money?" inquired Maud, slathering her toast with marmalade.

It was the wrong thing to say. Hyacinth made a little moue of distaste. Victoria looked at Maud as if she were a dead mouse in the pantry. "Really, Maud!"

"Why shouldn't she ask about the money?" broke in Judith. "What we do, we do for money. The child's part of it now. She might as well speak plainly."

Maud flashed Judith a look of astonished gratitude. She could scarcely believe that Judith, the strictest of the sisters, was taking up for her.

"Very well, then." Victoria pushed her plate away. "We will speak plainly. Mr. Burckhardt gave us the money—enough to pay for doctors that Hyacinth doesn't need and a bit more so that Hyacinth can travel to Cape Calypso for sea air. It seems that Mr. Burckhardt has forgotten that we own the cottage in Cape Calypso—"

"I didn't remind him," Hyacinth put in nimbly.

"—and gave us money for rent," concluded Victoria. "So yes, Maud, we got the money. Quite a lot of it, since Burckhardt is as openhanded as he is foolish."

Maud regarded Victoria warily. The older woman looked as if she had scarcely slept. Her hair was bundled up any old way, and her collar was open. Usually she wore a cameo with a lady's head. Maud missed it. She wished Victoria would go upstairs and tidy herself up.

"Speaking of the cottage in Cape Calypso," Hyacinth said silkily, "why don't you tell Maud how we came by it, Victoria? Your morals weren't always as dainty as they are now—were they?"

Victoria gave her sister one murderous glance. Then she rose so violently that her chair rocked back and fell over. Without another word, she swept out of the room.

Judith righted the chair. She frowned at her sister. "You go too far."

"It's such a waste," said Hyacinth. "She used to be a perfectly good medium. Now she's turned pious. It's such a bad example for Maud."

Judith jerked her head in Maud's direction. "Do you really think she can play Caroline Lambert?"

"I'm sure of it," Hyacinth said staunchly. "You should hear her read the part of Lord Fauntleroy — you wouldn't think it, but she's sweet. She's quite the little actress."

"Do you really think that reading *Little Lord Fauntleroy* will prepare her?"

"I don't see why not," Hyacinth answered serenely. "As long as she's properly rehearsed, she ought to be able to play any number of angel children — female or male. She's quite convincing as a boy, actually — makes Fauntleroy a bit less precious. It's a pity no one's lost a little boy."

Maud leaned across the table. "Is that why we read Lord Fauntleroy? I thought we were just playing."

Judith said slowly, "Hyacinth doesn't play."

"No," agreed Hyacinth. "I wanted you to make a special study of Fauntleroy because he was an angel child. Sweet and pure and polite. Grieving parents always fancy they've lost a little angel child."

Maud sat back in her chair, crestfallen. So that was what Hyacinth had meant in her letter: *She will be our perfect little angel child.* She had been alluding to Maud's acting ability. It had been foolish to imagine that anyone, even Hyacinth, would consider Maud angelic. Maud felt her cheeks getting hot. She was glad no one knew the mistake she had made.

"Is she too boyish to play Caroline?"

"No," answered Hyacinth, "and besides, Caroline Lambert was a little hoyden. Otherwise she wouldn't have drowned."

The word *drowned* got Maud's attention. "Why did she drown?"

Hyacinth gazed across the table, out the window. Her eyes were dreamy.

> "'O Mary, go and call the cattle home,
>   And call the cattle home,
>   And call the cattle home,
>   Across the sands of Dee.'
>   The western wind was wild and dank with foam,
>   And all alone went she."

There was a brief silence, followed by Maud's "What?"

"A very sensible question," Judith said approvingly. "Don't be poetical, Hyacinth—it tries my nerves and the child doesn't appreciate it. Hyacinth is reciting poetry about a girl who drowned, but poetry doesn't come into it. Caroline Lambert died because she went bathing when her mother forbade it."

"She was alone." Hyacinth took up the story. "It was the last day of her holiday in Cape Calypso, and there'd been a storm the night before. Caroline wanted to go to the ocean one last time, but her mother—Eleanor Lambert—was too busy packing."

"Eleanor Lambert spoiled that child."

Hyacinth shrugged. "Undoubtedly. At any rate, that was one morning when Caroline didn't get her way. Her mother was too busy to take her to the ocean, and Caroline wasn't allowed to go by herself. Then Caroline changed her tune. She wanted to ride the flying horses—"

"What flying horses?" asked Maud.

"The horses on the carousel." Hyacinth saw that Maud had not yet understood. "Gracious, child, haven't you seen a carousel?"

Maud shook her head.

"It's a ride at the amusement park. The carousel, the flying horses, the merry-go-round—"

"I've heard of merry-go-rounds," Maud said, eager to regain ground. "Only I've never seen one."

"There's a fine one in Cape Calypso. The wood

carvings are splendid—horses and tigers and zebras. There's even a giraffe—and a tabby cat—all kinds of animals. Caroline's favorite was a sort of sea monster. Odd to think of that now, isn't it?"

Maud had a hazy but dazzling image of herself on the back of a tiger. She wore the white dress trimmed with lace, and her scarlet sash fluttered in the breeze. "Will I ride the merry-go-round?"

"It isn't likely," answered Judith, dashing her hopes. "Remember, in Cape Calypso, you'll be even more of a secret than you are here. You'll be spending most of your time in the attic."

Maud digested this news in silence.

"Eventually"—Hyacinth raised her voice and went on with the story she was telling—"Caroline Lambert switched her plea from *one last swim* to *one last ride*. The carousel was close to the hotel where they were staying. Caroline knew the way—she was in the habit of riding every day. So Mrs. Lambert emptied her purse into Caroline's greedy little paws and told her to come back when the money was spent. Only she never came back."

Maud's imagination conjured up another picture: another little girl, almost her twin, vanishing into thin air. "Maybe she didn't drown," she said tentatively. "Maybe someone kidnapped her. Or she ran away."

"She drowned," Judith informed her. "First she went to the carousel and spent her mother's money. Then she went in the water—in her street clothes, not her bathing dress. They found the body. She was her mother's only child."

"*They row'd her in across the rolling foam,*
The cruel crawling foam,
The cruel hungry foam,
To her grave beside the sea."

"Hyacinth," Judith said disdainfully.

Maud considered the fate of Caroline Lambert. It frightened her that a child had died. It was sadder and scarier than Mr. Burckhardt's silly Agnes. "What did she look like?"

"Tall for her age—she was eight. Exceptionally pretty, by all accounts. Long curls. An angel child," Hyacinth answered.

Maud's sympathy for the victim wavered and dissolved.

"She'll need a wig," Judith reminded her sister.

"I know that." Hyacinth sounded offended. "I've

ordered one from a theatrical costumer." She directed her attention back to Maud. "Eleanor Lambert offered five thousand dollars to any medium who could produce a genuine manifestation of her child."

Maud's head jerked up. "Five thousand dollars?"

"Five thousand dollars. Enough to pay off the mortgage with a comfortable balance left over." Judith looked straight into Maud's eyes. "You see how much is at stake."

"It won't be easy," Hyacinth warned Maud. "Unlike Burckhardt, Eleanor Lambert is no fool. And she's been tricked before. Last year, she employed a certain Madame Zauberlicht. She caught the medium pretending to be Caroline."

"How could a grown-up pretend to be a little girl?"

"She was walking around the room on her knees," Hyacinth explained. "The idiot! Eleanor Lambert reached for her child and found a grown woman kneeling by her chair. It was grotesque. Zauberlicht was ruined, and a good thing too. People like that give the profession a bad name."

"Hyacinth has spent the last year trying to gain Mrs. Lambert's trust," Judith told Maud. "That's why she's spent so much time in Cape Calypso. She's managed to persuade Eleanor Lambert that there *are* honest mediums—and that she's one of them."

"She trusts me," Hyacinth said. "She is fond of me, even. She's almost ready . . . and now we have Maud." She brushed her palm against Maud's cheek. "You see, Maudy? Do you see why we need you so badly?"

Maud nodded, grave-faced. She saw.

CHAPTER THIRTEEN

Hyacinth was restless. Maud had come to see the power of Hyacinth's moods: if she was merry, the household seemed brighter; if she was angry or bored, the house fell silent, and the silence was ominous. In the days that followed the séance, Hyacinth's moods changed a dozen times. Sometimes she darted about like a moth, astonishing Maud with her energy, teasing and flattering so deftly that Maud danced on air. At other times, she withdrew to her room, wanting only to be alone. Maud knocked at her bedroom door, but no one answered, and the door stayed locked.

It was not only Hyacinth who seemed on edge. Victoria had not forgiven her sister for what she had said about the cottage in Cape Calypso; her manner was stiff and cold. Even Judith seemed to have altered a little. She was more matter-of-fact than usual, signaling that she was not going to be drawn into the quarrel between her sisters.

Maud felt the tension like an itch. She had spent a good bit of her life battling grown-ups—there were even times when she found it stimulating—but she didn't like it when grown-ups quarreled among themselves. After all the fuss they made about children quarreling, they ought to be able to get along. Maud took her cue from Judith and tried to act as if nothing were the matter.

On the days when Hyacinth remained behind closed doors and Victoria brooded, Maud was left to amuse herself. She continued to tinker with the glockenspiel, and she made a set of alphabet cards for Muffet. It wasn't easy to persuade Muffet that capital letters and small letters were two versions of the same thing—like tablespoons and teaspoons— but once the hired woman grasped the concept, she tackled the cookery book afresh. Maud spent a lot of time in the kitchen, acting out recipes for Muffet's benefit. When the bell rang, she dropped everything to run upstairs to Hyacinth. On one occasion, Hyacinth sent her away the moment she arrived; on another Maud was encouraged to peacock about in Hyacinth's old ball gowns while Hyacinth sat on the bed and applauded.

Most often Maud was summoned to rehearse. Now that she knew that the readings of *Little Lord Fauntleroy* were more than a game, she found them a little nerve-racking. Hyacinth was strict about her speech. "*Lit-tle,* not *liddle,*" she said sharply. "And *pret-ty,* not *priddy.* And don't singsong! You sound like an Irish nursemaid!"

"I am Irish," Maud said proudly. "My mother was Irish."

"Me mither was Eye-e-rish," mimicked Hyacinth.

Maud's eyes flashed. "I didn't say it like that!" *And you'd better not make fun of my mother,* she thought, but she held her tongue.

Hyacinth seemed to sense she had gone too far. She twinkled her fingers in a gesture that might have been an apology. "*Did-ent,* not *dint.*"

"I bet Caroline Lambert didn't say *did-ent,*" said Maud.

Hyacinth's face broke out in a smile. "I bet she didn't, either. Nevertheless, after she drowned, she became an angel child, and angel children speak prettily. *Pret-till-lee,* if you please."

"Pret-till-lee," Maud echoed, pronouncing the word so crisply that spittle flew from her lips.

"Very good. Open your mouth, please."

Maud opened, worrying that her teeth were not clean. She had brushed them that morning, but Hyacinth's standards were very high. All at once she felt something round and soft against her tongue.

"Have a caramel," Hyacinth invited her. "You didn't see my fingers move, did you? That's called sleight of hand—I'll teach you later. As for now, run along, and don't let me see your little face till after dinner."

Maud withdrew, obedient to the letter. As she tiptoed upstairs to her bedroom, she wondered what else she could do to make Hyacinth love her. According to her own standards, she was being very good, but Hyacinth seemed less impressed by goodness than other grown-ups were. Maud thought about the little girls she read about in books, who nestled into the hearts of adoring friends and relations. They were usually very pretty, with long curly hair. Maud had no curls, and though her eyes were blue, it wasn't the sort of blue that people got excited about. The faint hollow in one cheek that she had hoped might be a dimple didn't seem to work properly. What could she do if she lacked the equipment to win Hyacinth's heart?

She supposed she might fall ill. Children in books were often ill, or they had dreadful accidents that left them unable to walk. Maud imagined herself in Hyacinth's bed, with Victoria and Judith weeping and Hyacinth stroking her forehead. "My poor darling," Hyacinth would say softly, while Maud was most beautifully ill, delicate and pale like a little white snowdrop. . . . Unfortunately, children who were ill often died. Maud felt that this was taking things too far. She preferred to model herself on Lord Fauntleroy, whom everyone loved even though he was healthy. She wondered if there was anything Fauntleroy did that might endear her to Hyacinth.

A week stretched to twelve days. Then a telegram arrived for Hyacinth: Eleanor Lambert, who had been visiting relatives in Boston, had returned early to Cape Calypso. She looked forward to seeing the Misses Hawthorne again.

Hyacinth made up her mind at once. She and Judith would return to Cape Calypso immediately.

Would Maud be a darling girl and help Hyacinth pack?

Maud agreed to be a darling girl, but her stomach knotted. Nothing had been said about her going with Hyacinth, and she dreaded being left behind. She wrapped waists and skirts in tissue paper and counted out gloves, hoping that Hyacinth would see that she was too useful to be abandoned. At last she could bear the suspense no longer. "Mayn't I come with you?" she begged, careful of her grammar. "Please?"

"You'll come soon," Hyacinth assured her, "but not yet. Mrs. Lambert has invited Judith and me to stay at her hotel. We'll go first and get the cottage ready for summer, and then you'll come, with Victoria and Muffet. Only remember, once we're in Cape Calypso, we mustn't be seen together. Mrs. Lambert must never suspect that you're my little girl."

Maud was slightly softened by that "my little girl," though her heart was heavy. Faster than she wished, the trunks were packed and she trailed Hyacinth down the stairs. She knew that once the hired carriage arrived, she would be banished to the third floor. In the days to come, she would have no one to talk to but Muffet, who couldn't talk back, and Victoria, who would think of new ways she ought to be improved. She descended the stairs as slowly as she could, leaning away from the balustrade and dragging her feet.

Judith frowned at her from the front hall. "Don't pull on the banister. And pick up your feet. You'll wear out the carpet."

Maud looked daggers at her.

"Maud!" said Hyacinth. "Come and kiss me!"

Maud hesitated. Then she obeyed. If Hyacinth was leaving, she wanted to say good-bye properly. "Do you want me to write to you?"

"Certainly," answered Hyacinth. "Write and tell me everything."

"There won't *be* much 'everything,'" Maud said darkly. "It's dull here without you."

"That's polite," remarked Judith. She nodded toward the parlor door. Victoria stood in the doorway. She had come to bid her sisters good-bye. Maud hadn't seen her there.

Maud knew she had been rude. She glanced apprehensively at Victoria, and her heart sank. "I'm sorry, Aunt Victoria," she said.

"It doesn't matter," replied Victoria, so gravely that Maud knew that her feelings had been hurt.

Maud knotted her fingers behind her back. "I didn't mean *you* were dull," she pleaded. "It's just that—" She risked a glance at Hyacinth, who was watching her with amused tenderness. All at once, Maud knew just what she wanted to say. "It's just that I love Dearest more than anyone else in the world."

She took a deep breath. The idea that she might call Hyacinth "Dearest" had occurred to her two days ago, but until now she hadn't dared speak the word. She was surprised by how sweet it sounded— exactly like Lord Fauntleroy. She waited for Hyacinth's response.

"Maud"—Hyacinth's voice quavered—"*what* did you call me?"

Maud licked her lips. "Dearest," she said tentatively.

"Dearest?" Hyacinth's face lit up. "Oh, Maud! Do you really think you're Little Lord Fauntleroy and I'm your mother?"

All at once Maud knew she had made a terrible mistake. "I meant—it was a joke," she said hastily.

But it was too late. "'Maud—pretending to be Lord Fauntleroy! 'Dearest'!'" Hyacinth chortled. "What a funny little girl you are, Maud Flynn!"

To Maud's horror, she felt her eyes fill with tears. "It was a *joke*," she insisted frantically, but Hyacinth's laughter drowned out her words. "Maud—trying to be Little Lord Fauntleroy!" Laughter trilled from her, and even Judith succumbed to a rusty chuckle.

Then Victoria said, "The hack's come," and Maud saw her chance to escape. She turned on her heel and rushed upstairs, not troubling to mute her footsteps.

She ran to her room and sank down on the floor. Her cheeks burned with embarrassment. She had never been more humiliated in her life—not even when Miss Kitteridge hauled up her petticoat and spanked her in front of the entire orphanage. *Do you really think you're Little Lord Fauntleroy and I'm your mother?* Oh! Maud wanted to crawl under the bed and hide, like a sick animal. She moaned with shame, covering her mouth with her hands.

The bedroom door creaked. Maud raised an anguished, blotchy face and glowered at Victoria.

"Maud?" Victoria said. She broke off. "I've never seen you cry before."

Maud's eyes darted around the room, seeking a missile. The closest thing at hand was a discarded stocking. Maud grabbed it and hurled it at Victoria.

It was not an effective weapon. Victoria was not even annoyed. She sat down on the bed. With some difficulty, she began to lower herself to the floor. "I'm sorry Hyacinth hurt your feelings," she said. "Sometimes Hyacinth makes fun of things that other people . . . don't. My dear, it isn't so bad as all that! Don't cry so!"

"I *hate* Hyacinth," stormed Maud, and all at once, it was true. She thought of her unanswered letters and unanswered questions, of the times when Hyacinth pinched or slapped playfully and it hurt. She remembered a hundred slights she had managed to ignore because she wanted Hyacinth to be perfect.

"No, you don't," soothed Victoria, and Maud felt her heart twist: that was true, too. She adored Hyacinth, and Hyacinth had laughed at her and left without saying sorry or good-bye. Her sobs rose to a wail.

Victoria put her arm around Maud's shoulder. "It was very unkind of Hyacinth. It was cruel of her to laugh at you. Maud, listen to me. It isn't wrong to be affectionate. And it isn't funny, either."

Maud wiped her nose on her wrist and scowled at Victoria. She wished the old woman would put both arms around her and hug her properly. Victoria always got everything wrong.

"I think," Victoria said hesitantly, "I think *Dearest* is a lovely thing to call someone. I would love to have someone call me *Dearest*."

"I'm never going to call anyone *Dearest* again," Maud said savagely.

PART TWO

THE
DROWNED
CHILD

Summer 1909

CHAPTER FOURTEEN

On the morning of the journey to Cape Calypso, Maud rose before dawn and followed Victoria through the woods, retracing the path that had brought her to Hawthorne Grove three months ago. The morning was foggy and humid; the sun had not yet risen. Without Hyacinth, Maud found the semi-darkness of the wood less enchanting than before. She was glad to emerge from the shadow of the trees and take her place on the station platform. Victoria stooped and kissed her cheek.

"Remember," Victoria said, "Muffet and I will get on at the very next stop. We'll sit where you can see us. It's better if you don't speak to us, but if you think you can't manage, or someone frightens you, come to me."

"I can manage," Maud said curtly. Her stomach was upset. She wasn't used to eating breakfast in the dark, and her whole body felt queer.

Victoria glanced along the platform. "The farmers will be here soon," she said. "You won't be alone long. Remember—don't talk to strangers. Do you have your ticket and your money?"

"I've got it." Maud unclenched her fist and showed a knotted-up handkerchief. A rectangle of cardboard showed through the cloth.

"Don't lose it." Victoria seemed reluctant to leave her. She looked up at the sky. "I don't think it's going to rain, but if it does, your parasol—"

"It won't rain," Maud said impatiently. She knew what Victoria was going to say: if it rained, she could use her new parasol as an umbrella. As far as Maud was concerned, this was useless advice. The parasol was made of silk, and Maud had no intention of subjecting it to water spots. If it rained, she would fling herself on top of it in order to protect it. "Hadn't you better go?" It was the whole point of getting up early and coming to this place—that no one should see her with Victoria.

Victoria's lips tightened. "Don't be rude," she admonished Maud. "It's disrespectful to speak to me like that. I only want to make sure—" She broke off. "Muffet and I will get on at the next station," she repeated.

"Yes, ma'am," said Maud. Victoria studied her for a moment and then turned away. A moment later she had vanished into the mist.

The farmers' carts arrived a few minutes later. Victoria had explained to Maud that this was where the train picked up milk from the neighboring farms. Maud kept to the farthest corner of the platform, hoping that none of the men would speak to her. She had her answer ready: if anyone asked what she was doing there, she would reply that she was not allowed to talk to strangers.

But nobody asked. If the farmers noticed her, they were too busy to be curious. Before the sky was fully light, the train came. Maud was glad to board it. She felt exposed, standing on the platform, surrounded by fog and dingy sky.

"Ticket?" asked the conductor, and Maud

unknotted her handkerchief and handed it over. "This is a grown-up ticket, missy. Children under ten are half fares."

Don't let anyone ask you questions, Hyacinth had warned in her letter. *They'll feel sorry for you because you're little, and try to make you talk. Don't let them.*

"I'm eleven," Maud said pertly. "I guess I know what sort of ticket I ought to buy."

The conductor wrinkled his nose. Maud could tell he had changed his mind about her. She was no longer a helpless innocent who ought to ride half-price. She was a stuck-up little thing who could be trusted to look after herself. Maud selected an empty seat and turned her face to the window. *Don't talk to strange men,* Victoria had warned her. *Little girls have been kidnapped because they talked to strange men.* Maud was inclined to scoff at the idea of kidnappers—if people really wanted children, there wouldn't be so many leftovers at the Barbary Asylum—but she couldn't forget Victoria's words.

The train began to move. Maud fixed her eyes on the scene outside the glass. After spending three months confined to the Hawthorne house, the red barns and wide pastures appeared almost exotic. She craned her neck to watch a collie dog chase a squirrel.

The train slowed again. It had come to the station in Hawthorne Grove. On the platform was Victoria, clad in her best fawn-colored suit—and Muffet. Maud goggled at the hired woman. She had never seen Muffet wear anything but a print housedress. Now she saw that Muffet owned a jacket and skirt in a plaid so bright it was almost scarlet. Her hat was covered with what looked like hundreds of blood-red cherries. Maud was guiltily grateful that it was Victoria who traveled with Muffet and not herself. She could see the other passengers turning to stare at the hired woman; no doubt Muffet was making the noises Maud had learned to take for granted.

The two women took seats several rows ahead of Maud's. Maud let out her breath. She was safe. Later, when they came to the next station, she would follow Victoria at a distance. "We'll buy our tickets and watch to make sure you've got yours," Victoria had promised. "Then we'll make sure you get on the right train, and get on after you."

Changing stations went according to plan. The second station was large and crowded, but Maud elbowed her way into the line where Victoria and

Muffet waited. The gentleman behind her subjected her to an offended stare, but he didn't say anything. Maud avoided his gaze and raised her chin. She felt that she was getting away with something akin to murder. At the Barbary Asylum, "butting in" was a serious crime.

The second train was more crowded than the first. Maud looked for a seat by a window and found none. She passed Muffet and Victoria without looking at them and sat down beside a large, fat man who was smoking a cigar. It seemed to Maud that this was exactly the sort of stranger Victoria had warned her against, and she responded to his cheerful "Foggy this morning, ain't it?" with a chilling silence. She sat as far away from him as she could, with her elbows held in and her buttocks tight. An hour later, when he got off the train, she slid over to the window with a sigh of relief.

The view outside the window had changed. The land was flatter than it had been, and the mist had burned off. Half of the sky had turned from gray to blue; it was going to be bright after all. She would be able to raise her parasol to keep off the sun.

"Are you all alone, dear?" A motherly-looking woman with a little boy in her arms leaned across the aisle to speak to Maud. "Where are your mama and papa?"

Mama and Papa. How babyish. Maud's nostrils flared as she pronounced the words Hyacinth had supplied. "If you please," she said, with the utmost distinctness, "my mother would rather I didn't converse with strangers."

The lady drew back, shifting the little boy in her lap. Maud saw that she felt rebuffed. *Make sure you say "converse" instead of "talk,"* Hyacinth had cautioned. *You look younger than you are. You'll need to sound older.*

Hyacinth. In a little while, she would see Hyacinth again. The prospect filled her with longing and terror. She prayed that Hyacinth would be glad to see her, that she would kiss her or touch her cheek, that she would give some sign that she was the real Hyacinth, the one who was worthy of Maud's love. Maud's stomach tightened. Better to think of something else. In a little while she would see the ocean. Rumor had it that the ocean was well worth seeing, and today would be her only chance to look at it. Once she arrived at Victoria's cottage on Ocean Street, she would remain within. She could not risk being seen. Eleanor Lambert had promised five thousand dollars to the person who could produce a manifestation of her dead child.

Maud tensed in her seat. She knew how important it was to perform well during the séances. She had practiced the glockenspiel and memorized five pages of information about Caroline Lambert. Hyacinth had sent the information to Maud, accompanied by a letter and a package.

My darling Maud,

Why haven't you written, you wicked child? No, don't answer me—I know quite well why you haven't written, because Victoria has written me twice, dreadful scolding letters about what an unfit guardian I am. She says I broke your little heart when I said I didn't want to be your "Dearest." Did I? I hope I didn't. The truth is, I've never much cared for Lord Fauntleroy, and I can't endure his mother. They are both too sweet. If I'd wanted a sickly, sweetish, vapid little girl, I'd have adopted one. But I wanted a child like you—someone tart rather than sweet, and clever enough to help with the family business.

So don't be cross, my darling girl. I
can't bear it. And do accept the enclosed as
a peace offering. It will match your dress
with the rosebuds, and you will be a perfect
little picture when you saunter down the
boardwalk at Cape Calypso.

Now, about the journey. You must see
that it would be fatal for anyone to see you
traveling with Victoria . . .

Maud's eyes fell to the parasol that hung from a ribbon around her wrist. The ribbon had etched a line into her flesh, but she didn't mind that—the parasol itself was still immaculate; she had been right to hold it instead of leaning it against her knee. She recalled the thrill of unwrapping it. First the brown paper and string, then the ribbon, then the box with its rustling tissue paper, and last of all the parasol, striped green and pink and festooned with lace. Maud had not known that parasols for little girls existed. She had never thought to own such a luxury.

"That's Hyacinth all over," Victoria had said. "She just likes buying things—anything pretty. . . . Where on earth will you carry it? You'll be spending all your time indoors."

It was true. Maud's face fell. She sensed that

Victoria was hoping she would dismiss the gift entirely—stand on her dignity and refuse to be bought. It was a point that Maud could appreciate; it would be fine, somehow, to stay angry at Hyacinth and thrust aside the parasol as if she didn't like it. But she did like it. She felt that she had never seen anything so pretty in her life, and she wanted it dreadfully. She wanted to promenade down the boardwalk of Cape Calypso with her boots shined and her dress starched and the parasol raised above her head.

A flurry of wings outside the window drew Maud's attention away from the parasol. White birds, bigger than pigeons, with dark edges to their wings. Maud opened her mouth to ask the motherly lady what they were, and then shut it. The conductor was shouting "Cape Calypso!" and the train was slowing to a stop.

Maud never forgot her first walk down the board-walk. The sky had cleared and the wind had risen. Maud felt the pull of the breeze against her parasol; the scalloped edge trembled violently. She felt that if she let go of the handle, the parasol would sail off like a kite. Beyond the circle of cloth, the sky was intensely blue.

And wide. Over the ocean, the sky was immeasurable. Maud gazed at the two vastnesses in wonder. The brilliance of sun on water made her blink. Before her was a world she had never thought to imagine: the pale, clean-looking sand, the foaming water, the jeering white birds against the blue.

Maud stole a glance over her shoulder. Victoria and Muffet were behind her, strolling arm in arm. Slowly, drawing out her steps, Maud processed down the boardwalk. She had a map of the streets in her head. When she came to Ocean Street, she would turn left and go two blocks. *Our cottage is sage green,* Hyacinth had written. *You must look up and down the street to make sure no one is looking and then dart between the left side and the hedge. Knock on the back door. I'll be waiting to let you in.*

The signs on the boardwalk vied for Maud's attention. FRANKFURTERS, SALT WATER TAFFY, ICE-CREAM SODAS, PING-PONG. What, Maud wondered, was Ping-Pong? It sounded delicious. The smell of frankfurters made her nostrils quiver; she wished she had money to buy one, or ice cream, or Ping-Pong.

She spun the handle of her parasol between her fingers and watched the stripes blur. She dawdled: she was going to make it last, this one lovely saunter down the street. She strolled slowly, admiring herself in the mirror of her imagination. Around her was a loosely connected crowd: ladies and gentlemen and children, all enjoying the breeze for which Cape Calypso was famous. The women wore parasols and enormous hats; many were dressed in white. It dawned upon Maud that they were different from the grown-ups she had known. They had no work to do. They had left their cares behind, in Philadelphia, Baltimore, and New York; they had come to this town for pleasure. It was oddly uplifting to be among such idle, genteel people. Maud tried to fancy she was one of them. There were children down by the water, wading and splashing; she envisioned herself with the ocean frothing around her ankles. She felt a pang of surprise when she realized that she would never be allowed to wade in the ocean.

All at once, she could not bear it. With quick fingers, she collapsed her parasol and took off across the sand, heading straight for the water.

Or such was her intention. Running in sand was harder than she had expected. She stumbled and almost fell. Righting herself, she scuffed on, not looking back. What could Victoria do to her, after all? She couldn't call after her. She would just have to wait until Maud came back.

The sand beneath her boots grew firmer. Maud looked down and saw that it had changed color. It was grainy, dark gold, smudged as if with charcoal. She was almost at the edge of the water. She could smell the salt and feel the coolness of the spray against her shins. Her eyes followed the movement of the waves.

She had never seen waves before. Her eye rested upon them, fascinated; how much time passed, or how many waves she tracked, she had no idea. Farther out to sea, they weren't waves at all, only mounds, like furrows in a field. Then, somehow, each mound rose to an edge, thin as the blade of knife. The knife-edge tilted, the wave coiled, and there was a moment when it seemed as if it must break—and yet it did not. Then a line of brightness, crooked and notched like paper catching fire, rippled across the top edge of the wave. The water crashed and erupted, droplets spurting straight up and leapfrogging off the surface of the foam.

"Do you want to play?"

Maud dragged her eyes away from the ocean. A girl her own age had come to stand beside her. She was holding out a spade. "We're making a castle. Do you want to play, too?" The girl gestured toward a patch of sand several yards back. Two little boys labored over a series of sandy hillocks and low walls. Maud understood at once that this was what was meant by a castle. Her eyes searched the girl's face. It was a round, sunburned face, with clear green eyes. The strange girl wasn't trying to trick her. She was inviting her to play. Of course, Maud realized, the girl had never visited the Barbary Asylum. She had no way of knowing that Maud was nasty. All the same, it was a remarkable thing, as unexpected as the ocean itself.

For a split second, Maud entertained the invitation. She could put her parasol somewhere safe, so that the ocean couldn't carry it off. Perhaps she might remove her shoes and stockings—the other girl had done so; it must be a thing one could do. She pictured herself kneeling in the moist sand. Her fingers almost closed around the handle of the spade. Then she snatched back her hand. "I can't," she told the other girl, and fled.

CHAPTER FIFTEEN

Victoria's cottage was a four-story house with a porch that wrapped around three sides. Maud had little time to study it; as Hyacinth had ordered, she checked to make sure it was the right house, glanced up and down the street, and lunged for the shelter of the hedge. From the hedge, she darted to the back porch. The kitchen door opened before her fingers touched the knob. "There you are!" hissed Hyacinth, seizing her by the forearm. "What took you so long? I've been waiting and waiting."

Maud kissed the cheek that was held to her lips, catching a whiff of violets. She had a confused impression of an untidy kitchen: torn linoleum, shuttered windows, and a sink full of dirty dishes. Hyacinth whisked her past the kitchen table, and up a flight of stairs—steep, narrow stairs, like the ones at the Barbary Asylum.

"You must always use the back steps," Hyacinth whispered as she guided Maud ahead of her. "And whisper—always whisper. We have to keep the windows open, because of the heat. You mustn't forget." She paused at the first landing and leaned against the balustrade.

"It's hot," whispered Maud.

"It is," admitted Hyacinth. She lifted her skirt and resumed the climb. "Hot air rises. Something to do with science, I believe. However, one grows used to it, and there's often a breeze at night." She nodded for Maud to go on ahead. They mounted a second flight of stairs and a third. The final flight had no handrail, but ran straight through the floor of the attic. Both Maud and Hyacinth were panting when they emerged from the stairwell.

"Here's your room," gasped Hyacinth, "at the back of the house. The other side of the wall's—the box room—where we keep our trunks—and then Muffet—has the front."

Maud surveyed her new quarters dubiously. She saw a high iron bed with a white counterpane. The dresser was carved oak, with a tarnished mirror that showed only the top of her head. On the washstand was a pitcher decorated with daisies, a matching washbowl—and, on the bottom shelf, a large chamber pot. Maud raised her eyes to Hyacinth's face. She was afraid to ask.

Hyacinth read her thoughts. "My poor child, don't look at me like that! Of course we have a water closet!" She fingered the lace at her collar. "It's on the first floor, off the back hall. Mr. Llewellyn—the man who left the cottage to Victoria—had it put in years ago, along with the electric lights. I just wanted to prepare you for when we have visitors—you mightn't be able to go downstairs—" She paused apologetically.

Maud sank down on the bed and looked up at the ceiling. The roof slanted down on either side. Both walls and ceiling were papered: red diamonds on a snuff-colored background. It was not a pattern that appealed to Maud. She was hot, thirsty, and disheartened. She had risen before dawn, taken two trains, seen the ocean, and narrowly avoided making a friend. She was in no state to bear up against chamber pots and ugly wallpaper.

"We'll show you the rest of the house tonight," Hyacinth assured her. "It's better downstairs. The only thing is, we're closer to the neighbors than we were in Hawthorne Grove, and the windows are open. You'll have to be twice as quiet as before."

Maud nodded. She glanced at the windows, half expecting to see bars against the glass.

"The curtains are sewn together down the middle and tacked to the window frame," Hyacinth explained, "which helps keep out mosquitoes." She sat down next to Maud and slipped an arm around her shoulders. "Maudy," she said softly, "what's the matter? Are you homesick?"

Maud nodded a second time. She could not have said what home she was missing, but "Poor Maudy," murmured Hyacinth, and Maud closed her eyes and leaned against her. She wished she could curl up against Hyacinth and fall asleep, like the little boy on the train. But the attic was hot. If she leaned too long or nestled too close, she ran the risk of being pushed away. She straightened up, opened her eyes, and blurted out, "I don't like the wallpaper."

Hyacinth looked shocked. "Oh, you mustn't like the wallpaper!" she flashed back. "It's quite un-speakable! I should be ashamed of you, Maud Flynn, if you liked the wallpaper."

Maud felt a surge of relief. Once again, Hyacinth was on her side, sympathizing with her even when she was rude. She could not keep from smiling. "I like the parasol you sent me," she said huskily, "but I missed you."

"And I missed you." Hyacinth flicked a lock of hair away from Maud's ear. "But we'll talk tonight." She rose from the bed. "I've left you my little clock. I want you to come downstairs at seven-thirty. By then it will be dusk, and we won't have callers. I'll show you the house and tell you about the next séance." And with that promise, she slipped down the stairs, sinking from sight as if through a trapdoor.

Maud overslept. After supper, she lay down to rest, meaning to keep one eye on the clock. In ten minutes, she had fallen asleep. When she opened her eyes, the room was dim, and it was quarter past eight. She scrambled to her feet and splashed water on her face.

Groggily, on tiptoe, she descended the stairs. All the doors in the back hall were closed. Maud turned the knobs stealthily, opening each one a crack. The first led to the kitchen, the second to the water closet.

The third door opened into a room scarcely six feet wide. A streetlight shone through the single window, illuminating a row of glass-fronted bookcases. There was a globe in one corner, and a marble bust of a man in a wig. Maud realized that the room had been a library. It had been chopped in half to make room for the water closet.

A voice spoke from the far side of the wall. Maud stepped forward, listening.

"You assured me this would be the end of it," accused Victoria. "That was what we agreed—"

"But we're just getting established!" Hyacinth sounded exasperated. "This summer alone, I've been asked everywhere. Not just for séances, but to speak—I've half a dozen engagements in the next month. And if Eleanor Lambert—"

Victoria interrupted. "You said we'd get the money for the mortgage and stop," she insisted. "Judith, you were there. We said—"

It was Hyacinth who answered, not Judith. "Eleanor Lambert is just the beginning. Only consider, Victoria! Once we've convinced Eleanor

Lambert, we'll meet others in her circle. People who wouldn't trust an ordinary medium, people who are discreet—"

"People whose children have died," Victoria said harshly. "Judith, this is *wrong*."

"Of course it's wrong," Judith said flatly. "But we need the money. During the last two weeks, we've had the expense of two households—"

"We could economize," pleaded Victoria.

"You could and I could. Hyacinth won't. The mortgage must be paid. Muffet doesn't cost much, but we have to give her something. Even Maud is an expense."

Maud felt her stomach twist in terror.

"Maud is a godsend," Hyacinth said vehemently, to Maud's unutterable relief. "Really, Victoria! Have you no imagination? Can't you see the possibilities now that we have Maud? Besides, it's a waste—to adopt her and train her and stop after—"

"We should never have taken her," Victoria said bitterly. "To force her to go on and on . . . This is the worst possible home for her." She sounded close to tears. "It's not just that she's a child; it's the kind of child she *is*."

Maud let out a yelp of outrage. Her hands came

up to cover her lips. She stood rigid, hoping the sisters had not heard her cry.

Victoria went on passionately. "If we can't take her back to the Asylum, we ought to send her away to school—"

"And how will we pay for the school?" Judith gave a short, mirthless laugh. "For heaven's sake, Victoria! I don't like Hyacinth's schemes any more than you do, but I don't see how we are to live without money."

"There must be something—" Victoria began.

"Are we likely to marry, do you think?" Judith's sarcasm was withering. "Do you suppose anyone wants to hire a seventy-year-old housekeeper? Or a factory worker?"

Maud had heard enough. She stepped out of the half library and headed for the door at the far end of the passage. She turned the doorknob and stalked inside.

The three women turned to face her. Hyacinth's cheeks were becomingly flushed; Victoria's were mottled with anger. Judith might have been sitting for a portrait, her face was so calm and still.

"There you are!" Hyacinth sounded as merry as if the three sisters had been having a party.

"Welcome to the back parlor. The front parlor's larger, but this is where we'll have the séances." She extended her hand as if she were about to lead Maud into a dance.

Maud took stock of the room. There was stained glass in the side windows and a chandelier overhead. The walls were hung with dark blue paper and oil paintings of ships. Maud nodded toward the round table in front of her. "Is that where I'll be hiding? Under there?"

Hyacinth shook her head. "No. That's where we sit. We have something much better for you." She crossed the room and ran her fingers over the carved mantelpiece. "Watch."

The side of the mantelpiece swung outward, revealing a closetlike space.

"You see?" Hyacinth flickered her fingers inside the dark cavity. "This house was built as a summer cottage. The fireplace isn't real and the mantelpiece is hollow. Mr. Llewellyn used to keep his maps inside. It's the perfect place to hide you." She nodded encouragingly. "Come closer."

Maud peered inside, intrigued. The space was roughly twenty inches deep and twenty inches wide.

"She's too tall," Judith said waspishly.

"She isn't," contradicted Hyacinth. "Show her, Maud. Go in and pull the door shut after you. See, there's a handle on the inside of the door."

Maud stepped into the cavity. "I told you," Hyacinth said triumphantly. "I knew she'd fit the first time I saw her."

Maud shifted uneasily. The fit was tight. If she stood on tiptoe, her head thumped against the top of the mantel; if she put her hands on her waist, both elbows touched wood. She wished she hadn't read about Oliver Twist sleeping among the coffins. The image came back to her now, and she had a feeling it would come back to her when she was shut up inside and the cupboard was dark.

"Try closing the door," Hyacinth encouraged her.

Maud took the handle and pulled the panel shut. In the darkness, her eyes searched for the crack of light around the panel. It was hair thin. "How do I get out?"

"Just push." Victoria's voice sounded close by; she must have left her chair and come to stand by the mantel. "Anywhere. The door fits snugly—we glued felt on the sides—but it doesn't latch. You can always get out."

Maud pressed her fingertips to the door panel and pushed. As Victoria had assured her, the door opened with a soft *shhh* of wool against wood. Maud emerged from the cabinet. She shook herself, like a cat coming out the rain. "How long does it take for people to run out of air and die?"

Hyacinth looked insulted. "Have you lost your mind? Do you think we'd put you in that closet if there wasn't any air?"

Maud hesitated.

"There's plenty of air," Judith assured her. "The back of the mantel faces a bookcase on the other side of the wall. We drilled airholes behind the books."

"If she's frightened, she could wait in the hallway and slip in when it's dark," Victoria said worriedly.

Maud looked daggers at her. "I'm not frightened," she said scornfully. "But I can't play the glockenspiel in there. There isn't room."

"Oh, the glockenspiel!" Hyacinth shrugged, as if the glockenspiel were no longer of importance. "We won't be using that." She reached past Victoria to capture Maud's hand. "Come and see what you'll be wearing."

Maud followed Victoria to the table. Before her were a number of objects, only one of which made sense to her. Her fingers stole out to touch the yellow wig. "Is that mine?"

"Yes and no." Hyacinth smiled. "It's Caroline Lambert's."

Maud drew her fingers back. Her shoulders twitched in an involuntary shudder. "You mean—they cut off her hair after she drowned?"

"No." Hyacinth and Victoria spoke at the same instant. Victoria looked as horrified as Maud felt. "Even Hyacinth wouldn't—"

Judith spoke up, drowning out the voices of her sisters. "The wig came from a theatrical costumer. You needn't be afraid to touch it."

"What I meant," Hyacinth sounded both offended and amused, "is that it was Caroline Lambert who had long curls, not you. Really, Maud! I sometimes think you have a morbid streak. You must strive to overcome it. Cultivate wholesome thoughts."

Maud scowled. She hated it when she couldn't tell whether Hyacinth was making fun of her. She picked up the wig and draped it over her fist. The ringlets bounced and rippled.

"Try it on," Hyacinth said eagerly. "It's a very good wig. I insisted on the best quality."

Maud pulled the wig over her head. She tucked her own hair under the edges and asked, "How do I look?"

If she had hoped for admiration, her hopes were dashed. All three sisters regarded her with the same startled expression. Maud searched the room for a mirror and saw one over the mantel. She pulled a chair over and climbed up to gaze at herself.

It was a severe disappointment. Ever since she could remember, she had yearned for hair like the hair she had just put on. She had always thought that if she had ringlets, the rest of her would improve; somehow her pointed witch's chin would grow round and dimpled, and her forehead wouldn't look so bony. Instead, she appeared plainer than usual. The yellow curls robbed her skin of color, and her face looked small and pinched.

"In the dark—" Hyacinth said, making the best of things.

"Yes, of course. In the dark she will do very well." Judith cleared her throat. "Maud, stop preening and put the wig back. There's no need to wear it now."

Maud stuck her tongue out at the mirror and yanked off the wig. She put it down on the table, on top of a thin wooden board. The board was inscribed with the letters of the alphabet, pictures of the sun and moon, and the words YES, NO, and GOOD-BYE.

"What's this?"

"Don't point," Judith said crisply. "It's a Ouija board. People use them in séances. Mrs. Lambert wants to try one."

"This is the planchette—" Hyacinth directed Maud's attention to a small three-legged table shaped like an arrowhead. "It moves over the board and points out the letters." She placed the tips of her fingers on the planchette and pushed the little table over the board. M-A-U-D spelled the planchette.

Maud eyed the board with interest. She was thinking of Muffet. She had finished Muffet's alphabet cards, but there were only twenty-six of them, not enough for words with double letters. The Ouija board would make it easier to spell out sentences.

"Maud." Hyacinth was recalling her attention. "Have you ever seen a Ouija board used?"

"No, ma'am."

"Then pay attention." Hyacinth drew aside a chair and sat down. "Two people sit with their fingers on the planchette. One asks a question and the planchette spells out the answer. Quite ordinary people use the Ouija board—one needn't be a medium. The planchette will move for almost anyone."

"How does it move?"

Hyacinth laughed. "Oh, someone pushes it!" She

put up her hand to silence Victoria, who looked as if she was about to object. "People don't realize they're pushing. That's the best thing about it. The only trouble is, the board says such silly things."

"What kind of things?"

"Nonsense. The sort of things people say in dreams." Hyacinth lifted her wrists and let her hands fall back in her lap. "That's why I don't like it. You don't have much control over what it says."

"Then why—" began Maud.

"Because Mrs. Lambert insisted," Hyacinth answered. She picked up a dark, shiny object and pushed it across the table to Maud. "What do you make of that?"

Maud studied it. It was a large toy cricket, made of tin. Hyacinth's smile seemed to imply that there was something special about it, but Maud thought it was ugly. She hoped it wasn't meant to be a present.

"Press it against the table. No—not the whole thing—the tail end."

Maud snapped the cricket's tail. The thin metal let out a loud, sharp *Rap!* It was a sound Maud had heard before. "Oh!" she exclaimed. "So that's how—at the séance!"

"Yes." Hyacinth's smile was dazzling. "Of course, Judith can make rapping sounds, too—with her heel, with her thumbs—but the clicker toy is particularly useful at séances. I always have one—sometimes I wear two." She lowered her voice to answer Maud's unspoken question. "Underneath. Under my petticoats."

Maud averted her eyes, embarrassed. She didn't want to criticize Hyacinth, even in her thoughts, but it seemed to her that there was something very unladylike about wearing a tin bug under one's petticoats. "Do I have to wear one?"

"No. But you do have to do your very best in the days to come." Hyacinth leaned across the table and looked into Maud's eyes. "You must remember Mrs. Lambert has been tricked before. Our performance must be perfect."

Maud nodded earnestly. "Yes, ma'am."

"When Mrs. Lambert first came to me, she was suspicious. I could tell—and I knew not to rush her. I knew it would be a mistake to make Caroline appear too soon. People don't believe when things happen too fast. So I held back. Every time we tried to contact Caroline, we failed. And every time we failed, Eleanor Lambert became more convinced that she could trust me. Now it is time to succeed." Hyacinth lifted one hand and brushed her fingers against her palm. "I have arranged it so that she is exactly ready."

She opened her fingers. A seashell lay in the hollow of her hand. Maud blinked.

"We'll begin with a present." Hyacinth handed the shell to Maud. "Caroline Lambert collected shells. On the night of the first séance, you'll leave this on the table for her mother to find. A gift from the dead."

Maud warmed the shell in her hand. Her mind drew away from the dark room and the séance that was to come. All at once she seemed to see the sharp blueness of the sky and the white gulls over the water. She envisioned Caroline, lucky Caroline, dabbling her feet at the edge of the ocean, stooping to pick up shells. Maud felt a surge of envy. Caroline had been curly-haired and lovely and spoiled. She had played by the ocean and ridden on the merry-go-round. . . .

"Maud," Hyacinth said gently.

Maud jerked her attention back to the room. She pulled out a chair and sat down so that her back was to Judith and Victoria. She folded her hands on top of the table and lifted her eyes to Hyacinth's face. "Tell me what to do," she said, and Hyacinth smiled her sweetest smile and began to instruct her in the art of the séance.

CHAPTER SIXTEEN

Now, Muffet," said Maud in her bossiest voice, "pay attention."

It was a foolish thing to say. Muffet was already paying attention. The hired woman leaned forward, her palms flat against the kitchen table. Her eyes were fixed on Maud's lips.

"See, Muffet," Maud continued, "this is the planchette, and it spells. Watch." She moved the alphabet cards to spell out M-I-L-K and repeated the word with the planchette. "*Milk*. You know that one." She went to the icebox, took out the bottle of milk, and hoisted it into the air. "Milk."

Muffet glowered. She crossed the room, snatched the bottle from Maud, and slammed it back in the icebox. Maud, who had grown familiar with Muffet's language of gesture and expression, had no trouble understanding this: *Put that back. It'll go sour.* Maud glanced around the kitchen, spied an empty jar, and carried it over to the Ouija board. "Jar, Muffet. J-A-R."

Muffet took the planchette and flipped it upside down, so that the three peg legs were up in the air. Then she smacked her palm against the cookery book.

Maud sighed. The cookery book had become an obsession with Muffet. Every day she circled words that she wanted Maud to explain. Maud did her best and had managed to convey the meanings of *slice, fry,* and *boil,* of *put in, take out,* and *sprinkle over*—but now Muffet wanted to know what *the* meant. Maud feared that *the* would be her Waterloo. She was surprised to realize that she had no idea what *the* meant.

"That's not a real word, Muffet," she said earnestly. "It's a stupid word. It doesn't mean anything."

Muffet pushed the book closer to Maud and

ruffled through the pages. Her forefinger jabbed the circled word. The. The. The.

Maud shrugged, miming, *I don't know.*

Muffet's eyes narrowed in suspicion.

"I can't tell you," Maud said. She threw out her arms and raised her eyes to the ceiling. *I give up.*

Muffet shook her head, frustrated. She put the jar back on the shelf, took the towel off the bread bowl, and brought the bowl to the table. One hand slashed the air, and Maud read the gesture. *Get that thing off the table. I need room to work.*

Maud removed the Ouija board and went to sit by the window. In the last week, she had come to spend more and more time in the kitchen. Summer had settled over Cape Calypso, and the temperature rose a little every day. By late afternoon, the attic was almost unbearable. Maud knew that if Hyacinth were to see her sitting by the window—where one of the neighbors might glimpse her shadow against the screen—she would be in trouble. Luckily, Hyacinth seldom descended to the kitchen. Maud thumbed through her copy of Andersen's *Fairy Tales,* in search of "The Snow Queen." The Snow Queen's palace, with its corridors of glittering ice, sounded distinctly attractive.

Muffet squealed, raised her fist, and buried it in the bread. The soft dough collapsed with a sigh of protest. For a moment, Maud watched as the hired woman folded and thumped the dough. The muscles in Muffet's hirsute arms were impressive. During the past week, the hired woman had scrubbed every inch of the slovenly kitchen and patched the floor with squares of linoleum from the attic. She had white-washed the walls and blacked the stove. In the back-yard, she was digging a garden; every night, after the dishes were done, she disappeared into the dusk and came back with an apron full of young plants. Whether she hypnotized the neighbors into giving them to her or dug them up without permission, Maud had no way of knowing, but the garden was coming along nicely. Muffet had tried to entice her out of doors to admire it, but Maud refused, shaking her head until the hired woman gave up.

Maud leaned toward the window, yearning for a breeze. In a little while, Muffet would light the oven and the kitchen would be as hot as the attic. Maud wished that Hyacinth would summon her upstairs to rehearse the séance. Rehearsal sessions were some-times followed by a carton of ice cream from the cor-ner store. The thought of ice cream, pure and cold and white, made her mouth water. She wished her part in the séance were more difficult; she would have been happy to rehearse for hours every day. Unfortunately, she had little to do. Hyacinth was taking no chances. Maud's part in the séance was small, and—Hyacinth had used the word—foolproof.

The map closet was stifling. Maud shifted her weight from one foot to the other and waited for the séance to begin. She was wearing her white dress with the lace frills: dress, petticoat, drawers, stockings, and wig. "Why do I have to be all dressed up if nobody's s'posed to see me?" Maud had protested, and Hyacinth had replied, "In case something goes wrong." Maud saw no reason why anything should go wrong. She was well rehearsed. She was eager to begin and miserably hot.

She heard a ripple of laughter from the dining room. What did people laugh about before a séance? She reached up and scratched at the edge of her wig. A trickle of sweat ran down her chest. She gulped air like a panting dog and shoved her hand into the ice bucket fastened to the inside of the cupboard.

The ice bucket was Hyacinth's idea. Maud was supposed to keep her right hand submersed, so that when she touched Eleanor Lambert her fingers would be eerily cold. Maud was grateful for this somewhat macabre inspiration. Without the little pail of ice, the closet would be even hotter. She dribbled a little water down her face and sucked her fingers. Through the clear flavor of water, she detected the salt of her sweat.

The parlor door opened. Maud pricked up her ears at the sound of an unfamiliar voice. Mrs. Lambert—it must be she—sounded like a foreigner. Her pronunciation was clear, but there was a queer tune to her sentences. Her accent reminded Maud of Marta, the Swedish laundress at the Asylum.

"—Your servant has always been deaf?"

"Since childhood, I believe," Victoria answered. "I know very little about her. The pastor of St. Thomas's church recommended her to us."

"I—wondered how you managed to talk to her." Mrs. Lambert sounded flustered. "Nowadays, there are schools to teach such people—I myself have sponsored students at a school in Washington. . . ." Her voice trailed off, as if she was afraid the sisters might take offense.

"Victoria manages to talk to her with signs," Judith explained. "I don't quite understand how she does it, but she's very good with poor Muffet."

"I'm sure she is." Mrs. Lambert paused. "I have

an interest in such things. My dear mother was deaf the last years of her life. She suffered greatly from loneliness."

Maud could not catch Victoria's answer, but Hyacinth's voice was clear as a bell. "I think Muffet is a bit old to attend school. Old dogs and new tricks, you know. Poor thing, she's rather simple."

Simple meant stupid. Maud stiffened with indignation. She opened her mouth to defend her pupil. *Muffet's not stupid,* she wanted to cry out. *She learns everything I teach her!* But Hyacinth's tone had changed, and the subject with it.

"Dear Nell, you are not thinking of our hired girl." There was a hint of steel in the bell-like voice. "You are thinking of Caroline and wondering how long we must talk of trivial things before we try to contact her."

There was a brief moment of silence. Then Mrs. Lambert said, "I suppose I am."

"Of course you are," answered Hyacinth. "And you're quite right. There's no need to delay. Let us begin."

Yes, let's, thought Maud. The sooner the séance began, the sooner she would get out of the map closet. The bright edge around the door panel disappeared. Judith had switched off the electric lights. Now she would light the candles in the chandelier.

"If you wouldn't mind," Mrs. Lambert said hesitantly, "I should like Miss Victoria to take the planchette."

There was a startled pause. Maud knew that Hyacinth, not Victoria, had planned to control the movement of the planchette.

"I have heard your sister is a very powerful medium," Mrs. Lambert explained. "Forgive me, Hyacinth, but you and I have tried so many times—"

"Of course." Maud heard the rustle of fabric; the women were sitting down. "Don't look so downcast, Eleanor! I am not offended." Hyacinth's voice was tender. "Victoria, if you will—"

Evidently Victoria complied. More rustling, the creak of a chair, and then silence. Maud knew that Victoria and Mrs. Lambert were sitting very still, gazing at the planchette. She envisioned them: Victoria facing the mantel, Judith by the window, and Hyacinth closest to the door. *During the time when we wait for the planchette to move, you mustn't budge,* Hyacinth had warned her. *She'll be alert for the slightest sound. You must be absolutely still.*

Maud tried to obey. Another drop of sweat

crawled down her back. She could smell herself—a musky, sweetish smell, like a sweating horse. She wrinkled her nose fastidiously.

Rap!

Maud heard a gasp, and then Judith's voice: "Is there a spirit present?"

Rap!

Mrs. Lambert cried out. "Caroline?"

There was a pause. Maud listened for the tinkle of the prisms of the chandelier. She heard Mrs. Lambert repeat, "Caroline?"

"The chandelier's moving," said Hyacinth in a low voice. "The candles are going out."

"The planchette!" Mrs. Lambert sounded as if she were about to cry. "The planchette is moving—but I can't read! It's too dark!"

"Caroline Lambert!" Judith's voice rang out authoritatively. "Caroline Lambert, are you here?"

Rap!

"Caroline, please—" Mrs. Lambert's voice was infinitely pleading. "Please—if you are here, speak to me! Don't leave—oh, don't—" Her breath caught. "I can't read in the dark! Oh, God! My dear one, wait, only wait—"

"Light another candle," Judith commanded, and Maud heard a chair scrape back.

"It began with an L, I think," Victoria said breathlessly. "Perhaps she means to spell out *love*—"

"Do you think so?" Mrs. Lambert said. Her voice rose hysterically. "Do you think it could possibly be?"

Maud heard the *scritch* of a match, followed by the thud of a candlestick on the table. "Now," whispered Mrs. Lambert. "Caroline, come back!"

Silence. Maud waited. *People don't believe when things happen too fast,* Hyacinth had said. Maud understood that to give Mrs. Lambert only a taste of her daughter's presence was excellent technique: it increased the rich woman's faith in Hyacinth and fed her longing for her child. What Maud hadn't understood was that the technique was harrowing. She could hear the woman sobbing, and she felt a prickle of discomfort that had nothing to do with the heat of the cupboard. Maud knew what it felt like to cry that hard, so that every muscle seemed to jerk and her breath caught in her throat. She swallowed.

"Caroline," begged Mrs. Lambert, "are you there? Please!"

"The planchette is moving," Victoria assured her. "*L-O-*"

"*Ssssh,*" Hyacinth cautioned her sister. Maud caught the resentment in her hiss. It wasn't part of

Hyacinth's plan that Caroline should spell out *love*. Victoria was improvising.

There was another loud *rap!*

"The table—" Judith gasped. "The table—"

The table was rising into the air, and Maud knew how. Judith had wedged one foot under the lion-claw legs and was hoisting it up, steadying it with her palms. There was a loud clomp as she let it fall. Candle, candlestick, and planchette were supposed to hit the floor. Hyacinth gasped, "The planchette!" and "The candle's out!"

Judith raised her voice to a shout. "Caroline Lambert, are you here, in this room? If you are here, rap once for yes and twice for no."

Those words were her cue. Maud fished the seashell from the bottom of the ice bucket. Cautiously, she pushed open the door and stepped out of the cupboard. The freshness of the air made her smile in spite of herself. After the map cupboard, the parlor seemed spacious, cool, and bright. She could see the pale rectangles of the two stained-glass windows and the bulky shapes of the women near the table.

Maud glided forward, her stocking feet noiseless against the carpet. She took a brief moment to get her bearings. Mrs. Lambert was where Hyacinth had assured Maud she would be. Hyacinth was ransacking the room for another candle in the chest by the window, and making as much noise as she could over it. Victoria was reciting the Our Father. "And lead us not into temptation—" *Now,* thought Maud, and headed for Mrs. Lambert. She placed her hand against the woman's cheek. In a soft, piteous voice, she whispered, "Mama?"

Mrs. Lambert gasped. Blindly she reached for that small, chill hand—but Maud was quick, as Hyacinth had told her she must be. She pushed the shell across the table and stepped straight back. Mrs. Lambert groped wildly at the air. Maud retreated toward the cupboard and pivoted to dart inside.

Ouch. She had left the panel ajar and collided with it in the dark. Maud ducked into the map cupboard and pulled the door shut. Once inside, her hands went to her face. A warm wetness coated her fingers, running down her chin and into her mouth. She reached down to wipe her hands and stopped, fingers flexed. Her good dress, with the lace . . . ! But already the blood was soaking through the bodice of her dress. Grief for lost finery gave way to panic. Maud whimpered, close-mouthed.

Faint as the noise was, it frightened her. Mrs.

Lambert would hear. The séance would be ruined and Hyacinth would be furious. Maud pressed her bloody fists against her lips. The blood tasted like pennies.

It's only a nosebleed. The words floated into her mind, and all at once she was back in the Asylum. Irma had tripped on the ice and bloodied her nose. Maud had watched, repelled and fascinated, while Irma shrieked and Miss Clarke fished two dirty handkerchiefs from the bosom of her shirtwaist. "It's only a nosebleed," Miss Clarke had said. "People don't die of nosebleeds." Maud seized upon the memory gratefully. With it, came another, less comforting: "People can die from loss of blood, though, can't they, Miss Clarke?" She couldn't recall the answer. Her fingers fluttered toward her nose—the blood was still gushing forth. She wondered how much she had lost.

Outside the door, the lights were on. Victoria and Hyacinth were trying to comfort their client.

"—if she was here, why wouldn't she stay? I felt her—I felt her hand. But why wouldn't she speak to me? And why did she leave the seashell? What does it mean?"

"Hush." Victoria sounded close to tears herself. "Now that she has come, she will surely come again."

"She didn't sound like herself." Maud tensed at the criticism. "She sounded frightened. Oh God, what have I done, that she should be afraid of me?"

"Eleanor, take comfort," Hyacinth said tenderly. "The important thing is that she was here tonight. All of us sensed her presence."

"Her little hand was like ice," wailed Mrs. Lambert. "It even felt wet. Dear God! She is buried; the salt water should be dry by now—"

Ice! Maud stopped listening. She fumbled for the lump of ice in the pail. She lifted it, dripping, and pressed it against her injured nose. Cold water joined the river of blood and tears. She wondered if she was going to faint. She imagined herself falling down in a pool of blood. Perhaps Hyacinth would see the blood oozing from under the mantel and come to her aid. Maud imagined Hyacinth flinging open the door and catching her up in her arms.

But Hyacinth did not come. Maud sagged against the wall of the map cupboard in a stupor of pain and stickiness and heat. Outside the door, the Hawthorne sisters continued to soothe their wealthy client. Mrs. Lambert must have a glass of sherry or a cup of tea. Mrs. Lambert must not go home by herself— Victoria must accompany her. Hyacinth would call the next day to make sure that she was well. . . . The leave-taking seemed to go on for hours. When at last Victoria and Mrs. Lambert had departed and the door of the map cupboard opened, Maud stumbled out so eagerly that she almost fell.

The light in the room was dazzling. The room looked bright and tidy and civilized. Hyacinth and Judith were staring at her.

"Goodness gracious!" cried Hyacinth. "What on earth—?"

"Had a dosebleed," mumbled Maud, clasping the ever-diminishing block of ice to her face. "I wocked indo de door—"

"Great heavens!" Even Judith's sangfroid was ruffled. The look on her face told Maud just how grotesque she must look.

"For heaven's sake! The poor child will bleed all over the carpet," said Judith, while Hyacinth sympathized, "Oh, *poor* Maud!" But there was something wrong with the way she said it, and she didn't rush forward to clasp Maud in her arms. Maud understood why—no sensible woman would want bloodstains on her best tussore silk—but Hyacinth's aloofness was the last straw. Maud opened her mouth and wailed as if she were three years old.

"Take that wig off her and help her into the kitchen," ordered Judith. "She's better off bleeding on the linoleum. It's a mercy she didn't black her eye, walking into that door. Gracious, child, don't cry!" The last three words were more command than comfort, but they were spoken with unwonted kindness. "It's only a nosebleed, after all. Do calm down."

"I *am* calm," sobbed Maud. She felt that under the circumstances, she had been heroically calm. She hadn't ruined the séance; she hadn't cried out when she hurt herself; she had waited patiently while the Hawthorne sisters cosseted Mrs. Lambert. Now she was through with being calm. She wanted to cry until she felt like stopping, and she wanted Hyacinth to take care of her.

"Who would have thought the child had so much blood in her?" marveled Hyacinth. She advanced within an arm's length of Maud and plucked off the wig. Then she turned her toward the back hall, steering with the tips of her fingers. "I don't blame you for crying, you know—it's too gruesome. I thought I heard a bump when you went back in the closet. It's providential you didn't cry out. I'm sure Mrs. Lambert didn't notice a thing."

Maud hunched her shoulders. She was sick of hearing about Mrs. Lambert.

Muffet was in the kitchen. Maud, who had a hazy sense that it was the middle of the night, noted this with surprise. The hired woman was seated at the kitchen table, playing a game of solitaire. Even in her agitated state, Maud wondered who had taught Muffet to play cards. Then the woman looked up. She stood up, darting a fierce look at Hyacinth. Three steps and Maud was buried in Muffet's arms.

It seemed that nosebleeds, like solitaire and gardening, were among the things that Muffet understood. Maud was not aware of Hyacinth's leaving or of exactly what was happening to herself. She only knew that one moment she was bleeding down the front of Muffet's apron and the next she was seated at the kitchen table in nothing but her petticoat, with a wet rag on the back of her neck. The white dress was soaking in cold water, and Muffet was holding Maud's nostrils shut with one hand and wiping the blood off her chin with the other. The horny, callused hands were soft as feathers.

Maud gave a shudder of relief. The wet dishtowel felt good against her skin. It was good to feel the space of the kitchen all around her. She looked up at Muffet, meaning to signal gratitude. The hired woman had never looked grimmer. Maud's forehead puckered. She couldn't think of anything she had done to make Muffet angry.

Muffet pressed Maud's fingers around the sore nose, directing Maud to keep her nostrils shut. Then she got up and fetched pencil and paper. Maud watched as the drawing took shape.

It was a drawing of Maud in her white dress. Then another figure emerged. It was a spider, and not a spider; it wore a stylish shirtwaist and had an elegant, pointed face. Maud emitted a cry of recognition and surprise. Somehow Muffet had drawn a spider that was also Hyacinth. And the spider was reaching out one of its legs, striking the little girl.

Maud looked to Muffet, perplexed. Then she understood. "No, Muffet!" She shook her head emphatically. "No. She didn't hit me."

Muffet pushed the pencil and writing pad toward Maud.

Maud sighed. Muffet knew she couldn't draw. Still, she managed a stick figure with a wide skirt. She drew a rectangle and added a circle on one side for the doorknob. "I walked into the door, that's all." She pointed to the door and stood up, miming the collision. Then she remembered that *door* was one of Muffet's words. She printed carefully, MAUD WALK INTO DOOR.

Muffet cupped her hands around Maud's cheeks,

forcing Maud to look her in the eye. *Are you telling the truth?*

Maud nodded. With the pencil, she underlined <u>DOOR.</u>

Muffet nodded in return. Then she went to the icebox. She poured a glass of milk and opened a tin of anise cookies. She put the glass and the cookies in front of Maud and tapped her left hand lightly, giving her permission to let go of her nose.

CHAPTER SEVENTEEN

Early the next morning, Maud was awakened by a series of thuds.

It was not yet dawn. The light was dim. Maud sat up and ran her fingers over her hurt nose. It was sore, but the blood caked inside her nostrils was dry. It was not pain that had wakened her, but noise. Another thud sounded from the other side of the wall.

Someone was in the next room, where the boxes and trunks were kept. Lamplight flickered in the open doorway. Maud slid out of bed and peered inside. Victoria, fully dressed in hat, gloves, and traveling suit, stood between two suitcases. Muffet, clad in her nightgown and barefoot, faced her. At the spectacle of Muffet, Maud rubbed her eyes. The hired woman's nightdress was elaborately pintucked and adorned with scarlet ribbons. At one end of this confection were Muffet's feet—short, square, with thick ankles—and at the other was Muffet's face, which was wearing an obstinate expression.

"What's the matter?" demanded Maud.

Victoria looked over her shoulder. "Go back to bed."

"You woke me up," Maud said defensively. "What are you doing here?"

"We're leaving," Victoria said shortly. "We need to catch the early train."

Maud's eyes went to the suitcases on the floor. Victoria's bags were already packed. The trunk that Maud shared with Muffet lay open and empty on the floor. Maud's clothes had been taken out and set aside. "Am I going?"

"No. Only Muffet and I." Victoria darted a frustrated glare toward the hired woman. "Only she won't."

Maud's gaze shifted to Muffet. The hired woman's hands were half clenched, and there was something about the way her feet were planted that proclaimed that she would not be moved. Maud's attention was caught by Muffet's toenails, which were barbaric enough to erase all other thoughts from her mind. They were dull yellow and curved like the claws of a bear. Maud resolved that no matter how long she lived, she would never have toenails like that.

Victoria seemed to come to a decision. She stalked past Muffet into the hired woman's bedroom, opened the chest of drawers, and took out a selection of stockings. Muffet pursued her, reclaimed the stockings, and shut them back in the drawer. Maud was intrigued. She sidled away from the doorway and leaned against the wall, where she had an excellent view of the battle that followed.

It was a brief tussle, but vigorous. Once Muffet headed back to bed, Victoria yanked open a second drawer and removed two aprons, a corset, and an armful of petticoats. Briskly she headed for the box room, only to be waylaid by Muffet. Once again, Muffet snatched back her clothes and returned them to the chest. Victoria, changing tactics, went to the box room and brought in a suitcase. She laid it on Muffet's bed and pointed to the empty interior. Muffet shook her head. She began to replace the items of clothing in the chest. Victoria attempted to reach around her, and Muffet uttered a cry of rage. She slammed the drawer shut so violently that the chest rocked and banged against the wall.

Victoria's face puckered despairingly. "She'll wake the whole house!" In her perplexity, she turned to Maud. "What is the matter with her? She's never behaved so before. Whenever we go traveling, I begin packing, and she understands what I want. What's possessed her?"

Maud had no intention of entering into a quarrel between grown-ups. "Why are you going away?"

Victoria looked back to Muffet. The hired woman had finished putting her clothes away. Now she thumped back to bed—her limp was more pronounced than usual—and climbed in with the air of a woman who meant to stay there. As she settled herself between the bedclothes, her feet kicked the suitcase off the bed. The message was clear.

"It's no use," Victoria said helplessly. "She won't come. I'll have to go without her."

Maud felt a little sorry for Victoria. She went to retrieve the empty suitcase. "Where are you going?"

Victoria went back to the box room. Once the suitcase was back in place, she spoke to Maud. "I hear you hurt yourself last night. How do you feel this morning?"

Maud touched her sore nose. "S'better," she said cautiously. She didn't want to fend off any sympathy that might be coming her way. "It still hurts, though."

Victoria nodded briefly. Her hair had come loose during the quarrel with Muffet, and her hat listed to one side. She tried to tuck her hair back into place. "I'm leaving Cape Calypso. I'm going back to Hawthorne Grove."

"Why?"

"Because—" Victoria took a deep breath and started over. "After the séance last night, I went back to the hotel with Mrs. Lambert. We talked together for a long time. Maud, I felt so sorry for her! She poured out her heart to me. She can't get over Caroline's death. She goes over and over it in her mind, thinking what she ought to have done that last day. . . . Do you know what she told me? She goes to the merry-go-round almost every day. She watches the children circling on their horses and thinks that if only she'd gone with Caroline the day she died . . . Sometimes she thinks Caroline will be there, riding the merry-go-round with the other children, and she'll be able to reach out her hand and say, 'Come home!' And Caroline will slide off her sea monster and come. She won't be dead any longer."

Maud felt a prickle of superstitious dread. She didn't like the idea of Caroline coming back from the grave. It would be one thing if there had been some mistake and Caroline were still alive, but the drowned girl's body had been found. People who were dead ought to stay dead. Maud said flatly, and perhaps brutally, "That's stupid."

"Perhaps. Only if Mrs. Lambert had followed her that day—" Victoria spread her hands in a plea for understanding. "That's all she can think about, Maud—the impossible chance that she might see her child again. Last night, she thanked me. She *thanked* me, Maud. She thinks Caroline appeared last night because of me—because I'm such a powerful medium. She holds me responsible." Tears began to flow down Victoria's cheeks. "And if she holds me responsible, I must hold myself responsible. I can't do this any longer. It's too cruel. I can't stand by while Hyacinth torments her and takes her money."

"Did you tell Hyacinth that?"

"Hyacinth? No." Victoria took out a handkerchief and wiped her eyes. "What's the use of talking to Hyacinth?" She broke off. "Never mind Hyacinth.

The point is I won't do it. I'm going back to Hawthorne Grove."

Maud summed it up. "You're running away." She spoke as if Victoria were one of the children at the Barbary Asylum.

Victoria flinched. "Yes," she said, "I'm a coward, I know. I've no faith that I can withstand Hyacinth if I stay here." She cast a resentful glance over her shoulder. "Only Muffet won't go with me."

Maud considered Muffet's disobedience. She realized that she understood why Muffet was refusing to go. Muffet was learning to read and write. She wanted the words that Maud was teaching her.

"What if I come with you?" The words slipped out before Maud made up her mind to say them. She didn't know if she wanted to go with Victoria.

"I can't take you with me," Victoria answered in a voice that struck Maud as surprisingly harsh. "I have no legal right. I'm not your guardian. Hyacinth is."

"Oh."

"I *can't* take you," Victoria repeated, as if Maud were refusing to take no for an answer. "I was against adopting you. Hyacinth went behind my back. I don't have the power to take you away from her. And if I did, you wouldn't agree. I was never your 'Dearest.'"

The last word cut like a whip. Then Victoria's face crumbled. "Oh, Maud, forgive me! It's just that—all my life—" Her mouth wobbled. The elderly woman looked like a baffled child. "I've always tried to be good. Surely to be good is to be lovable? But no one has ever cared for me. And Hyacinth—Hyacinth never tries to be good and yet . . . The house in Hawthorne Grove belongs to her, did you know that? Our father left the estate to Hyacinth. Judith and I live there on her charity."

Maud felt a pang of sympathy. She knew all about charity. She searched for words of comfort. "But this house is yours," she pointed out. "Isn't this your house? Not Hyacinth's?"

Victoria slumped down on the nearest trunk. She reached up and removed the pins from her hat. Slowly, mechanically, she took off her hat and placed it in her lap. Then she began to re-knot her hair.

"It's true. This house is mine, to my shame. It's the fruit of my wickedness."

Maud was tired of standing. She dropped down at Victoria's feet and looked up expectantly, as if waiting to be told a fairy tale. Something about the posture made Victoria laugh, though her eyes were full of tears.

"Years ago, Maud, I used to dream of the dead. Judith says it's all nonsense, but I did, Maud, I did! I had a gift, you see. People would tell me about their loved ones, and I would dream of them. . . . It wasn't the kind of heaven you read about in books, with harps and cities of gold. But there were trees and rocks and the river—and oh, the light! The colors in my dreams weren't like earthly colors. The light shone through them, like stained glass. And in my dreams, I would talk to the dead and see their happiness, and then I could tell the people left behind that all was well. I comforted them. It really was a gift, but I suppose I grew conceited." Victoria toyed with the veil on her hat. "And then there was Mr. Llewellyn. He owned this house. His son died young—consumption. He used to send little Tom to the ocean, in the hopes that it would cure his lungs—but it was no use. After Tom died, Mr. Llewellyn used to come and ask me if I would dream of Tom, and I did dream and I told him—but it wasn't enough. You see, in the dreams, I just saw Tom—he didn't speak. And Mr. Llewellyn wanted him to say something."

"So you made things up," Maud said matter-of-factly. She felt that she might have done the same thing.

"No—yes. It wasn't just that. You see, Maud, Mr. Llewellyn owned a cotton mill, and he used child laborers. Little children—some of them younger than you—I visited him at the mill, and they almost broke my heart. They were so frail and dingy and crooked, and I thought it was a shame." Victoria's head was up now. "It was dreadful, Maud! He loved his son— but he couldn't see that those poor factory waifs were children, too. He saw nothing wrong with forcing them to work ten hours a day for two dollars a week, and I couldn't help myself. I told him"—she gulped—"I told him Tom came to me in a dream. I told him Tom wanted him to build a school for those children and pay them for learning their lessons. And he did. He built the school. The children worked half a day, and the rest of the time they studied and played."

Maud clapped her hands, tickled by the idea that decorous Victoria had thought of such a scheme. "But that was good!"

"That's what I thought." Victoria shook her head. "I told myself it was a good lie. I hadn't hurt anyone. And Mr. Llewellyn was greatly admired for treating the children well—for the first time in his life, people looked up to him. But it was a lie, Maud, and I was punished for it. After that lie, I lost my gift. I no longer dream of the dead."

"Do you miss it so much?"

"Yes." Victoria spoke the monosyllable very softly. "But it isn't just that. Mr. Llewellyn left me this house when he died—he had others, but this was the one where Tom died—and that made me feel dreadful, but that wasn't the worst thing, either. The worst thing was that after I stopped dreaming, people still came to me for comfort, and I had none to give. And then Hyacinth began to say she was a medium and to hold séances. . . . I never asked for anything, ever, but she accepted gifts, and after a while we were making money. Oh, we needed it—Hyacinth spends so recklessly—but it wasn't right. And so we became what we are now. Liars and the cruelest sort of thieves." With great gentleness, Victoria laid her fingertips against Maud's nose. "And now there's you. Hyacinth took you from the Asylum so that you could learn the family business. Can't you see that what she is making you do is wrong? Think of Eleanor Lambert—think of all she's suffered! What will become of you, Maud?"

Maud lowered her eyelids. She didn't like the question. In her opinion, the problem of what was to become of her had been solved, and solved to her full satisfaction. She had a good home and a guardian. If there was a price attached to both, she was willing to pay. As for Eleanor Lambert, she was a grown-up—and rich. She would have to look after herself. "Don't worry about me," Maud said gruffly. "I'll be all right."

Victoria sighed and got to her feet. She replaced her hat on her head and took up her suitcases. "I must be going," she said hopelessly. "I must catch the early train."

Maud took the kerosene lamp and walked the stairs to light her way. She held out her free hand. "Good-bye," she said. "I'm sorry—" She almost said, *I'm sorry I love Hyacinth better than you,* but stopped herself just in time. "I'm sorry you're going away. I'll miss you."

Victoria bent and kissed her forehead. She had had no breakfast, and her breath was unpleasant. "I'll write to you," she promised. Maud watched as she descended the stairs, casting her shadow before her.

That night Maud dreamed of Caroline Lambert for the first time.

CHAPTER EIGHTEEN

Four days later, the temperature rose to one hundred degrees, and Maud abandoned being perfectly good.

It was not only the heat that drove her to disobedience. Since Victoria's leaving, both Hyacinth and Judith were edgy and short-tempered. Hyacinth was giving a series of lectures on spiritualism at a nearby hotel, and she had little time for Maud. Muffet was cross because Hyacinth's outings demanded freshly ironed clothes every day, which meant that the kitchen stove had to be lit to heat the irons. Maud strayed back and forth between the airless attic and the steamy kitchen. She had nothing to read. When she complained, Judith provided her with one of Mr. Llewellyn's old books, which was supposed to be about a whale. Maud skimmed over a hundred pages of dense prose without encountering the promised monster. Feeling cheated, she flung the book aside in disgust. Her head ached. She was bored, hot, sticky, and lonesome.

In her quest for something to do, she explored the box room. Inside the trunk she shared with Muffet, she came across the striped dress she had sewn under Victoria's instruction. Maud had never worn this garment, which had not been a success. The gathers of the skirt were uneven, and one sleeve jutted out in a peculiar way. The cloth itself was thin and flimsy — Victoria was too frugal to waste good cloth on an unskilled seamstress.

Maud eyed the dress speculatively. It was a dress of no value, a dress she could get dirty if she liked. Maud had a sudden vision of herself cavorting by the edge of the ocean, wearing the striped dress. It would be terrible if she left the house and Hyacinth found out, but the risk was small. The Hawthorne sisters were at a dinner party given by a rich lady named Mrs. Fortescue. They would be spending the evening indoors.

Maud felt a surge of terror and delight. Her fingers trembled as she unbuttoned her rosebud print. She kicked off her shoes, peeled off her stockings, and removed almost all of her underwear. Then she yanked the striped dress over her head. A moment later, she padded barefoot down the stairs.

The kitchen was empty. Maud peered through the kitchen curtains and saw Muffet kneeling in the garden. Her back was to the door, and she was weeding. With luck, she would not hear—Maud almost smiled. Muffet *couldn't* hear the screen door slam. Maud opened the door and trotted down the porch steps. Once in the alley, she began to run.

It was months since she had been able to run and it felt good, in spite of the gravel that bruised her feet. She dashed past the neighbor's yard, ducked behind a bush, and rounded a corner. All too soon, she was out of breath. She slowed to a skip and then to a saunter. Her bare legs felt deliciously naked, and the air was fresh. She was free. It was dangerous. In five minutes she would be at the ocean. She spread her arms wide and skimmed between the buildings like a swallow.

She remembered the way. She crossed the board-walk, dodging its evening strollers, and ran over the rough grass. At last she stood on the strand, with the broad sky stretching around her in three directions. The ocean glistened and tumbled upon the shore. Maud stopped, breathing hard. She was hoping to see the child who had invited her to play the day she came to Cape Calypso. But it was seven o'clock, and most of the children had gone home.

No matter. It was joy enough to be out of doors, with a breeze making her skirt flutter and the ocean beckoning ahead. A ripple of foam seethed forward and receded within inches of her toes. With boldness and longing, Maud stepped into the water.

It was so cold it made her bones ache. Maud squealed, baring her teeth. Then the wave receded, and for the first time, she felt the pull of the ocean; the sand under her feet was being sucked away. She locked her knees and laughed. She loved the bubbles of the foam against her skin. She pinched her skirt daintily and waded in deeper.

The hour that followed was blissful. Maud jumped in rhythm with the cresting waves; she tried to out-run the foam as it breathed upon the shore. She hopped on one foot and kicked the ocean into spray.

She screamed with joy as the water splashed upward and wetted her thighs. For once Hyacinth was forgotten. Maud was drunk with salt water. She felt that she could go on playing by the ocean for the rest of her life and never have enough of it.

Suddenly it was dark. The water was no longer greenish brown, but ink-colored; the white foam no longer glittered, but shone in the dimness. She was alone on the shore, and the crowds on the boardwalk had thinned. Reluctantly, Maud turned her back on the glory of the ocean. Every adult she had ever met, save Hyacinth, agreed that danger lay in wait for children who were out past bedtime. She turned back toward the boardwalk.

Once under the streetlamps, her wanderlust returned. It seemed a pity to return to the house after only an hour. Other people were still enjoying themselves; why shouldn't she? Maud brushed the sand off her legs and surveyed the passersby. She eyed a crowd of older girls, who were sharing a bag of taffy. They were noisy and merry, and Maud found them attractive. She tagged after them.

Her instincts were good. The girls led her up the boardwalk, to lights even brighter than the streetlamps. Two white fences flanked an entrance with a sign shaped like a rainbow. The sign read ODYSSEY AMUSEMENT PARK. The girls strolled in.

Maud's heart beat fast. They hadn't stopped at the entrance. They hadn't reached into their purses for money. Perhaps it was free; perhaps anyone could go inside. Maud flicked her fingers through her hair and straightened her wet skirt. Then nonchalantly, without looking right or left, she passed under the rainbow and into the park.

Once inside, her senses reeled. There were strings of electric lights between the trees, and their brilliance was dazzling. She could smell frankfurters and cotton candy and popcorn. Ahead of her were booths and pavilions with gaudily painted signs. And there was music—a hooting, languishing oom-pah-pah that made Maud want to dip and sway. Straight ahead of her—making the music—was the merry-go-round. Maud flew to it like a phoenix toward the sun.

It was as spectacular as the ocean. Maud knew that a merry-go-round was a circle of wooden horses, but she had not dreamed of horses like these: spirited, glossy creatures with manes that soared upward like tongues of fire. Nor were the horses all; they were partnered with creatures that Maud knew only through the rumors of geography. She saw a tiger, brazenly orange and baring his teeth; the haughtiest of camels; a bear with a dotingly friendly smile. The animals were richly caparisoned, and their saddles were adorned with sphinxes and gargoyles and jewels. There was a painted backdrop with mountains and castles; there were mirrors and lights and stars and rosettes. Maud was struck dumb. She did not even envy the children who rode. She was content to stand and watch.

The music was slowing. A coal-black horse passed her. Then a pig with the garland of flowers around his neck. An ostrich, a stag, a hare. The children slid off their mounts, and others came forward to ride.

Maud did not intend to steal a ride. She was simply unable to help herself. Before she knew it, she had ducked under the striped canopy and clambered up the side of the merry-go-round. She was weaving her way between the horses, choosing a mount, when a large man caught her by the shoulders. "Whoa, there!"

Maud looked up. She had known very few men in her life, and she was a little afraid of them. This man was peculiar-looking. He was red-bearded, and he had an enormous belly, which he followed as if it were a dog he was taking for a walk. His hands were huge, and she could smell his sweat, but he held her away from him respectfully. "You need a ticket," he told her. "Do you have a ticket?"

"A ticket?" echoed Maud.

"You need a ticket," the man said patiently. He pointed to a red-painted booth beside the carousel. "It costs a nickel. You stand in line and get a ticket."

Maud looked down at her toes. They were still caked with sand—she had wanted to stop on the boardwalk and pick between them, but she was afraid this action would brand her as a vulgar child. "I haven't got a nickel."

"Well, then, you can't ride." The man spun her around and steered her off the carousel platform. "It's crowded tonight, duckling. I need every horse for the customers." He closed one eye. "When it's rainy, now, that's different. I can sometimes give away a ride on a rainy night."

It took Maud a moment or two to take in the fact that he had made her a promise. By the time she had puzzled it out, he was gone. She took her place among the spectators and watched as the carousel began to spin. A waltz began, oom-pah-pah. If she had been alone, she would have held out her skirts and danced to it.

It was some time before Maud realized that her mood had changed. She kept her eyes on the carousel, but her enchantment was marred by the sense that there was something she ought to notice, something she didn't especially want to see. Against her will, her attention shifted from the carousel to the face of a woman.

She was a tall and slender woman, dressed in half-mourning and the sort of hat that Maud instinctively classified as "good." Under her hat, her hair was fair and windblown. Her face was freckled, and there was something wrong with her expression. Unlike the other spectators, she didn't smile or wave; there was a fearful hunger in her face as she watched the carousel. All at once, and without a shadow of a doubt, Maud knew who she was.

Instinctively, Maud turned to hide, dodging behind a fat woman in a sailor hat. Once out of sight, she reasoned with herself. There was no chance that Mrs. Lambert would recognize her. Mrs. Lambert didn't know she existed, let alone that Maud had impersonated her daughter during the séance. Maud risked a second glance. The woman's gaze was fixed on one of the carousel animals, a jade-green creature with the foreparts of a lion and the tail of a fish. *That must be Caroline's sea monster,* thought Maud. A little boy was riding it, lashing it monotonously with the reins.

Maud studied Mrs. Lambert. The rich woman had taken off one glove and was twisting it between her fingers. Her shirtwaist was untucked and a long strand of flaxen hair had fallen to her shoulder. Maud pursed her lips disapprovingly. Grown-ups ought to be able to pull themselves together.

The carousel was slowing. Maud decided to go. At the same instant, Mrs. Lambert turned from the merry-go-round. For a split second, their eyes met. Mrs. Lambert fumbled at the handle of her purse.

Maud retreated, almost colliding with the fat lady. As the crowd changed shape, she made her escape. Once on the boardwalk, she broke into a run. She knew she would come again, in spite of Mrs. Lambert. Tomorrow, she promised herself. Tomorrow, and every night when Hyacinth was away, she would steal from the house. She would see the ocean and the carousel again.

CHAPTER NINETEEN

The day that followed was hot and overcast. Maud scanned the mournful sky with mounting hope. The red-haired man in charge of the merry-go-round had hinted that children sometimes rode free, if the weather was bad and the horses lacked riders. If the Hawthorne sisters went out and it rained—not too much, but a drizzle—Maud might ride the carousel. Maud realized that she was listening for the sound of Hyacinth's leaving as eagerly as she had once awaited her return.

But the Hawthorne sisters stayed home. Evening came and supper was served. Hyacinth and Judith dined upstairs, in the dining room that overlooked the street. Maud ate in the kitchen with Muffet. She seethed through the meal and cleared the table with bad grace. As she stacked the plates from the dining room, a roll of thunder announced the arrival of a storm.

Maud could have wept with frustration. Outside the window, the trees were bending, and angry raindrops spattered the dust, leaving it pockmarked. A thread of lightning glittered against the clouds. Maud pressed her hot forehead to the window glass and closed her eyes. Judith and Hyacinth had no carriage. They would never go out in a storm.

The linoleum creaked faintly. Muffet had come to stand at the window. One calloused hand cupped Maud's shoulder, turning her until they stood face-to-face. Muffet had noticed Maud watching the sky all day, and she knew something was up. Maud shrugged and pulled away. She crept upstairs to sulk, leaving Muffet to wash the dishes.

The attic windows were open. The rain splashed through the curtains, making a pool of water on the floor. Maud glared at it. She was in no mood to wipe up puddles. Another roll of thunder sounded, so much closer than the last that she scurried to the safety of her bed.

Lightning illumined the room. Maud dragged her pillow from under the bedclothes and hugged it to her chest. The wet curtains billowed inward, pulled taut by the wind. The air was dim—the storm clouds seemed to have invaded the attic. Maud wished she had thought to bring a lamp from the kitchen. Selfish old Mr. Llewellyn, who hadn't bothered to put electric lights in the part of the house where the servants lived.

Muffet's bedroom would be brighter. There were more windows at the front of the house. Maud slid off the bed and tripped through the box room to the hired woman's bedchamber. Muffet's windows, like her own, were open—Maud shut them and smeared the water across the floorboards with her foot. She wished Muffet would finish the dishes and come upstairs.

She settled down on the rug beside Muffet's bed. She was not afraid of the storm—only little children were cowed by thunder, she reminded herself—it was just that Muffet's room was nicer than her own. Besides being brighter, it was tidy. There were two bouquets of flowers from Muffet's garden—marigolds and petunias—and their spicy fragrance offset the mustiness of the attic. Muffet had hung chromos on the wall: Gibson Girls and kittens and Jesus walking on the water. There was a crazy quilt on the bed, patched in red and violet and bottle green.

Two rectangular shapes caught Maud's eye. Books. They lay on a footstool, under a workbasket: one plush covered, the other black. Maud stared at them, perplexed. Muffet had books? Automatically, she reached for them.

The black book was the Bible—a disappointment, but not a surprise. Big black books generally turned out to be Bibles. Muffet's Bible, however, was a puzzle. It had thin paper and black numbers at the beginning of each section, but it was full of foreigners: Giovanni and Pietro and Giacomo. The name on the flyleaf was "Vicenzo Cerniglia."

Maud tried to pronounce it. Then she turned to the other book, which was a photograph album. That, too, was a disappointment—Maud didn't care much for pictures, particularly pictures of homely-looking people in old-fashioned clothes. Nevertheless, she leafed through them. There was a hollow-cheeked man with untidy whiskers and a woman whose hair was pulled back so tight that it made her ears stick out. There was also a child.

In Maud's opinion, the child was the only person in the album who might lay claim to being pretty. She was doe-eyed, with a wide brow and curls that looked as round and dark as purple grapes. Maud pictured her in modern clothes and decided she would look nice. She turned over another page, and there was the child again: the woman was wearing the same dark, ill-fitting dress, but the child had grown taller. Her curls tumbled past her shoulders.

Maud turned another leaf, but there were no more pictures. The album was less than half filled. Between the last two pages was a piece of paper, much yellowed and folded in thirds. Maud unfolded it and read:

The Statement of Anzoletta Cerniglia,
wife of the late Vicenzo Cerniglia
November 12, 1871

I have asked Father Domenico to write
these words for me because I cannot write
English. The doctor says my heart is not
strong. It is about my daughter Anna that I

wish to speak, because she cannot speak for herself.

My husband and I came to America in 1850. Six years after, our only child was born. We called her Anna Maddalena. She was as beautiful as an angel and as good as gold. When she was almost four years old, she caught the whooping cough. She almost died. Afterward, she was deaf. When I first understood that she would never hear or speak, I was angry with God and I wept.

But I was wrong, because Anna was always a blessing. God gave her a good heart and she was intelligent. As she grew older, we made up our own language and we spoke to her with our hands. She understood everything. She learned quickly. I taught her to work hard.

I have taught her everything I know. She can sew and knit and do fine needlework. She can cook and keep house. Our neighbors let her work in their homes, and they showed her the sewing machine and the gas stove. She can cook with gas or

coal. My husband taught her a little
carpentry and how to count money.

  I have tried to make sure she knows
every useful thing, as I think no man will
marry her. I write this letter to say that she
is a good and useful girl. She is honest and
will work very hard. I beg you who read
this letter to treat her well, and I pray that
God will reward you.

Maud refolded the letter and placed it between the pages. Her mind was so busy with what she had read that a sudden roar of thunder caught her unawares. She leaped to her feet, and the two books fell to the floor.

She gazed at them in consternation. The Bible had fallen open, and the thin pages were wrinkled; the cover to the photograph album, loose before, had ripped and hung crookedly. Maud knelt to repair the damage. She smoothed out the pages of the Bible, reversing the creases. It was unlikely that Muffet would open a book she could not read. Maud turned back to the child in the picture. That sweet-faced girl was Muffet—*Muffet*—whose mother had thought her beautiful.

Maud shut the book and set it back on the footstool. *I beg you who read this letter to treat her well.* She felt a twinge of discomfort. She had left Muffet with the supper dishes and damaged her books.

Someone was coming up the stairs. Not Muffet—her clumping, uneven footsteps were unmistakable—but light, staccato steps. Maud froze. Then she jumped up and rushed back to her room. She had left her striped dress by the washstand. There was sand in the pockets—Hyacinth must not find it—Maud grangled the dress into a knot and shoved it under the bed.

Maud heard Hyacinth's whisper. "Maud! Maud! Maud!"

Hyacinth was carrying a lamp and a clock. She placed both on the dresser and came to clasp Maud's hands.

"What is it?"

"Mrs. Lambert's here." Hyacinth's eyes glittered with excitement. "Do you remember how to play the glockenspiel?"

Maud goggled at her. "You told me not to practice here," she reminded Hyacinth. "You said the neighbors might—"

"Hush! Never mind." Hyacinth dropped Maud's

hands and went to the dresser. From the top drawer, she took the golden wig. "You can sing—it will do just as well. Quickly, get dressed! Mrs. Lambert's here, and I mustn't leave her long."

"Are we having a séance?" There had been no preparation. "How will I get in the map cupboard if she's already here?"

"We won't use the map cupboard," Hyacinth said briskly. "Now, Maud, don't make difficulties."

"I'm not making difficulties," Maud said, stung. "I'll do anything you want, but you have to tell me what it is."

Hyacinth held up her palms, silencing her. "Do stop arguing! Mrs. Lambert was out calling and was caught in the rain. She came here because she was nearby—that's what she says, but that's not the real reason. She wants a séance—that's what fetched her. Judith's helping her into dry things—it's a perfect night, with the storm—but we must move quickly, quickly." Hyacinth reached behind the curtain where Maud kept her dresses. "You'll wear the white dress and the wig. It's not likely any of the neighbors will see you out the window, but if anyone sees, you must look like Caroline."

Maud wrinkled her nose at the white dress. The

bloodstains had been bleached to a dingy beige color. They wouldn't show up in the dark, but Maud's pleasure in the dress was much diminished. "Where will I be?"

"Outside the window. Wait ten—no, fifteen minutes." Hyacinth turned Maud away from her and began to unbutton her dress. "Five minutes of useless chatter—what a dreadful storm, et cetera—another five to bring up the idea of a séance and talk her into it—two to dim the lights and set the chairs . . . another three or four before you begin to sing. . . . Yes. Fifteen minutes should do nicely. Go downstairs, through the kitchen, out the back door—climb up the side porch and crouch under the stained-glass windows. The parlor lights will be off. If for some reason the lights are still on, don't sing. And when you do sing, take care you keep down—if the lightning strikes, I don't want to see your shadow against the glass. Do you know what to sing?"

"'Shall We Gather at the River,'" Maud answered promptly. It was Caroline's favorite hymn. She also knew Caroline's favorite color (green), her favorite food (cinnamon toast), and the name of her favorite toy elephant (Turrible).

"Yes, that'll do. Two verses, I think. It's possible

Mrs. Lambert will rush out in the storm once she hears Caroline's voice, so you must be ready to flee if you hear the front door opening. Luckily it sticks— that'll give you an extra few seconds. Two verses at the most—then off the porch, in the back door, and back to the attic. It couldn't be simpler."

Maud thought it could. "It's thundering and lightning," she pointed out. She knew quite well she would do what Hyacinth commanded, but she wanted full credit for going out into the storm.

"Pooh!" Hyacinth swooped down and kissed Maud's cheek. "You're not afraid of a little rain, are you? You'll be on the porch almost the whole time— people are *never* struck by lightning when they're on a porch."

Maud gave her a skeptical glance.

"Fifteen minutes." Hyacinth nodded toward the clock. "Mind you open the kitchen door softly—and shut it—and don't run into it, for goodness' sake! You'll be perfect—I count on you." Hyacinth kissed her fingertips and blew her a kiss that smelled of violets.

It was a stroke of good luck, Maud thought as she passed through the kitchen, that Muffet was in the water closet. Muffet understood that for some reason

Maud was not allowed to leave the house, and she had never seen Maud in her golden wig. Maud knew that the hired woman was quite capable of blocking the doorway and questioning her as best she could. Maud lifted the hook that latched the screen door, took a firm hold on the glockenspiel, and stepped out onto the porch.

The rain fell in gleaming sheets. Maud clutched the glockenspiel to her chest. The glockenspiel was a surprise for Hyacinth; during the fifteen minutes before Maud came downstairs, she had practiced the hymn, hammering the air above the bars. She remembered it well—she was sure that she could play it without mistakes. For a moment she stood poised on the back porch, gathering her nerve. Then she squinted, hunched her shoulders, and plunged out into the rain.

In a matter of seconds, she was drenched. Wig, dress, and skin ran with water; her bare toes squeaked against the wet grass. With one leap, she was up on the porch. She hunkered down under the window ledge.

As Hyacinth had promised, the windows were dark. Maud took in her breath. This time she would not hurry. It was important to get everything exactly right. Methodically, she wiped her face on her sleeve and shoved back the sodden wig. She experimented with crouching positions until she found one that was comfortable—half squatting, half kneeling. From this position, she could get to her feet in an instant.

She listened. She thought she could hear Judith's voice intoning a prayer. The words were blurred by the tumult of rain. Maud grasped the little hammer and began to play the glockenspiel. The chimes rang out sweetly, unevenly, and Maud began to sing—

"Shall we gather at the river,
 Where bright angel feet have trod,
 With its crystal tide forever
 Flowing by the throne of God—"

She waited a split second, listening. Judith's voice had stopped. Maud could sense the excitement on the other side of the wall. She struck a single wrong note and made haste to cover her error:

"Yes, we'll gather at the river,
 The beautiful, the beautiful river—
 Gather with the saints at the river
 That flows by the throne of God."

The glockenspiel jangled along with her voice, not quite in time. Maud's fingers tingled with cold and nervousness. Better to stop playing now, before she made another mistake. She gathered the instrument to her chest and shifted position, squatting on tiptoe.

> "Ere we reach the shining river,
>   Lay we every burden down;
>   Grace our spirits will deliver,
>   And provide a robe and crown.
>
> Soon we'll—"

She heard the forceful sound of the front door sticking—a sound not unlike a sneeze. She leaped to her feet. Without looking back, she jumped from the porch and rushed to the back lawn. Once around the corner of the house, she flew to the door and opened it. At the last moment, she remembered not to slam the door—her muddy foot lashed out and caught it before it banged shut.

For a marvel, Muffet was not in the kitchen. Maud tore off her wig, seized a dishtowel, and wiped her feet. Then she trotted upstairs, quick and self-possessed as a little goat.

She had done it! She half heard, half fancied, the sound of female voices raised in wonder and distress. The sound reminded her to step lightly. In fits and starts, she climbed the stairs, arriving at last in the attic.

Caroline was taking off her boots. She perched on a promontory made of huge dark stones, which stretched from the ocean to the shore. Maud knelt on the sand and watched her. Caroline's dress was sandy and damp. It was a deliciously pretty dress: pale blue batiste embroidered with forget-me-nots. Maud would have cherished a dress like that, but Caroline was reckless. Caroline didn't mind if she mussed her dress or whether the wind whipped her hair into disorder.

Maud spoke. "You have a green smear on your skirt."

Caroline didn't answer. She rolled her stockings up in a ball and threw them into the air. She had a good arm: the balled-up stockings landed in the mouth of the boot she had just discarded.

"Maud," whispered Hyacinth, "are you asleep?"

Maud dragged herself out of her dream. The memory faded as she sat up in bed. For the second time that night Hyacinth stood before her. This time she carried a candle and a bowl of ice cream. A whole pint of ice cream, with two spoons stuck in it. Maud blinked in astonishment. "I'm not asleep," she assured Hyacinth.

"Good!" Hyacinth set the candle before the mirror. The faint light doubled. By the light of glass and candle, Hyacinth appeared supernaturally young. She was wearing what Maud thought of as a "negleyjay," lavishly embroidered and foamy with lace. Maud feasted her eyes upon it. Someday, perhaps, she would have a "negleyjay."

Hyacinth held out the ice cream. "The shop was out of vanilla, so I bought peach."

Maud cupped her hands around the bowl. The china was beaded with cold water, and the ice cream was pure and sugary, with shreds of peach that rasped against her tongue. "Mmmn."

Hyacinth sat down on the bed. "The rain's stopped."

"What time is it?"

"About nine thirty." Hyacinth leaned forward, skimming her spoon over the mountain of cream. "The shop was closed, but I hammered on the window—I was determined you should have a treat. Maud, you were perfect! The glockenspiel was a masterstroke. You should have heard it—the chimes against the rain—the effect was beyond everything! I felt my own skin prickle, and *I* knew it was you. You couldn't have done better if we'd rehearsed for hours."

"Was the singing all right?"

"The singing was exquisite," said Hyacinth approvingly. "Neither too loud nor too soft. Eleanor Lambert went white as a sheet—Judith thought she was going to faint."

"Did she?"

"No. She ran to the window—she stood there with her cheek against the glass—crying and crying. And then she rushed for the door, and Judith and I tried to stop her—while you, my nimble darling, vanished into thin air! Oh, it was perfection! She was certain it was Caroline. Though"—Hyacinth's eyes crinkled with amusement—"she did say as how Caroline generally sang a little flat. Now, you, pettikins, were absolutely on pitch."

"I can't help that," Maud protested. "You never told me to sing flat."

"My precious child, I didn't know! Luckily, it took no time at all to persuade Eleanor that everyone sings on key in heaven—if they didn't, how dreadful for poor God! Yes, it was an absolute triumph."

Maud prompted her, "So I was good?"

"My darling child, you were better than good—didn't I say so? I never thought we should find a child who could improvise so brilliantly." Hyacinth put down her spoon and pushed the bowl closer to Maud. "There. Finish that."

Maud spooned up an enormous lump of ice cream and put it in her mouth. She was almost too happy to speak. The circle of candlelight seemed to contain everything she desired. She had done well; Hyacinth was sitting at the foot of her bed; they were eating ice cream in the middle of the night.

"What'll we do next?"

Hyacinth frowned a little. "I'm not sure. Judith and I disagree. She wants you to materialize soon, so that we're sure of the money. For myself, I think it better to proceed slowly. Caroline died on August the fifteenth. It would be poetical to have you materialize on the anniversary. Perhaps, between now and then, we'll have another séance using the map closet. You can speak, but you won't materialize."

"What happens when I materialize?" asked Maud. "Won't she be able to see I'm not a ghost?"

"It's a problem," agreed Hyacinth. "We haven't done much with apparitions—there are tricks with mirrors I'd like to try—but I think Eleanor wants to hold you in her arms. You must be prepared for her to clutch you and kiss you and cry." She gave a little shudder. "I detest that sort of thing, don't you?"

"Um," said Maud. One of her knees was touching Hyacinth's side. Stealthily she drew it back. "I wish they wouldn't cry."

"Dear Maud, they *all* cry." Hyacinth threw up her hands in comic despair. "We go to such trouble to make them happy, but they always cry. One simply has to get used to it. It's their money, after all. If Eleanor Lambert's willing to pay five thousand dollars to cry all over you, who are we to judge?"

Maud took another spoonful of ice cream, dribbling it down her front. "Five thousand dollars is a lot of money."

Hyacinth gave a low laugh. "Dear Maud! Did Victoria get at you before she left?"

Maud hesitated. "I don't know what you mean."

"Of course you do. She told you we were wrong to take the money, didn't she?"

Maud risked a glance at Hyacinth and saw that her eyes were dancing. "She said something like that."

"Of course she did. Now, listen to me." Hyacinth leaned forward and touched Maud's cheek, guaranteeing her attention. "If Eleanor Lambert wanted to know that her daughter was dead, who would tell her so?"

"Most anybody, I guess."

"Exactly so. The doctor. The undertaker. Anyone. She could have the truth for free. But Eleanor Lambert isn't in the market for truth, and she's not in the market for religion, either. Any minister worth his salt would tell her she would see her daughter in heaven. But Eleanor Lambert doesn't want to see her daughter in heaven. She wants her *now*. Do you follow me, Maud?"

Maud nodded.

"In short, she wants to resurrect the dead—which is impossible. And the impossible is bound to be expensive. Why, look at the money we've spent! Your white dress, the glockenspiel, the Ouija board, the wig—not to mention the amount of time we've spent working to perfect the illusions. Do you really think, Maud, that we could afford to do all this for nothing?"

"No." Maud had a sense that Hyacinth's reasoning was faulty in some way, but she had no further desire to argue. "When she pays us, may I have a new book?" She was frightened to hear herself say the words, but Hyacinth rewarded her with the sweetest of smiles.

"You shall have a dozen new books," she assured Maud, "and a new dress—and enough ice cream to sink a ship. There! Are you satisfied?"

"Yes," Maud said, happily, guiltily.

"Then kiss me good night." Hyacinth lowered her cheek. "And finish your ice cream and go to sleep. You've done a good night's work."

CHAPTER TWENTY

The following night, Maud stole from the house to play on the shore. The ocean was rough after the storm. Even Maud, who had seen it only twice before, could see the change. The foam from the shallow breakers splashed her to the waist. Maud rejoiced. An evening of freedom stretched before her. Hyacinth and Judith were dining out—Muffet had gone off with her spade and her basket—Maud had escaped. The only flaw in her happiness was that she had little hope of riding the merry-go-round. Last night's thunderstorm had cooled the air, and tourists thronged the boardwalk, enjoying the breeze and the sunset. The amusement park would be crowded.

Still, there was the ocean. For the first hour, Maud played tag with the waves. Then she settled down to make a sand castle. A large shell served as a spade, and she scooped and patted until she had achieved three mounds of diminishing size, one on top of the other. She clawed a circular moat around this structure and was charmed when the water welled up beneath her fingernails. She had not known there was water under the sand. A vision dazzled her: a complex city of castles and canals. On her hands and knees, she dug for it, not looking up till the air was dim.

Night was falling. Maud sighed and rose to her feet, brushing her dress. A moist crust of sand coated everything—dress, fingers, toes, and knees. The sand had even infiltrated her underclothing. When she reached up to scratch her ear, she found it gritty. Stiff-legged, fingers splayed, she headed for the waves to rinse herself clean.

The chill of the ocean was a shock. Maud squealed as the water climbed to her waist. She ducked so that it came up to her shoulders and fanned out her skirts. All at once the next wave was upon her, curling like the top of a question mark. Maud hopped upward, trying to catch the surge. Her timing was wrong. The wave slapped her face, knocking her headlong into the water.

Maud flailed. Salt burned her throat; she could not breathe; she was choking to death. Instinctively she worked her arms and kicked, but the force of the wave had disoriented her. With increasing desperation, she pawed and thrashed, forcing herself deeper into the water. Her mouth opened for air. Her mind shrieked that she could not be drowning: nothing so disastrous could happen so fast. But her toes had lost bottom, and the water was dark; no matter how frantically she punched and kicked, she could not get free of it. At last her muscles went limp. She stopped propelling herself sideways. In that moment, a wave bore her up, and her face touched the air.

She was saved. Her toes scrabbled, seeking the touch of sand and finding it. Coughing, spluttering, sobbing, she stumbled back to the shore and collapsed. The salt in her sinuses was agony, and she thought she was going to be sick. She snorted and spat, rubbing her eyes with fists of sandpaper.

Little by little, the salty anguish subsided. "I almost drowned," Maud said to the darkening sky. She had always heard that it was possible to drown in a small amount of water. Now she knew it was true. For the first time, the horror of Caroline Lambert's death struck home. She had imagined it wrong. Whenever she thought about it, she had pictured Caroline floating on her back and falling asleep, while the water slid over her face like a blanket. Now she knew better. Caroline had died fighting, her body battered by a power too fierce to resist. The words of Hyacinth's singsong came back to Maud:

> *They row'd her in across the rolling foam,*
> *The cruel crawling foam,*
> *The cruel hungry foam,*
> *To her grave beside the sea.*

Maud shivered. She thought of the figure in her dreams—the ghost-child Caroline. It frightened her that she, who was impersonating Caroline, had nearly shared her fate. She wanted Caroline to leave her alone—she wanted to stop thinking about her—she wanted the dead girl to get out of her dreams.

Maud leaped to her feet. She would leave the ocean and the solitude of the shore. She wanted lights, people, noise, Hyacinth—or Muffet. . . . But Hyacinth was not at home and Muffet mustn't see her all sandy and wet. She couldn't risk either of them knowing what had happened that night.

The Amusement Park. Maud broke into a run. Even if she couldn't ride the carousel, she would be among people. There would be crowds, laughter, the smell of good things to eat. Caroline's ghost would not haunt her there.

She felt better the moment she passed under the brightly lit arch. As she had guessed, the park was crowded, and the crowds seemed particularly merry. Maud eavesdropped and lollygagged, wending her way toward the merry-go-round.

By the time she reached it, the sky was black and the stars were coming out. Maud wormed her way to the front of the crowd and drank in the music of the calliope. Lips parted, she gazed at the animals: which would she ride, if she had a nickel?

She had daydreamed through four rides when the red-haired man beckoned. He was holding up a fragment of cardboard. Maud plunged forward, agog with hope.

"What's that?" demanded Maud, though she knew.

"That's your ticket," answered the man. "A nice lady saw you watching and bought you a ticket."

A nice lady. Maud's heart sank. She had forgotten all about Mrs. Lambert. Her eyes raked the crowd, catching sight of a fashionably wide-brimmed hat. Yes, Mrs. Lambert was there. It would be Mrs. Lambert. She was watching expectantly, waiting for Maud to betray some sign of pleasure. Maud imagined what Hyacinth would say if she knew that her partner in crime was in the company of their chosen victim. She thrust the thought aside. This might be her only chance to ride the carousel.

"All right," she said tersely. She nipped the ticket out of the man's fingers and turned her back on Mrs. Lambert, heading for the tiger. There was only one tiger, and she meant to ride him—but a long-legged boy was already astride him. All around her, children swarmed, claiming their mounts. Parents lifted the smallest children to the horses' backs. Maud was terrified that all the most beautiful animals would be chosen and her ride would be wasted on an animal she didn't like. She didn't want to ride the pig or the leaping frog, and the zebra in front of her was baring his teeth in an uncouth fashion. She heard the first notes of music and scrambled into the saddle of the nearest horse.

He was a beautiful horse. Maud let out her breath. He was as white as sugar, and his mane swirled and peaked like icing. He had glass jewels on his harness: rubies and sapphires and emeralds. If she leaned sideways, she could admire the curving arch of his neck and the sweet expression on his face. He was serene, magnificent. As the music grew louder, he leaped into the air and eased downward. Maud floated. She was weightless, soaring, splendid. She squinted a little so that the electric lights wavered and swelled.

For several blissful minutes, she circled and flew. All too soon, the music slowed. At last the white horse halted, halfway up his pole. Children slid off their mounts and parents surged forward, calling their names.

Maud pressed her palms on either side of the horse's neck. "I'll always ride you," she promised rashly. "I'll always like you best, and I'll name you—" She hesitated. She knew if she chose the right name, he would be hers forever. "I'll call you Angel."

It was the right name. He was white and benevolent, and he flew. Maud slid off and looked at him from the side. There was a sculpted hollow at the edge of his lips, which made him look as if he were smiling. Maud caressed it, smiling back tenderly. She was still smiling as she walked to the platform's edge.

"Just a moment." The red-haired man caught her as she stepped off. "Wait a minute, duckling. Aren't you forgetting something?"

During the ride, Maud had forgotten everything. Now her eyes grew wide with dismay.

"I'm talking about 'thank you,'" said the red-haired man. "Don't you want to say 'thank you' to the nice lady who bought you the ticket?"

Maud's mouth fell open. *No,* she wanted to say, but the red-haired man was steering her straight for Mrs. Lambert. His hands on her shoulders were strong and purposeful. She had an idea that she could drag her feet or squirm but it wouldn't make any difference.

"Rory, don't force her!" Mrs. Lambert's voice was disagreeably familiar. "I don't need her to thank me. Leave her alone—you'll frighten her."

Maud risked a glance at Mrs. Lambert. The rich woman appeared flustered, and Maud felt a surge of irritation. A grown-up, especially a rich grown-up, should have more self-confidence.

"She ought to say 'thank you,'" insisted the red-haired man. He leaned down, addressing Maud. "Somebody does something nice for you, you say 'thank you.' Didn't your mother teach you that?"

"My mother's dead," flashed back Maud.

She saw Mrs. Lambert wince. "Rory, let her go."

The heavy hands remained in place. "If she don't know any better, she ought to be taught."

If she don't know any better. Maud took in the critical words and saw Mrs. Lambert's pitying glance. All at once, she understood: they thought she was poor. Mrs. Lambert had paid for her as if she were a beggar. Rory was trying to teach her manners as if she were only half-civilized. Maud felt a stab of shame that changed swiftly to outrage. She was conscious that she was barefoot, that her dress was tawdry, that she was wearing the absolute minimum of underclothing. Nevertheless, she was respectable — she was not a street child. She flung back her head, cheeks scarlet.

"Thank you, ma'am." She spoke with the exquisite crispness that Hyacinth required of an angel child. She borrowed a leaf from Lord Fauntleroy's book and quoted, "I'm ever so much obliged to you."

She had the satisfaction of seeing the pity in Mrs. Lambert's eyes turn to astonishment. She caught hold of her damp skirts and sketched a curtsy, pointing her grubby toes. "Thank you," she repeated. "I enjoyed the ride — tremendously. Good-bye." With one violent twist, she jerked herself free of Rory's hands and sprinted for the safety of the crowd.

In the dreams, Caroline's hair was brown, not golden.
The girl was kneeling beside her, patting the sand of
Maud's newly built castle. Caroline's head was bent,
and her curls tumbled down, concealing her face.
They were glorious curls: lush, tangled, silky, the sort
that Maud had envied all her life. But they were not
golden. They were the color of molasses—several
shades lighter than Maud's sparse locks, but distinctly
brown.

"I almost drowned today," Maud told Caroline.
She groped in the sand, searching for the shell she
used as a spade.

Caroline handed it over. "You didn't drown," she
contradicted. "You got water up your nose. I've had
that lots of times."

Maud shut her lips tightly. It was just like Caroline
to contradict her. Caroline thought nothing important could happen to anyone but herself.

"It's an awful feeling," Caroline said kindly, "getting water up your nose. Did you cry?"

"No," denied Maud, doubly annoyed because
Caroline hadn't realized she was being snubbed.

"I always cry," Caroline confided, as if there were
nothing wrong with that.

"You're a crybaby," Maud said disagreeably. She

looked up from the sand castle. It was early morning, and the gulls were swooping over the water, gleaning for food. There was no one on the beach but the two children. The freshness of the morning reminded Maud that she never left the house by day, which in turn told her she was dreaming. "I don't see why you're always bothering my dreams," she told Caroline.

Caroline didn't answer.

"Why don't you haunt your mother's dreams?" demanded Maud. "She'd like that, probably. *I* don't want you."

"I can't," replied Caroline. "She's too miserable."

"She's miserable because you drowned," Maud said accusingly.

"Yes, but I didn't do it on purpose." Caroline pulled one leg up to her chest and fingered a scab on her knee. Her petticoats were snow white and frothy with lace—*real lace,* Maud thought savagely. What a waste.

"I wish you'd tell her about my shoes and stockings," Caroline said.

Maud frowned at her sand castle. "I don't know about your shoes and stockings," she retorted. "Why should I tell her about your shoes and stockings?"

She waited for Caroline to reply. Then she saw she was alone. The sand lay around her in smooth hills. There were no marks, no footprints—not even a hollow where Caroline had been sitting.

CHAPTER TWENTY-ONE

Maud twitched in her sleep. The sheet she held to her throat was moving. Someone was pulling it away from her. Maud opened her eyes and saw that the someone was Muffet. It was early morning and the hired woman was glaring at her. Maud sat up, blinking. Even half-asleep, she grasped that she was in trouble.

Muffet pointed to the window. Before it was a chair, draped with the striped dress Maud had worn the night before. Maud had placed it there to dry.

Muffet stumped over to the dress, held it up, and rubbed the fabric between her thumb and fingers. *Sandy,* the gesture proclaimed. *Wet. You've been down to the ocean.*

Maud groaned. She pressed the heels of her hands against her eye sockets and racked her brains for an answer. She wondered if she could persuade Muffet that, even though she never left the house by day, it was all right if she played outdoors at night. It wouldn't be easy. Of all the people in the household, Muffet was the most difficult to mislead. It was really too much, Maud thought with a stab of self-pity, the number of lies she had to keep track of now that she lived with the Hawthorne sisters.

Muffet had not finished stating her case. She marched over to the bed and pointed to a few grains of sand that had ended up in Maud's bed. She fingered a lock of Maud's hair. Her gaze was intensely critical.

"I know," Maud agreed. "My hair feels awful— I think it's the salt water. Do you suppose I could wash it today?"

Muffet took out her tablet. She scrawled MAUD NOT GO IN WATER OR MAUD DEAD.

Maud read the message, appreciative of the fact

that Muffet was using the word *or,* which was new to her. It had taken Maud some pains to teach the meaning of *or.* Maud wrote MAUD NOT DEAD, tapped her chest as if to prove it, smiled placatingly, and returned the tablet to Muffet.

Muffet snorted, exasperated. She sat down on the bed and proceeded to draw. Maud gazed over her shoulder, fascinated as the seascape took shape—a long line of rocks leading from shore to sky, the curving waves, last night's waning moon. Between the waves there was a head, and two arms raised in desperation. Muffet put down her pencil, lifted her hands, and began to gasp for air. It was a vivid and ugly pantomime of a person drowning.

Remembering the night before, Maud felt her skin prickle with gooseflesh. Had Muffet seen . . . ? No. The shore had been deserted. Maud pushed the thought aside. The ocean had frightened her the night before, but she had every intention of going back to it. She took the tablet and tried to draw a picture of herself playing in the sand. She mimed making a castle, pulling the bedsheet into peaks. She assumed her most pleading expression. *I only play in the sand.*

Muffet's eyes narrowed.

Maud pinched the grains of sand from the sheet and let them trickle onto the tablet. Beside them, she wrote the word SAND. Then she wrote MAUD WORK IN SAND—Muffet hadn't yet learned the word for *play.*

Muffet snatched the pencil and wrote MAUD IN WATER. She went back to the dress and wrung out the hem, producing a few drops of moisture. *You weren't just playing with the sand; you were in the water.*

Maud threw up her palms, asking for mercy.

Muffet jotted down MAUD IN HOUSE and held the tablet so Maud could see.

Maud shook her head. She took the tablet and wrote HOT IN HOUSE. MAUD GO OUT HOUSE. She stopped with the pencil in her hand. She wished she had the words to tell Muffet how much she wanted to go out. The attic was not just hot; it was suffocating. She was sick of being a secret child, of feeling lonely and invisible and forlorn. Outside was the freshness of the wind and the ocean and the magic of the carousel. An idea came to her. She seized the pencil and began a sketch more complicated than any she had tried before.

She began with an upside-down triangle, for the carousel's canopy, and drew four stick horses, two up and two down. She drew herself standing to one side and made a dotted line going from her eye to the merry-go-round. Surely Muffet would understand that staying in the house was hopeless when there were things like that just beyond the back door.

Muffet was interested. She sat back down on the bed and watched the drawing take shape. After the fourth horse appeared, the light of recognition came into her face, and she raised one hand, miming the up-and-down motion of the flying horses. Evidently she had seen the merry-go-round.

Maud nodded. She wrote MAUD GO OUT HOUSE. MAUD GO SEE—she drew an arrow and printed CAROUSEL under the flying horses.

Muffet took the tablet from her. Her pencil moved rapidly, fleshing out the horses, changing the upside-down triangle into a cone. She often corrected Maud's drawings—Maud suspected that her stick figures were as distressing to Muffet as Muffet's clothes were to Maud. She watched respectfully as Muffet rounded out Maud's self-portrait with sleeves, a sash, and hair.

Muffet finished correcting the drawing and wrote MAUD GO SEE CAROUSEL. Then she wrote MAUD WORK IN SAND. And afterward, with such pressure that the tip of the pencil broke, MAUD NOT GO IN WATER OR MAUD DEAD.

Maud took away the tablet. With the nub of the

pencil, she drew a pair of feet, with a wavy line just up to the ankles. MAUD GO IN LITTLE WATER.

Muffet shook her head. She wrote MAUD NOT GO IN WATER.

Maud realized this was an ultimatum. She bowed her head. In smaller letters, she conceded, MAUD NOT GO IN WATER. MAUD WORK IN SAND. MAUD GO SEE CAROUSEL.

Muffet nodded, patted her shoulder, and pointed toward the bedclothes. *Make your bed.* Obediently, Maud stood up and began to pull the sheet taut. The hired woman withdrew to her own room, only to reappear, holding out a closed fist. There was a tentative smile on her face. Slowly she uncurled her fingers, showing five dimes on her palm.

Maud gazed at her blankly.

Muffet took Maud's hand and tipped the dimes into it.

"Mine?" breathed Maud.

Muffet bowed her head like a soprano acknowledging bouquets thrown from the balcony. She took up the tablet and wrote proudly MAUD GO IN CAROUSEL.

Maud's brain reeled. Five dimes. Fifty cents. Ten rides on Angel, or nine rides and an ice-cream cone. . . . Why, the boardwalk was full of things that could be bought for fifty cents! She had seen the signs. She could see a moving picture show, or buy a little bottle of cologne. She could have a frankfurter or a grilled sandwich or an egg cream or a whole big bag of candy. "Oh, *Muffet*." She knew that the hired woman earned little more than a dollar a week.

Muffet's smile spread to a grin. She held out her hands and Maud leaped forward, wrapping her arms around the hired woman's waist.

"Caroline," begged Hyacinth, in the heartbroken voice of a mother who had lost her child, "where are you? Why did you leave me?"

Maud lifted her eyes to the ceiling. The questions that Hyacinth had just asked were numbers seven and twenty-one on the list she had memorized. She knew the answers, of course, but it was the first time Hyacinth had combined separate questions, and she wasn't sure which to answer first. "I am right beside you, dear Mama," she answered in her sweetest voice. "I am closer than your shadow."

"Why did you leave me?" persisted Hyacinth.

"Dear Mama," Maud replied, "I didn't leave you. I never shall. It was time for me to leave your world— that is all."

"Why haven't you spoken to me before?" demanded Hyacinth.

"Dear Mama," Maud began, "I tried to speak, but you couldn't hear me. Tonight it's different. The other lady makes it easier for me to come to you." She scratched her nose. "Do I have to say the 'dear Mama' part every time?"

"Every time." Hyacinth kicked a footstool into place beside her chair, put up her feet, and lolled backward.

"It's the same thing over and over," complained Maud.

"It's affectionate," said Hyacinth. "Mrs. Lambert will want you to be affectionate." She glanced at the list she had written out for Maud and chose another question. "Do you forgive me?"

Maud sighed. That was number four. "Dear Mama! There is nothing to forgive! Are you sure she's going to ask that one?"

"They all ask that one." Hyacinth sighed mournfully. "Oh, Caroline! If only I could hold you in my arms!"

"Perhaps you may, sometime," Maud said evasively.

"Dear Mama," prompted Hyacinth.

"Perhaps you may, sometime, dear Mama," Maud said.

"Good." Hyacinth ran her finger down the list. "Where are you, Caroline? Are you in heaven?"

Maud pitched her voice so that it sounded high and faraway. "I am in a country that is called by many names," she answered plaintively. "Oh, Mama! How beautiful it is! I wish you could see it—the sparkling sunlight and the lilies and the streets as clear as crystal!"

"Are you happy there, my child?"

"Oh, Mama, so happy!" Maud grimaced. "I hate that line. It makes me feel silly."

"Well, of course, a good deal of this is silly," conceded Hyacinth. "However, that's neither here nor there. When can I hold you in my arms, my darling child?"

That was an easy one. "Soon," Maud promised. "Dear Mama, I hope it will be soon! You must ask the lady to help us."

"Excellent." Hyacinth folded the list. "Very nicely done."

"When is the séance?" demanded Maud, flopping down on the carpet close to the footstool. "Wednesday or Thursday?"

"Thursday, perhaps. Judith and I are still working out the details. She's nervous." Hyacinth tapped the folded paper against her palm. "A great deal rests on your shoulders."

Maud was aware of this. "I know my lines."

"Of course you do. Besides, people are dreadfully predictable—they all say the same sort of thing, and I have prepared you particularly well. However—if there should be some question you can't answer—"

Maud recognized this for the cue it was. She rose on her knees and clasped her hands piously. "Dear Mama, I can't hear you! It is as if there were a gulf between us. . . . Oh, Mama, I can no longer feel your presence. Farewell, dear Mama! I will come again!"

Hyacinth corrected her. "Farewell, dear Mama. I love you. I will come again. You tend to leave out the 'I love you.'"

Maud sat back on her heels, crestfallen.

"However"—Hyacinth's voice made her look up again—"on the whole, your performance is remarkable. Quite perfect. I have absolutely no fear that you won't pull the thing off."

"I'll do my best."

"Of course you will." Hyacinth lounged against the back of the chair, her eyes half-shut. "You are really the most extraordinary child . . . so clever . . . *such* a little actress. . . ." Her voice trailed off, and Maud wondered if she were falling asleep. She hoped she wasn't. It was the first time in a week that Hyacinth had spared time to talk to her, and she wanted to hear more about how clever she was. She wondered if she dared rouse her by touching her hand.

Before she could make up her mind, the door opened, and Judith came in with a letter. "Hyacinth, Mrs. Fortescue's written to you."

Hyacinth sat bolt upright and put out her hand. Rapidly, she tore open the envelope and read the letter.

"Does she want a séance?" demanded Judith.

"Better than that." The eyes that had been half-shut glittered with anticipation. "She's having a house party in Philadelphia—all next week—and we're invited to come."

"Which one is Mrs. Fortescue?" asked Maud. She had heard the name but paid little attention to it. Mrs. Fortescue, Mrs. Sheffield, Miss Quigley, Mrs. Lugwig. All of them were Hyacinth's clients, but they were of no importance to Maud. Their dead relations were all grown-ups.

"The wife of a millionaire," answered Hyacinth. "Judith and I helped her contact her twin sister, who died thirty years ago. She lives in a veritable mansion—she knows all the most fashionable people in Philadelphia—the house will be full of them! No doubt Judith and I will be the entertainment."

"Séances?" asked Maud.

"Certainly." Hyacinth put down the letter. "Judith, it's a splendid opportunity. We'll see people we'd never meet anywhere else."

Judith nodded. "We'll take the steamer, I suppose?"

"It's an easy journey—five or six hours, I believe—so much pleasanter than the train. Oh, Judith, it's perfect!" Hyacinth's eyes were shining. "Think of the clients we can acquire! Rich as Croesus, every man Jack of them!"

"What about me?" asked Maud.

The two women looked startled. They had forgotten her.

"We can't *not* go," Hyacinth said breathlessly.

"I suppose we might ask Victoria to look after—" Judith began.

"No!" Hyacinth's voice was sharp. "I won't have Victoria here. Really, I'm surprised at you, Judith! She could put all sorts of morbid ideas into Maud's head! Why, she could ruin everything!"

Judith glanced meaningfully at Maud. "We can't

leave the child by herself. And I can't stay with her. You'll need me for the séances."

"Can't I come?" begged Maud. She knew it was futile, even before the sisters chorused, "No."

"She'll be with Muffet," Hyacinth began.

"No." Judith repeated. "The woman's close to a half-wit. What if there were a fire—or a burglar? She can't hear, and Maud—"

"Muffet's not a half-wit," interjected Maud.

"Of course not," Hyacinth said silkily. "She may be deaf, but she's perfectly well able to look after Maud. Besides, Maud's not a baby. She's accustomed to amusing herself, aren't you, Maud?"

Maud could not think. Her stomach was churning and she didn't know why. She imagined a week with Hyacinth and Judith gone. She saw herself free, able to walk all over the house, even to sleep on the first-floor sofa, where it would be cool at night. She pictured herself by the ocean every evening, or prowling up and down the boardwalk with Muffet's dimes in her fist. Nevertheless, she felt a lump in her throat. A moment ago Hyacinth had been saying how clever she was. Now she was leaving.

"How can we tell Muffet?" asked Judith. "We can't leave her in charge of an empty house, with no one to tell her what to do. How will she know we're coming back?"

"I can tell her," Maud said. She was tired of hearing the Hawthorne sisters talk about the hired woman as if she were some kind of animal. "Muffet understands me."

"There, do you see?" Hyacinth smiled radiantly. "Maud and Muffet will do very well together—and a week isn't long. Why, it's no time at all!" Her face clouded. "I wonder if I should buy a new dress. I daresay they will all be very fashionable—my silver moiré is quite—"

"*No,*" Judith said grimly. "You've already spent a fortune on clothes."

"My dear Judith, if one wants to go among fashionable people, it is essential—"

Maud scowled. They were forgetting her again. "What about Mrs. Lambert?"

Judith looked uneasy. "Oh, gracious, that's right. We had promised—"

"Yes, but we can put her off."

"A bird in the hand—"

Hyacinth shook her head. "Now, don't fuss, Judith! Delay increases desire—you know that. I can tell Eleanor that Mrs. Fortescue needs my help—

urgently—she will *quite* understand if I do it properly, and we'll have the séance as soon as we come back. Provided"—she inclined her head—"provided our darling Maud practices her lines every day. Will you, Maud?"

"I know my lines," Maud said gruffly.

"Every day," Hyacinth said sweetly. She clasped the letter to her breast. "It won't be long, Maudy. Just a week. Will you miss me so terribly, terribly much?"

Maud stood up. Her eyes met Hyacinth's. "Actually," she said slowly, "I don't expect to miss you at all."

There was a brief, dreadful pause, during which Maud quailed, certain that she had gone too far. But Hyacinth did not take offense. Her eyes did not even flicker. She ran one finger down Maud's cheek. "Oh, well said, Maudy!" The whispered words trembled on the brink of laughter. Without another word, she rose from her chair and glided out of the room, leaving Maud torn between relief and something like fear.

CHAPTER TWENTY-TWO

Three days later Judith and Hyacinth took the steamer to Philadelphia, leaving Maud to the freedom she craved. It was, Maud found, a limited and disappointing freedom. She had the run of the house, but the front rooms were shuttered and still; though she would not admit it to herself, the silence made her nervous. She walked through the house on tiptoe and whispered when she played. After a day or so, she withdrew to the rooms that had never been forbidden: the attic and Muffet's kitchen.

She never left the house in the daytime. She had been a secret child long enough to develop a fear of being conspicuous; she could not imagine going out in full sunlight. Instead, she waited until the dinner hour, watching the neighbors' yards from an upstairs window. Stealthily she crept to the kitchen, opened the screen door, and ran barefoot across the grass.

Then the world was hers, and she was off to the ocean. Each night, it was different: warmer or colder, more or less rough; it changed color as the light changed in the sky. Maud could not resist it. In spite of her promise to Muffet, she waded in the shallows, taking care not to get her skirt wet. Once she followed the shore till she came to the rock wall that stretched from the sand to the horizon. Two boys were out on the rocks, wrestling and shoving each other. Maud watched them until their mother shouted at them to come off that jetty before they broke their necks.

So. The rock wall was called a jetty. Maud was intrigued. Something about the jetty struck her as vaguely familiar. She pictured herself walking on it, striding to the very end, with the sunset around her and the frenzied waves lashing her feet. She would feel like a heroine; people on the beach would marvel at her brave silhouette against the sky. As soon as the boys were out of sight, she clambered up onto the rocks. Climbing was harder than she expected. The rocks were slick and sharp, and there was nothing to hold on to. Almost at once she fell, bruising her leg and skinning the palm of one hand. She took half a dozen steps and fell again. This time, she didn't get to her feet right away, but sat still, licking the blood off her palm. It was easy to imagine slipping off the jetty into the rough waves. She didn't know how deep the water was, and she had no one to forbid her to break her neck. Slowly she got up and retraced her steps, anchoring each foothold before shifting her weight. When she reached the shore, she let out her breath. Another time she would walk on the jetty. Not tonight.

She left the jetty for the boardwalk, which she had never had time to explore. The next night she strolled from one end to the other, perusing every sign and peering through doorways. She learned that Ping-Pong was not a delicacy but a sort of parlor game. She risked a nickel on a bag of buttered popcorn and found it tasted even better than it smelled. Once it was gone, she scolded herself—Muffet's gift was too precious to be squandered on food. She must make it last. The next evening, she happened upon a pushcart where damaged books could be had for a nickel. Maud pawed through it and emerged triumphant with a copy of *Ragged Dick: Or, Street Life in New York with the Boot Blacks.*

She rode the merry-go-round every night. It was balm to her injured pride to utter the words "One ticket, please" at the ticket booth and to present her ticket to Rory. The carousel keeper greeted her laconically, "Rob a bank?"—to which Maud replied, "No, sir," in her primmest voice. She was faithful to Angel and rode him night after night, turning a blind eye to the tiger and the stag. It took all her self-control not to ride twice in a row. Each evening, she slid from the saddle with greater reluctance.

There was risk in riding the merry-go-round. More often than not, Maud caught sight of Mrs. Lambert in the surrounding crowd. The rich woman's gaze was no longer fixed on Caroline's sea monster. Instead, her eyes followed Maud. One night, as Angel dipped and soared, Maud yielded to impulse: she raised one hand in Mrs. Lambert's direction and flickered her fingers.

Mrs. Lambert's face lit up. Her face expanded in a smile; she lifted her gloved hand and waved back so vigorously that Maud could not help herself. With every rotation, she waved at Mrs. Lambert, and Mrs. Lambert beamed and wagged her hand.

It was a mistake—Maud knew it. Once the merry-go-round stopped, she jumped off Angel and fled to the other side of the carousel. As soon as her toes touched the ground, she ran. She didn't look back until she reached the edge of the ocean. The rich woman stood on the boardwalk, beneath the electric lights. Her eyes scanned the dusk without seeing.

Maud turned away and began to walk at the water's edge. She told herself she would never wave at Mrs. Lambert again. She would keep away from the carousel the next few nights. There were plenty of other things to do, after all. She would save her crusts and feed them to the seagulls. She would gather shells for the collection she was hiding in the box room. Even as she planned for the next night's amusements, she was wading deeper and deeper into the water, enjoying the fizz of the foam about her knees. Before long, her dress was soaked to the waist.

Maud sighed. Now she had disobeyed Muffet. She would just have to hope that the hired woman wouldn't be in the kitchen when she returned. She supposed that she might as well go on bathing. She played alertly, bobbing up and down with the waves, retreating whenever they rose to her armpits. When she skipped home, it was with the smug conviction that she had learned how to handle the ocean.

But her luck was out. Muffet met her at the kitchen door. At the sight of Maud's wet dress, the hired woman's face turned to stone. Maud flinched. No one had struck her since she left the Barbary Asylum, but Muffet looked angry enough to slap her. Maud dodged past the hired woman and flew upstairs. Muffet pursued her with such vigor that Maud wondered if the steps would give way.

Muffet did not touch her. Nevertheless, she made it clear that Maud was in disgrace. The next morning, when Maud got out of bed, she was unable to find her clothes. There was no point in sketching them and shoving the drawing pad under Muffet's nose: Muffet ignored her. Maud spent the day in her nightdress, feeling slatternly and frustrated. She sulked as hard as she could, but the look on Muffet's face spoke volumes. *We struck a bargain. You broke your promise. It serves you right.*

Maud was greatly relieved the following morning, when she found her dresses back on their hooks. The striped dress lay at the foot of her bed. Maud flew to the hired woman with her arms held out. Muffet returned the embrace, but her eyes were skeptical. Maud knew that when she returned that evening, Muffet would be lying in wait, alert for any sign that Maud had disobeyed.

On that night, Maud realized that Mrs. Lambert was following her.

She didn't expect to see Mrs. Lambert away from the Amusement Park. Maud was building a sand castle when she saw the rich woman approaching. Even at a distance, Maud recognized her. No one else would wear such a ravishing hat at such an awkward angle. Mrs. Lambert's skirt was fashionably narrow, and her high-heeled boots were the worst possible footwear for walking on sand. Her parasol lurched as she strove to keep her balance. She was risking a turned ankle with every step.

It occurred to Maud that nothing would be easier than to run away from her. Oddly enough, it would be too easy—Maud couldn't bring herself to do it. She bent over her castle and pretended she was invisible.

"I saw your castle from the boardwalk," Mrs. Lambert said breathlessly, "and I wanted to see up close. May I?"

Maud sat back on her haunches and spread her sandy hands, as if to say, "Go ahead and look." She recognized Mrs. Lambert's excuse for the ploy it was. She had made a study of sand castles during the past week, and she knew that her own were rather crude.

"It's very nice," Mrs. Lambert said.

Maud bowed her head. Mrs. Lambert's slow progress down the beach had given her time to think. She had made up her mind that she wouldn't speak more than a word or two. The last thing she wanted was for Mrs. Lambert to become familiar with the sound of her voice. She was glad that Rory wasn't there to wring another thank-you out of her.

Mrs. Lambert surprised Maud. She cast herself down on her knees, stabbing her parasol in the sand. Shocked, Maud reviewed her clothes. A shirtwaist adorned with minute tucks; a starched linen skirt, immaculate boots and gloves. *Good* clothes, Maud thought—not clothes for groveling on the sand. She was even more surprised to see the rich woman remove her hatpins, her hat, and her gloves.

"Did you ever make a crocodile?"

"What?" blurted out Maud. She blushed for herself. It was horribly rude to say "what." Hyacinth would be appalled.

"Sand crocodiles," explained Mrs. Lambert. "My—
I used to make them. I'll show you." Already the un-
gloved hands were scooping the sand into a mound.
Mrs. Lambert was kneeling in the sand, playing like
a child.

Thrown off-guard, Maud watched. She saw that
Mrs. Lambert's crocodile was a beast of some size—
the mound taking shape was as long as she was, with
a sinuous curve at one end that must be the tail.

"You can't make many animals in the sand," Mrs.
Lambert told her, as if Maud had asked, "because of
the necks. Most animals have heads that stick up, but
a crocodile lies flat on the ground."

"Um," said Maud, and began to help with the
mound.

"The eyes are the hard part. You can mold little
balls of very wet sand and put them on top of the
head, but generally it's better if you find two pebbles
the same size." Mrs. Lambert looked directly into
Maud's eyes. "Could you find me two round pebbles,
perhaps? And a shell with a curved edge?"

Maud nodded and got to her feet. Still perplexed,
she headed down to the water. It was another opportunity to escape. She could run away before Mrs.
Lambert noticed she was gone. She turned to look

over her shoulder. Mrs. Lambert was sculpting the back leg of the crocodile. Her hair was coming undone; flaxen wisps unfurled in the breeze. Maud began to search for pebbles.

By the time she found two the same size, three of the crocodile's legs were finished. Maud held out the pebbles and the shell. "What's the shell for?"

"Scales," answered Mrs. Lambert. She demonstrated, sinking the edge of the shell in the sand, making a curved line. Then she handed the shell back to Maud. Maud squatted down to continue the pattern.

She went on scaling the crocodile as Mrs. Lambert nestled the pebbles into the eye sockets. Now that the beast had eyes, it looked alive. An idea came to Maud. She picked up a water-rotted stick and held it out.

"What's that for?" asked Mrs. Lambert.

"Teeth," mumbled Maud.

"Ohhh," Mrs. Lambert said appreciatively. She began to break the stick into inch-long pieces, pressing them into the crocodile's jaws. Satisfied that she was doing a good job, Maud resumed making scales. When the crocodile was scaly from nose tip to tail tip, Maud sat back on her heels and watched Mrs. Lambert. She was applying the finishing touches — poking the left nostril, which was shallower than its mate, pinching a finer claw on the left foreleg.

"Why are you following me?"

During the making of the crocodile, Mrs. Lambert had relaxed. Maud's question caught her off-guard. "I hope I haven't frightened you."

Maud shook her head.

A faint flush stained Mrs. Lambert's cheeks. She looked younger, bareheaded. *She's bashful,* thought Maud. She had come to think that Mrs. Lambert was foolish, or a little mad. Now she saw that the woman was shy.

"I—noticed you." Mrs. Lambert was almost stammering. "I used to have a little girl, so I notice little girls—especially the ones the same age as my daughter."

"I'm eleven," Maud said rashly.

"I wondered," Mrs. Lambert went on, "if you were—all right. I've seen you playing in the water by yourself—always at night—and it's worried me. It really isn't safe for you to bathe by yourself. And I've been afraid—because you said your mother was dead—that you didn't have any home." The last words came in a rush. "That's why I've been watching you. I've been worried that you had no one to look after you."

Maud uttered an "oh" of pure surprise. She had never imagined that anyone could think she was a street child, like Oliver Twist or Ragged Dick the Bootblack. Her eyes fell to the striped dress she had sewed. It was worse than she thought if it made people think she had no home.

"There are places for children who need someone to look after them," Mrs. Lambert continued. "Some of them aren't very nice, but some are good places. There's a small orphanage just outside Cape Calypso— it's very friendly, and the children have toys and ice cream and regular outings—I know the people who run it and—"

At the word *orphanage,* Maud rebelled. "I don't need an orphanage," she flared. "I have a home. I live with—my father. So there!"

"I see," Mrs. Lambert said. She looked unconvinced.

"Yes," Maud said firmly, "with my father. And my little brothers—I have to look after them, because I'm the oldest and"—triumphantly—"that's why I only come out at night. All day long I have to stay home and look after my brothers because they're babies—and my father works all day in—" She hesitated only a second. "In a canning factory." She did not know if there was a canning factory in Cape Calypso, but she knew about canning factories; the girls at the Barbary Asylum often ended up at the canning factory. "So he doesn't get home until late, see, and when he does, he tells me to go out and get some fresh air. But I can't bring my brothers with me, because they're too little. They'd drown," finished Maud, and grimaced at the word.

"How old are they?"

"They're little," Maud said recklessly, "and their names are Dick and Oliver."

"And your name?"

Maud hesitated. Some instinct led her to hold back her first name. "Mary," she said, skipping to her middle name. Then she bit her tongue. Caroline's middle name was Mary, too. "Mary Fagin."

Mrs. Lambert brushed her palm against her skirt and offered her hand. "Mine is Mrs. Lambert."

Maud didn't want to take her hand. She plucked at her dress. "You prob'ly think I've only got this one dress, but that's not true. I have lots of dresses—real pretty dresses—but I wear this one in case I might want to bathe. It's kind of—a bathing dress. I sewed it myself. My mother made me. She was teaching me to sew."

Mrs. Lambert nodded. A shadow had passed over her face. "Then—your mother died only a little while ago?"

Maud's stomach knotted. She wished she had run

away earlier, when it was possible. Already she had talked too much. She had not made any fatal errors—not yet—but she dared not trust herself. It had been over a week since she exchanged spoken words with anyone, and she wanted to go on talking.

She saw a drop of moisture fall on the sand, turning the ivory grains to amber. Mrs. Lambert's eyes were overflowing. "I'm so sorry." She fumbled in her bosom for a handkerchief and offered it to Maud. Maud handed it back. She wasn't the one crying, after all.

Mrs. Lambert gave a little gulp of laughter. "I'm afraid—I cry—very easily—since my daughter died." She wiped her eyes. "What was your mother like?"

No one had ever asked Maud what her mother was like. She had even been told that she couldn't remember her mother. It was true that her memories were hazy and few. What she remembered best was lying in bed and listening for her mother's footsteps. If they made one sound, her mother was happy and it would be a happy day. Another sound, and it was a workday, when her mother flew from one task to another so energetically that Maud could not keep up with her. She remembered snatching at her mother's skirts, trying to capture her attention.

"She was a schoolteacher before she married my father," Maud said slowly. She was sure about that. She had been told. "And she used to read to me. Mother Goose and fairy tales." She squeezed shut her eyes, trying to see the book with her mother's thumbs at the sides. "And one day I just started reading—I was four years old, but I knew how. She told everyone I was clever. She was proud of me."

Mrs. Lambert was smiling. Maud cast her mind back a second time. Her memories included scoldings as well as fairy tales—Maud had an uneasy knowledge that her mother's love had been fierce as well as tender. All the same, she never doubted that her mother had loved and prized her.

"We had red geraniums," she said tentatively. She remembered the peppery smell. "There were . . . pots of them and I used to water them and she used to tell me when to stop." The image came clear: a red-brown pot with a bead of water swelling to a bulge at one side. She had been blissful, watering the flowers while her mother stood by. "I think she thought I was pretty."

"I'm sure she did," Mrs. Lambert said simply.

Maud felt a lump in her throat. Something about those four words pierced the scorn that she felt for the rich woman. *She's nice,* Maud thought unwillingly, and her heart sank. She didn't want Mrs. Lambert to be nice. "What was your little girl like?"

"Caroline?" Mrs. Lambert spoke the word very gently. She gazed out over the waves, as if expecting to see Caroline out to sea. "Caroline was very bold. That was one of the things I loved about her—that she was so free and candid and brave. I was such a timid child. My father and mother were strict, and I was always afraid of doing something wrong. But Caroline was fearless."

Maud squinted into the sunset. The blue of the sky was turning violet, with streaks of mauve and tangerine. The green of the ocean had darkened. "How was she brave?"

"Oh, in so many ways! For one thing, she was never shy—she always thought everyone would like her, so of course, they did. All kinds of people—and she liked them. She made friends with a beggar-man who lived in the street. He was very dirty and he smelled of beer, but Caroline thought he was funny; she would sit on the steps and talk to him for hours, if I didn't stop her. She was brave in other ways, too. One time there was a snake in the cellar stairwell— the servants were frightened to death of it. It was over a yard long, but Caroline said she'd read about black snakes in her animal book and they weren't poisonous. She marched right down the steps and picked it up with her bare hands. I nearly fainted."

Against her will, Maud was impressed. She knew she would never pick up any snake, poisonous or not. "I guess that was brave," she said grudgingly.

"People said I spoiled her." Mrs. Lambert spoke as if she had forgotten Maud. "I suppose I did. I didn't want to break her spirit, and heaven knows there was money for the things she wanted. After her father died, she was often naughty. I sometimes think she misbehaved on purpose, to keep from missing him too much."

Maud pricked up her ears. "What did she do that was bad?"

"She was very willful," Mrs. Lambert said reluctantly. "She was used to having her own way, and when I didn't give in, she teased and coaxed. She never gave up. I found her—difficult." Once again she took her handkerchief from her bosom. She pressed it over her lips and held it there, as if she were stifling her own cries.

Maud combed the sand with her fingers. She knew Mrs. Lambert was about to cry, and when she cried,

Maud guessed, she would cry hard. Maud wished she wouldn't. It was embarrassing when grown-ups cried. After a few moments, she changed her mind. Mrs. Lambert was trembling; her body was rigid; she was suspended halfway between self-control and wild grief. Watching her hang in the balance was unnerving. Maud ventured, "Was she pretty?"

The words broke the stalemate. Mrs. Lambert let out her breath. Tears brimmed from her eyes, but she wiped them away in a perfectly sensible manner. "Very pretty. She was rather vain about all that."

Maud had expected more loyalty from Caroline's mother. "Vain?" she echoed.

"A little," Mrs. Lambert said judiciously. "She loved pretty clothes—dainty, frilly things—and she was vain of her hair. She wasn't patient—she hated standing still—but she let me comb out her ringlets every morning, because she loved having such beautiful curls." Mrs. Lambert smiled at Maud's shocked face. "I try to remember her exactly as she was. If I were to forget, that would be like losing her again, don't you see?"

Maud thought about this. It went against what Hyacinth had told her. It seemed that Caroline Lambert had not been an angel child after all.

"Rory Hugelick used to say—" Mrs. Lambert paused. "You've met him, he's the man who takes tickets at the carousel. . . . Rory used to say that Caroline was as vain as a peacock and as brave as a lion." Her smile faded. "Only that was the trouble, you see. Caroline was never afraid of anything. She never believed that anything bad could happen to her. She wasn't allowed to go bathing by herself—I was strict about that—but she disobeyed me and she drowned." Her voice was suddenly harsh. "We must take care that doesn't happen to you. You mustn't go bathing alone."

"I won't," said Maud.

But Mrs. Lambert was not convinced. "Perhaps I could walk home with you and speak to your father? I don't want to get you in trouble, Mary, dear, but it does seem to me bathing alone is too dangerous. Perhaps I could meet you here and keep an eye—"

Maud scrambled to her feet. "I have to go now," she said. "I mean I have to go *now,* right this minute." She pointed to the sky. "It's dark."

Mrs. Lambert was gathering up her parasol. She had one glove and was groping for the other. Maud had no mercy. She had stayed too long, and now Mrs.

Lambert meant to follow her home. She snatched the second glove and threw it as hard as she could. Then she turned her back to the painted sky and fled, leaving the woman stranded and bewildered on the shore.

CHAPTER TWENTY-THREE

Maud dreamed. She was walking on the jetty, and the rocks were smooth as glass, slicked with a coat of bright green seaweed. Her toes curled at the touch of slime underfoot. She tilted from side to side like a tightrope walker, arms outstretched.

Someone was calling her name. Maud twisted, looking over her shoulder. The shore behind her had disappeared. She was in the center of the ocean, with the jetty rising from the water like the fin of a shark. Her head spun. In a moment or two, the rocks would lurch beneath her, and she would be lost forever.

Her name again. She looked down and saw without surprise that it was Caroline who called it— Caroline, who clung to the rocks of the jetty. Caroline's hair fanned out, floating on the surface of the water. One webbed hand pried itself loose from the rock, groping toward Maud.

Maud understood what Caroline wanted. She wanted Maud to draw her to safety, to pull her from the deep before she drowned. But the webbed hand repelled Maud; it was mucilaginous, transparent, sticky. Maud knew that once she touched that hand, it would adhere to her skin, cling and pinch, and she would lose her balance. Caroline would drag her to her death.

So she stepped back and let Caroline drown. The glistening fingers opened and shut, and the dark streaming hair crowned the waves like seaweed. Maud seemed to hear Hyacinth's voice chanting—

"*O is it weed, or fish, or floating hair—*
   A tress of golden hair,
   A drownèd maiden's hair,
   Above the nets at sea?"—

She woke. Her eyes darted from corner to corner of the dark room, trying to recover her sense of what was real and what was nightmare. Then heat lightning illumined the room with a blue flash. Maud saw her dresses hanging like ghosts from their hooks. She glimpsed the slanting ceiling and the flattened doughnuts of the bedknobs. She was in the attic, safe in her own bed.

She sat up. Little by little, her heartbeat slowed. Her eyes adjusted to the darkness. The terror of the dream left her, but her waking thoughts were no less frightening. A letter from Hyacinth had arrived that day, apologizing for her ten-day absence and promising her swift return. The Hawthorne sisters were coming back to hold the séance for Mrs. Lambert.

Maud swallowed. She dreaded the séance with all her heart. There was so much that could go wrong now that she knew Mrs. Lambert. If Mrs. Lambert recognized Maud's voice, all would be lost. The Hawthorne sisters would lose the money they were counting on. Hyacinth would find out that Maud had disobeyed her and escaped from the house by night. And Mrs. Lambert . . . the lump in Maud's throat swelled until she almost choked. Mrs. Lambert would see that once again she had been deceived. She would be bitterly hurt. Maud grimaced in the darkness. She wished she could stop thinking about Mrs. Lambert.

There was another flash of lightning. Maud stiffened, waiting for the thunder to frighten her.

But there was none. Maud let out her breath, grabbed the sheet, and lay back down. The creak of the bedstead frightened her. She spread out the sheet until it covered her whole body, in case Caroline was under the bed, reaching up with those sticky hands. The images from the nightmare returned. Maud was poised on the jetty and Caroline was reaching out to her. . . . Maud frowned, trying to remember. She thought she had dreamed of the jetty before. She wondered why the jetty should haunt her dreams. She had tried to walk it only once. Since the night when she made the sand crocodile, she had not left the house. She couldn't risk seeing Mrs. Lambert again. Mrs. Lambert, Maud knew, would be searching the beach and the Amusement Park, looking for the child she believed to be homeless.

Maud was thinking of Mrs. Lambert again. She shifted irritably, curling herself in a knot. For one brief moment Maud entertained the idea of betraying Hyacinth and confessing everything to the rich woman. She shook her head. Nothing would be worse than that. Hyacinth would find out and send her back to the Barbary Asylum.

It was stifling hot under the sheet. Maud kicked it off and sat up. She could not stand being alone a minute longer. She would go to Muffet's room.

She stuck her feet over the edge of the bed and lunged forward quickly, so that Caroline couldn't grab her ankles. Then she tiptoed into the box room. By day, the room was cluttered and ugly; by night, it was a storehouse of terrors. The bulky oblongs of trunks looked like coffins; the shadows in the corners loomed and smoked. Maud tried not to see them. Almost running, she passed into the next room.

Muffet was snoring. Maud crept to the rag rug and sank down beside the bed. She clutched two fistfuls of sheet and felt a little better. It struck her as queer that someone who was mute could make so much noise snoring. The hired woman lay on her back—in the dark her face was unfamiliar—and the sounds that came from her were as homely as a dishpan. There was a sort of snuffle, which sometimes erupted into a snort, followed by a drawn-out wheeze. No ghost could tolerate a sound like that. The specter of Caroline fled.

Listening to Muffet snore, Maud grew calmer. Perhaps the séance would go as planned. Then everything would be all right. The Hawthorne sisters would get the money they needed. Hyacinth would be overjoyed. Even Mrs. Lambert would be better off—in a way—because she would get what she wanted most. It was Mrs. Lambert, after all, who had offered five thousand dollars to anyone who would help her contact her dead child. Mrs. Lambert wanted to see Caroline more that she wanted anything else in the world. Maud set her chin. She would see to it that Mrs. Lambert got her money's worth. She would play the role to the hilt. She would make Caroline speak loving words to her grieving mother; she wouldn't omit a single "dear Mama." Her mind made up, Maud lowered herself to the floor. She braced one arm under her head and tried to go to sleep.

The Hawthorne sisters returned two days later. Maud rushed downstairs to greet Hyacinth with a forgery of her old affection. Hyacinth tweaked her hair and tickled her neck.

"So, you naughty child! Did you miss me after all?"

"Yes," Maud admitted unwillingly, "I missed you." It was not wholly untrue. She was glad to hear voices in the house again. She looked from Hyacinth to

Judith. Hyacinth had stood the journey well. Her traveling suit was only slightly creased, and her cheeks were flushed with wind and sun. By contrast, Judith looked twenty years older. Her face was a funny color, and her posture was slack.

"What's the matter?" Maud asked Judith.

Judith set down her valise. Hyacinth leaned over to whisper into Maud's ear. "She was seasick," Hyacinth said in a half whisper, as if Judith's being seasick were some kind of joke. "She's always seasick."

Maud wasn't sure whether to laugh or not. She compromised, smirking to please Hyacinth but speaking to Judith. "Do you want me to take your bag upstairs for you?"

"Thank you, Maud. No. Muffet can carry it." Judith put her hand on the balustrade, as if she still felt the ground swaying. "I'm going to bed."

"Poor Judith!" said Hyacinth, once her sister had lurched upstairs. "So dreary, being seasick. *You* won't be seasick when we travel, will you, Maudy?"

"No, ma'am."

"That's a good child. Let's go into the back parlor, where we can talk. You can help me unpack later. I brought you a box of chocolates—and you must see my new tea gown—it has a serpentine skirt and bishop sleeves. Judith was furious when I bought it, but I needed it dreadfully—Mrs. Fortescue's friends change clothes five times a day. One simply must *dress*." Hyacinth clasped her hands. "Oh, Maud! Such elegant people! By next year this time, we may be in Newport! That's where all the nicest people spend the summers. You can't think how many people we met—Mrs. Fortescue knows everyone, and we were immensely popular, Judith and I. It was all we could do to tear ourselves away."

Maud asked politely, "Did you meet any people with dead relations?"

Hyacinth laughed. "Dearest Maud, everyone has dead relations! The question is whether we met anyone who wants to talk to their dead relations—and—isn't it providential?—we *did*! There's even a job for you—a little boy who died of scarlet fever. Little Theodore was only six, but you are so tiny, I'm sure we can manage something for his poor grieving parents—and you will look delicious in a Fauntleroy suit." Her eyes crinkled with laughter. "I wonder if we shouldn't give you a tablespoon of gin every day. They say it stunts the growth. Of course, Judith would be shocked; she doesn't approve of spirits—not the alcoholic sort, anyway. Only we must finish up this

Lambert business, first of all." Hyacinth's quicksilver features underwent a change; she was no longer playful, but earnest. "Did you study your lines?"

"Yes, ma'am."

"Good girl. I'll write Eleanor this evening, and we'll rehearse tomorrow. Judith and I are agreed at last—I've come round to her idea that you should materialize *now,* so as to be sure of the money." A faint frown appeared between Hyacinth's brows. "Do you know you look rather frightened? I hope you're not going to develop stage fright now, when we're depending on you."

"I'm not frightened," Maud retorted. "It's just—" She felt her throat tighten. "It's just that it gets so hot in the map cupboard. I can't breathe. Can't Judith drill more holes in the back wall?"

Hyacinth considered the request. "I don't believe she could. The wood's rather thin as it is—it's cracked in spots. Too many holes and it'll splinter into bits. But never mind—you won't be inside the whole time. You'll be able to breathe once you materialize."

Maud gazed at her distrustfully. "Are you sure when she sees me—she'll think I'm Caroline?"

"How could I be sure?" Hyacinth sounded surprised that she had asked. "There's always a risk. But you must remember, Mrs. Lambert will *want* to believe you're Caroline. She will want that more than anything else in the world."

Maud swallowed. It was true. If she succeeded in deceiving Mrs. Lambert, she would be granting her heart's desire. It was just a question of pulling the thing off. "I know my lines," Maud said in a small voice.

"Of course you do." Hyacinth's gaze was searching. "And so you should. We're counting on you to do your very best. Remember that."

CHAPTER TWENTY-FOUR

On the morning of the séance, Maud woke to the sound of high wind and drenching rain. She left her bed and stood by the window, peering between the curtain and the window frame. The roof slates shimmered with water. Perhaps Mrs. Lambert would not come. Heartened by the thought, Maud tripped down to breakfast with a light step. She was even able to enjoy the pancakes Muffet set before her.

"Of course she'll come," Hyacinth assured her when Maud broached the subject. "She has a carriage.

Besides, she'd wade through high water to talk to Caroline."

Maud thought Hyacinth was probably right. She spent the afternoon going through her cues one last time. The Hawthorne sisters rehearsed for two hours before the electricity went out.

Hyacinth was pleased. "That's the one thing I was worried about—the streetlamps letting in too much light. Now, if only the power lines stay down until this evening—"

"They won't," predicted Judith. "The sky's clearing."

But Hyacinth got her wish. The lights stayed off. A little before suppertime, the wind blew the clouds into patches, revealing a sky the color of morning glories. Maud's last hope died. She borrowed Muffet's cards and played one game of solitaire after another, fretting all the while. When suppertime came, she could not eat. She picked up *Ragged Dick* but lost patience with it; Dick was so honest and manly and cheerful that Maud wanted to slap him. She shoved the book under her pillow and prayed that Eleanor Lambert would believe she was Caroline.

Mrs. Lambert arrived early. Maud was costumed and wigged when Hyacinth detected the sound of carriage wheels. "Tiresome woman!" Hyacinth hissed as she hustled Maud into the map cupboard. Maud agreed. How foolish of Mrs. Lambert to come early, to imagine that séances could be performed without prior preparation.

Ten minutes passed. Inside the map cupboard, Maud sweated and fumed. She could hear Mrs. Lambert and the Hawthorne sisters chatting in the front parlor, and she wondered how they could sound so lighthearted when so much was at stake. The twisted pain in her belly seemed to have risen to her throat. She had to go to the water closet. She crossed her legs tightly and opened her mouth to breathe. She could scarcely have said which was more miserable, her mind or her body.

The voices grew louder. The three women had come into the back parlor—Maud saw the line around the door brighten. Hyacinth had brought in the kerosene lamp, and the séance was about to begin. Maud caught a whiff of herself and wrinkled her nose. She stank of fear. She wondered what Mrs. Lambert would think when she embraced her long-dead daughter and found her hot and smelly.

"Shall we sing a hymn?" Hyacinth said. That was a signal that all was well. The women were seated around the table as planned.

The light dimmed. Mrs. Lambert began the

singing, and her voice shook. For a moment, Maud felt for her: Mrs. Lambert was nervous, too. Maud joined in.

> *"We shall sing on that beautiful shore,*
> *The melodious songs of the blest,*
> *And our spirit shall sorrow no more,*
> *Not a sigh for the blessing of rest.*
>
> *In the sweet bye and bye*
> *We shall meet on that beautiful shore —"*

Maud's voice was sweet and true. All at once the knot in her stomach dissolved, and she felt a thrill of excitement. The waiting was over—and she was very good at what she was about to do.

The women sang three hymns before falling silent. Maud listened for her cue. There was a series of raps, and Judith's whisper: "I feel something!" Those were the words Maud had waited to hear. In a moment, Hyacinth would fall forward in trance.

There was a low thud, and Hyacinth's voice murmured, "Mama?"

Maud counted to seven. She spoke the second line in unison with Hyacinth. "Dear Mama, can you hear me?"

There was another series of raps, and Mrs. Lambert whispered, "Caroline?"

Judith admonished her. "Don't touch her! She's in a trance!"

Good, thought Maud. She repeated her line, solo this time: "Dear Mama, can you hear me?"

A chair creaked. Mrs. Lambert said shakily, "Caroline? Is that—can that be you?"

"Dear Mama, I have come to you," Maud answered huskily. "Are you glad that I'm here, dear Mama?"

"I can't—see you." Mrs. Lambert sounded as though she were on the verge of tears. "I don't feel—oh, Caroline—don't leave me! Please stay and speak to me! I beg of you—"

Maud answered with lines from Hyacinth's script. "Dear Mama, I am right beside you. I am closer than your shadow."

Mrs. Lambert was weeping. Maud caught the words, "want to believe—" Then, sharply: "You've never called me 'dear Mama' in your life!"

Maud brought up one hand to cover her mouth. She grasped the fact that Hyacinth had misdirected her. Caroline Lambert had not been an angel child. The *dear Mama*s struck a false note. "But you *are* dear to me, Mama," Maud coaxed. "Can't I say so?"

The pause that followed was unnerving. Maud tensed, fearing that her voice had been recognized. Then Mrs. Lambert gasped, "Oh, Caroline!" with exasperation and tenderness. "Must you always argue?"

Maud didn't know what to say next. She kept very still. The silence was broken by Mrs. Lambert's sobbing. "Please—Caroline—don't leave me! Hear me out! I have to tell you—I've thought of nothing else but that terrible morning. I didn't mean it, my darling. I didn't mean what I said."

Maud grimaced. She wondered if she should recite the line about how she couldn't hear any longer, how a gulf had come between them. If she did, her problems would be solved. Hyacinth would come out of her trance, the séance would end, and there would be no more risks that evening. But Mrs. Lambert had begged Caroline not to go away, and the sound of her sobs was heartrending.

"I have thought, over and over, about what I said—God knows I have been punished for it! Caroline, my dear, I would cut out my tongue if I could take back those words. Forgive me—I didn't mean it, not one word—"

Maud interrupted. "I know you didn't mean it," she said warily. "It's all right."

"I ought to have gone with you—I shouldn't—" Mrs. Lambert's words were lost again. "Over and over . . . I've thought that was why—"

Maud remembered the script. "Dear Mama, there is nothing to forgive! If ever you spoke a cross word to me, I have forgotten it. Where I live now, Mama, all is forgiveness. All is love."

She finished the line, biting down on her lower lip to complete the *v* in *love*. Her consonants were exquisite.

"Then," Mrs. Lambert said bitterly, "you didn't drown yourself because of what I said?"

Maud was startled into saying, "No!" in her own emphatic voice. She made haste to correct herself, assuming the ethereal tones she had learned from Hyacinth. "Of course not, dear Mama."

"Stop calling me that!" Mrs. Lambert almost shrieked. "God forgive you, Caroline Mary, if you torment me now!"

Maud quailed. The grieving mother had become a fury; her voice coiled and struck like a cobra.

"How could you, Caroline? How dare you disobey and go into the water? You promised me—that very morning you promised—that you wouldn't bathe alone. And for spite—for very spite!—you lost your life and broke my heart, so that I will never mend, never love—"

Maud's reaction was instinctive. An adult had lost self-control and was castigating her. She forgot she was not Caroline and cried out desperately, "I didn't!"

"You drowned yourself—"

"I didn't do it on purpose," Maud pleaded.

Improbably, Mrs. Lambert laughed. Her laugh was a weird blend of hysteria and genuine mirth. "Oh, Caroline! What am I going to do with you?"

"I'm sorry," Maud apologized. "But I *didn't*. I didn't drown myself. It was an accident."

"But they found your shoes and stockings on the shore," argued Mrs. Lambert. "You *meant* to break your promise to me. You took off your shoes and stockings."

Shoes and stockings. Those were the words that Caroline had spoken. Maud felt herself grow cold. Her mind went back to the dreams: Caroline, barefoot, on the shore, Caroline stretching out her hand toward the jetty . . . All at once the words came easily, as if they were words Maud had learned by heart.

"I didn't take off my shoes to go in the water. I took them off to walk on the jetty."

Silence. The silence was so protracted that Maud wondered if the room outside the map cupboard was empty. At last Mrs. Lambert echoed, "The jetty?"

"I wanted to walk on the jetty," said Maud. "But it was slippery, so I took off my shoes and stockings." She remembered Caroline's boldness and added provocatively, "You never said I couldn't walk on the jetty."

"The jetty!" repeated Mrs. Lambert. "Oh! Caroline, you foolish girl! Didn't you know how dangerous that was?"

"I slipped," admitted Maud. "But I didn't do it on purpose."

Mrs. Lambert was weeping again. Her sobs were less violent. They sounded like sobs of relief. "Oh, my dear!"

"I'm sorry," Maud said meekly.

A rap from the table distracted her. *Rap, rap, rap!* Judith cried out, "Hyacinth! Eleanor—Hyacinth's stopped breathing!"

Maud pricked up her ears. They were about to begin the second part of the séance: her materialization.

"No, she's breathing," Mrs. Lambert contradicted. "I can feel her breath against my fingers."

"Yes, but she breathes so faintly!" Judith said. "There is danger in this. Her trance is so deep! We must stop. Hyacinth, wake up! My sister—wake up, wake up!"

Three cries of "wake up" meant that Mrs. Lambert had her back to the map closet. Maud pressed against the door and stepped out. Over by the table was a dark triangle—the two women bending over the collapsed Hyacinth. Maud took an extra moment to push the door panel back in place. She left it open by an inch. Then she whispered, "Mama?"

Mrs. Lambert turned. She glimpsed the white-clad figure in the dark. Almost imperceptibly the room brightened; Judith had raised the wick of the kerosene lamp, allowing a little more light. Mrs. Lambert lunged forward, arms outstretched.

Maud fell into them. "Mama," she whispered as Mrs. Lambert clutched her. Maud could feel the woman trembling; her heart thrummed in Maud's ear. "Oh, my dear girl," murmured Mrs. Lambert, and then, as if it were a miracle, "you're *warm*."

Maud had no idea why she was crying. She felt Mrs. Lambert's buttons dig into her cheek. She breathed in the scent of starched linen and lavender water. She wrapped her arms around the rich woman's waist and hugged back. "I love you, Mama." The words that had sounded false in rehearsal came easily now. "I love you!"

"Oh, Caroline, I love you, too," Mrs. Lambert whispered. "I love you, I love you—and oh, my dearest, forgive me those ugly words! I didn't mean them—"

"I know, Mama." Maud felt her wig lurch as Mrs. Lambert caressed her curls. She removed one arm from the woman's waist so that she could hang onto it. "I understand."

"Help me!" Judith's voice was a shock. She was almost screaming. "My sister! My sister! Help me!"

Maud felt Mrs. Lambert's arms loosen. Reluctantly she turned back toward the two spiritualists.

"She's dying! Help me!"

Slowly, Mrs. Lambert released her phantom daughter. Maud stepped to one side. As soon as she saw Mrs. Lambert lean over Hyacinth, she backed up, step by step, reached for door of the map closet, found it, and hid herself within. She pulled at her skirt, taking care that none of the cloth was caught in the door—

There was a tinkle of broken glass. Someone was screaming. Maud blinked in the darkness. Something was happening on the other side of the panel, something that had not been rehearsed. Hyacinth, who was supposed to be emerging from her trance, was shouting, and Judith, who never lost self-control, was shrieking like a banshee. The din was so terrible that Maud could not distinguish the words. The light outside the door increased—Hyacinth must have turned up the lamp—and the screaming went on. There was a sound like cloth tearing, a heavy thud, and several sharp cracks, different in timbre from Judith's rappings. "Quickly!" "No time!" "Look there!" "She's hurt!" and—from Mrs. Lambert—"Your servant—?" and from Hyacinth, sharply, "Out!"

The door slammed. Someone had come in, or gone out, the front door. Maud strained to hear. She heard a queer trickling noise, like a stream with a strong current—the sound of people shouting outside the house—was that Hyacinth?—and then a man, shouting about fire. *There must be a fire,* Maud thought, *and they've gone outside to look at it, but why?* It didn't make sense.

The light outside the door grew brighter. Maud's nostrils twitched. Something was burning—but supper was over and Muffet never . . . *Smoke.* Still disbelieving, Maud opened the door of the map cupboard.

The room was bright with fire. The kerosene lamp had fallen, and flames sprouted from the broken glass. The tablecloth lay rumpled on the carpet, cradling a lapful of fire. Fire danced on the threshold of the doorway, making the velvet curtains shrink and twitch. The women had left the house just in time.

Maud retreated. She had a crazy desire to rush back inside the map closet, squeeze shut her eyes, and hide until the fire went away. Then Hyacinth's words came back to her, as clearly as if she stood at Maud's side. *The wood's cracked. Too many holes and it'll splinter into bits.*

Maud whirled. Using her body as a battering ram, she flung herself at the back wall of the map cupboard. The wood panel creaked, but it didn't splinter. Maud cast a frantic look around the room. There was a bronze sailing ship on the mantel — heavy, with a sharp-pointed bow — and she seized it with both hands. Her arms sagged with its weight — it was heavier than it looked — but she gripped it tightly and beat it against the back wall.

At the first blow, the panel splintered. With the

second and third, she smashed a hole big enough to crawl through. She forced herself into the breach, wiggling like an animal trapped in a hedge. Her arms toppled the books on the other side of the wall and pushed open the glass doors of the bookcase. She kicked forward until her arms caught hold of the shelf's front edge. Then she began to pull through.

Only once, at the very beginning of her life, had she fought her way forward with such urgency. The splintered wood gripped her tightly, snagging her dress, gouging her skin. She felt no pain. Head first, she labored, pulling and kicking, until she toppled free and tumbled onto the floor of the library.

She leaped to her feet. She took one last look through the hole in the panel and saw the room was full of smoke. The fire was surging toward the front parlor. Maud raced through the library door, into the hall that led to the kitchen.

The kitchen looked surprisingly peaceful. The supper dishes were done. There was one place laid on the table. Muffet had left out Maud's supper; a covered plate stood between knife, fork, and spoon—

Maud froze with her hand on the door. Was Muffet in the house? Muffet almost always went for a walk after dinner—or out into her garden—Maud flew to the screen door and strained to see out, into the dusk. *Please,* she thought, *let me see Muffet.* But the hired woman was not in the garden. If she were upstairs, she would not hear the cries from the street.

Maud stood paralyzed. She knew what she wanted to do. She wanted to flee from the fire. Even if Muffet were upstairs, she wanted to run. She tried to imagine Muffet out walking. The hired woman would come back from her walk, with her basket of seedlings, and Maud would greet her and they would both be safe. Then the drama changed. Maud saw herself leaving the house. Only later would she learn that Muffet had died, trapped in the attic, burned to death. Maud tried to imagine life after that and found it impossible. She let go of the door handle and turned toward the back stair.

Her body rebelled. Just as she couldn't picture a future in which Muffet died, her legs could not accept the idea of turning back to the fire. Maud knew her time was short. If she was to go upstairs, she must go quickly. But her legs belonged to an animal that didn't want to die, and they would not budge. Maud forced herself to take a step. Another. Her body fought back every step of the way.

Up the stair she clumped. The smoke pursued her,

a ghost without a shape. Another flight—one jerk at a time, each foot a lump of lead. At last she reached the attic. She shrieked, "Muffet!" though she knew Muffet could not hear. She jogged stiffly through the box room and into Muffet's bedroom. "Muffet!"

The room was dark. Maud stooped and swatted the bedclothes. The quilt was smooth and cool. Muffet was not there.

With that knowledge, Maud's body underwent a transformation. All at once, she was free to leave the house, and every cell in her body leaped with joy. She flew down the steps with a grace and fluidity she had never known. Her feet scarcely touched the treads of the stairs; her hand soared five inches above the balustrade. Even when she reached the thick clouds of smoke on the second floor, she was euphoric. She soared through the smoke like an owl through the dark. She whisked through the kitchen, palms out, smacking open the screen door so that it slammed behind her.

Once outside, she began to cough. Her eyes watered; the smoke smell was so strong that she fancied that the insides of her nostrils were scorched. She was aware of the sound of great bells ringing and the brassy din of someone hammering a gong. She heard people shouting from the front of the house. There were hoofbeats—galloping horses—the firefighters were coming. Maud pulled off Caroline's wig and stashed it under the lilac bush. Then she fled, taking the path toward the shore.

She was halfway to the ocean when she stopped running. She halted, panting, one foot on the board-walk and one on the sand. Why had she come here? She sat down and pulled off Caroline's stockings.

What should she do? She tried to recover her wits, heartening herself. She was alive and Muffet was alive. That was good; that was better than good. Moreover, she had done well during the séance. But beyond that thought, another lay in wait. Maud shook her head to ward it off. She got to her feet. She had to know what was happening back at the house.

She started down the boardwalk. She slipped up the alley a street beyond her own. She would watch the fire from the opposite side of the street. If she kept to the shadows between the houses, she would not be seen.

A crowd had gathered. Some were neighbors, holding buckets. Others had come to watch. The street was crowded with vehicles: the steam engine, with its three gray horses; the fire chief's buggy; the ladder truck; the hose carts. The long ladder truck blocked her view of the house, but she could see the flames rising to the second-floor windows. *Judith's room*, thought Maud, and spared a pang of pity for Judith. She edged forward, careful to keep in the shade of a sycamore tree.

No one noticed her. Night was falling, and the fire drew every eye. The firemen rushed back and forth like actors in a play. The firelight played on the wet street, which seemed to be strewn with snakes; the flames hissed and steamed, brilliant against a background of dingy smoke. Maud tried to catch a glimpse of someone she knew. She almost jumped when a voice spoke on the other side of the tree.

"Anybody in there?" A boy in knickerbockers jerked his thumb toward the blaze.

Another boy, somewhat older, answered him. "Nobody." He sounded disappointed. "It's just old ladies that live there, and they all got out. One of 'em caught her skirt on fire. They said she fainted, but that's all."

"See that fellow there?" The younger boy pointed to one of the firemen. "That's Mr. Dowell from the pharmacy. He's one of the volunteers. He sold me an egg cream yesterday."

The other boy was unimpressed. "It's not much

of a fire," he said gloomily. "All that rain th's'after-noon." He took a step forward. "What's that?"

Maud heard the cry. She recognized it—it was Muffet's voice. The younger boy said, "What in thunder—?"

"Somebody trying to get in." The older boy was on his tiptoes. "One of the women—trying to get into the house. She must be crazy." There was a murmur from the crowd. "One of the firemen's caught her. There, he's got her."

"Mr. Dowell says that's stupid. He says if you get out, you stay out. It's different for the firefighters, because they *know*, but ordinary people—well, Mr. Dowell told me about this old maid who went back in the house to save her cat. The roof fell in and crushed her skull. Killed her like that." He smacked his palms together. "Just plain foolishness."

"I'd go in for a dog, but not a cat," remarked the other.

Maud cursed them with a look of hatred and disdain. What did they know about fires? They'd leave their own mothers to burn, probably. She made a wide circle around them, pushing to the front of the crowd.

Muffet sagged in the arms of the fireman. The fireman turned his head from side to side, as if he were searching for someone to take the burden off his hands. A tall woman hurried toward him. Maud saw Mrs. Lambert gesticulate, indicating a point somewhere down the street. The fireman heaved the unconscious woman onto one shoulder and followed Mrs. Lambert to her carriage.

Maud set one foot ahead of the other. She imagined herself sprinting forward, ordering the fireman to let her go with Muffet. Then she imagined Mrs. Lambert's surprise, and Hyacinth . . . Where was Hyacinth? She supposed they were all together— Mrs. Lambert and Hyacinth and Judith. Mrs. Lambert would take them back to her hotel. . . . Even as Maud pondered what to do next, the carriage began to move. Maud's mouth fell open. They were leaving her.

Maud spun in her tracks. She sped from the crowd, regaining the cover of the alley. Once in the alley, she increased speed, trying to outrace the demons in her head. She no longer cared what happened to the house. Let it burn. She ran until she crossed the boardwalk and stumbled down to the shore.

The moon was rising. It seemed to Maud that she had never seen so large a moon. A scrap of shining cloud crossed it and turned to smoke. The moon emerged, whiter than the cloud, flawless in its roundness, beautiful. Maud raised her face to the sky. Her mouth stretched wide and she howled.

She had never cried so hard in her life. The moon drew the sound out of her as if she were a dog. She cried because Muffet loved her and because Hyacinth didn't. She cried for Mrs. Lambert, who was nice, and for Caroline, who had died when she was eight years old. She cried because she had been left alone in a burning house and because she had not been good. She cried for fear, because she was afraid of the dark, and she cried for loneliness, because no one knew she was alive.

CHAPTER TWENTY-FIVE

When Maud awoke the next morning, the smell of smoke was still in her nostrils.

She sat up shivering. She had burrowed in the sand the night before, with a vague notion that it would keep her warm, but she was cold and damp as well as gritty. The skin over her right elbow felt stretched—when Maud ran her fingers over it, she discovered a mountain range of scabs. She thought that her back was scraped, but she couldn't reach the places that hurt. Her mouth was dry and her stomach was empty.

She got up, shook the sand out of her dress as best she could, and looked out over the water. The sun had risen behind her; the sea foam glistened, and the sky was streaked with mare's tails. The gulls swooped and screamed above the waves. Maud stumbled down to the ocean. She thought longingly of the water closet in Victoria's cottage. When she came out of the water, she was red-faced with shame. She pitied the tourists who would bathe in the ocean that day.

The boardwalk was almost deserted, which was a relief; Maud was fairly certain she looked awful. As a shabby child, she had passed among the crowds unnoticed; in Caroline's frilly dress, with its torn lace and bloodstains, she was a thing to be stared at. Maud ducked her head and walked briskly. Before long, she stood before Victoria's cottage, surveying the wreckage.

The cottage was still standing. Maud was surprised; she had expected to find it a heap of ashes. Nevertheless, the damage was substantial. The front of the building was scorched, and the porch had collapsed. The entire front was off-kilter, as if the frame of the house was buckling. The back of the house was still intact. Maud toyed with the idea of scurrying up the back stairs to see if any of her clothes had survived the fire. Then she shrugged. It wasn't worth it.

She headed back to the boardwalk and set off for the Amusement Park. When she reached the gates, she stopped. They were chained and padlocked. Maud's lip curled. It took her less than a minute to scramble to the top of the fence and leap down.

It was queer, seeing the park by day. The booths that seemed to glow in the dark were only wooden boxes; the painted signs, with their unlit lightbulbs, were lackluster, like stained glass after sunset. Maud made her way straight to the merry-go-round. Now that the park was deserted, she could see that the carousel stood at its center. All paths led to it. It was no accident that she had been drawn here, or Caroline before her.

She stepped up on the carousel platform, searching for Angel. Her eyes fell upon an eyesore: a great mound of a man, fast asleep on a heap of blankets. It was Rory. Maud could scarcely believe her luck. She had thought she would have to wait to see him, perhaps for hours. Instead, there he lay, his feet beneath the paws of the tiger.

Maud eyed him nervously. Grown-ups didn't like being awakened, and Rory Hugelick was a man.

Stalling for time, she went to Angel and put her arms around his neck. His glassy eyes were full of compassion. Maud fitted her fingers into the furrows of his mane. A fragment of memory swam to the surface of her mind. She had dreamed again last night, a surprisingly buoyant and blissful dream. She had been riding Angel, while Caroline rode the sea monster in front of her. From time to time, Caroline twisted around to wave at her, shouting with excitement. Together they had floated and whirled, calling to each another in shrill delight.

The carousel keeper stirred. His eyes blinked, passed over Maud, and came back to her. A short, interrogatory grunt came from him. "What the—?" He shifted sideways and propped up his head on his elbow. Drowsy irritation gave way to a look of concern. "God Almighty! What happened to you?"

Maud took in her breath to tell a lie and exhaled before she could think of one. She went straight to the point. "Do you know where Mrs. Lambert is?"

"Mrs. Lambert?" Rory sat up and rubbed the palm of his hand over his chin. He yawned. "She thought there was something the matter with you. I guess she was right."

Maud repeated, "Do you know where—"

Rory interrupted her. "What happened to you?"

Maud sighed. "The house was on fire, and I had to crawl through a hole."

"On fire." Rory took this in. "I heard the bells last night." He rubbed his eyes. "Anybody hurt?"

"I don't think so," Maud said patiently, "but I have to find Mrs. Lambert. Do you know where she lives?"

"Duckling," Rory said pathetically, "I haven't had so much as a drop of coffee." He fumbled in his trouser pocket. "Do you know Vicelli's?"

Maud shook her head.

"You go out the side gate"—Rory pointed— "few steps to the left, and across the boardwalk, that's Vicelli's. You tell them Rory Hugelick wants a sausage roll and a cuppa coffee." He handed her a quarter. "Bring back the change. After I've had my coffee, we'll talk about Mrs. Lambert. All right?"

"All right," conceded Maud.

She returned shortly afterward, balancing a tin plate on top of a mug of coffee. Rory Hugelick had tidied away his blanket roll and was polishing the brass on the carousel. When he saw Maud, he sat down and patted the platform next to him. "Good girl." He took a draft of coffee. "First things first.

You got some nasty cuts and scrapes. You put anything on 'em?"

"No."

"You been in the ocean this morning?"

"Yes." Maud felt her face grow hot. "I had to
wash off."

"That'll do, then." He took a bite of the sausage
roll. "There's nothing so good for cuts as salt water.
My mother used to say—" He broke off as Maud's
stomach emitted a growl. "You had anything to eat
th's'morning?"

Maud considered lying. "No," she said humbly.

"Poor little devil." Rory broke his sausage roll in
half. "You eat that and you'll feel better. And here—
take a sip of coffee."

Maud accepted gratefully. The taste of the coffee
was bitter beyond anything she had imagined, but after grimacing through the first mouthful, she wanted
another. The sausage roll reeked of garlic. Maud
wrinkled her nose at it, nibbled, and decided it wasn't
so bad after all.

"Now, what's this about Mrs. Lambert?"

"She's got Muffet." Rory looked bewildered. "I
don't mean she stole her or anything. Muffet's the
name of our hired girl. When the house was on fire,

Muffet tried to get back in the house, but she couldn't—and she fainted, I guess, and Mrs. Lambert took her away in the carriage. So I need to see her."

"Wait a minute." Rory held up a hand to stop her. "Where's the rest of your folks?"

"They're with Mrs. Lambert. The house was on fire so they went home with her, too."

"Why didn't you go with them?"

"They didn't see me." Maud averted her face. "They didn't know I got out."

"You mean to say there's people who think you died in that fire?"

"I guess so. I don't know."

Rory set down his coffee mug. "Look here, duckling. You're not telling me the whole truth. It's not that I don't believe you—I can smell the smoke on you—but there's something else going on, something damned queer from the sound of it, and I want to know what it is."

Maud said slowly, "It's a long story."

"I've got time," countered Rory Hugelick. "The park don't open till ten. Come on, duckling, out with it. Otherwise, you can forget about me telling you where Mrs. Lambert lives, because I'm not doing it."

Maud took another bite of sausage roll. She

chewed meticulously, trying to buy time. Rory would not be easy to fool. She fished for a lie that would account for her present situation and found that her mind was blank. She was all lied out. She couldn't seem to get interested in keeping any more secrets or protecting the Hawthorne sisters. The night before, she had learned too much. She had cried too hard.

So she surrendered the truth. Her account was a jumble, made worse by Rory's frequent interruptions, but eventually she got through most of the story. She told about her adoption and the mortgage that needed to be paid, and the séances and the life she had been leading as a secret child. The look on Rory's face told her just how bizarre her story was. It had been some time since she considered her life surprising. She had grown used to the peculiarities of the Hawthorne sisters.

"So," Rory summarized, when she had explained most of it, "you've been living like a prisoner with three old ladies that cheat grief-stricken people out of their money. They could go to jail for what they're doing, do you know that? And—in the middle of trying to swindle one of the sweetest ladies I've ever met—their house caught fire, and not one of them lifted a finger to save you. Ah, now, don't cry, duckling!"

"I'm not crying," Maud said, clenching her teeth and blinking rapidly.

"I wouldn't blame you if you were," Rory said back. "I'm just saying. You got out of the fire last night, you slept rough, and now you want to go find this hired girl, because she's the only one of those hell-hags that might care whether you're dead or alive."

Maud's temper flared. "Muffet's not a hell-hag," she threw back at him. "Muffet went into the fire for me. Hyacinth and Judith are bad, and so'm I, but Muffet's innocent."

Rory eyed her narrowly. Then he held out his freckled paw, inviting her to put her hand in his. "Then I guess we'd better go find Muffet." He helped Maud to her feet.

"Then you know where she is?"

"I don't know for sure." Rory squinted at the sky. "But Mrs. Lambert's a rich woman—she's probably at the Hotel Elysium. Either the Elysium or the Hotel Regina—they're the two best in town. But you've got to promise me something." He caught her other hand and gave her a little shake. "No more pretending to be Caroline. No more lying to Mrs. Lambert."

Maud squirmed to avoid his eyes. "We made her happy."

"You lied to her so you could cheat her out of her money," Rory said roughly. "That ain't happy. Listen to me, duckling. I knew Ellie Lambert when her daughter was alive. She and her daughter were regulars—they'd come by just about every day." He pointed to the hippocampus, with its acid-green body and curlicue tail. "That sea monster—that was Caroline's favorite. She was a nice little girl and she died. As for her mother, she was never the same since. She's too rich for her own good—and tenderhearted—but that doesn't mean people have a right to take advantage of her. Even Caroline—" He stopped. "The point is, I'm not going to let you cheat her anymore. If you don't tell her the truth, I will. You understand?"

"Yes," conceded Maud.

"That's a good girl." Rory laid a hand on the back of her head. His touch was surprisingly delicate. "Come on, then. We'll go find Mrs. Lambert."

CHAPTER TWENTY-SIX

The lobby of the Hotel Elysium was more magnificent than any place Maud had ever seen. She was overwhelmed by its splendor. She felt that her naked and dirty feet were an insult to its polished floors. She clung tightly to Rory's hand, expecting at any moment to be swept up and tossed out the door like a stray cat. But Rory was nonchalant. He followed his massive stomach past the doormen with such aplomb that they failed to question him.

Maud kept within his shadow. Before her was a grand staircase, carpeted in crimson; overhead was a forest of Greek columns and a host of chandeliers. A gentleman in a dark suit edged forward, the intention to evict them clear in his eyes.

"You're just the man I need to help me," boomed Rory, causing the tourists in the lobby to turn their heads. "I'm Rory Hugelick, and I'm here to see Mrs. Charles Lambert. This little girl"—he yanked Maud's hand—"almost died in the fire last night. Mrs. Lambert will want to see her."

The clerk cast a nervous look around the room. He saw that the hotel guests were eavesdropping. Maud heard a woman murmur, "Poor little thing!"

"If you'll come this way, sir." The clerk ushered them into a small room off the main lobby. "I'll tell Mrs. Lambert you wish to see her."

Maud squeezed Rory's hand in gratitude.

"Remember," Rory warned her, "no more lies."

"All right," agreed Maud, though how she was going to get through the next hour without lying she had no idea.

They waited only a short time before the hotel clerk held the door open for Mrs. Lambert. At the sight of Maud, the rich woman's face lit up. Then it knotted with concern. "Mary!" She stooped down, placing her hands on Maud's shoulders. "Gracious, look at you! You poor child!"

Maud felt her throat tighten. "I'm not Mary," she croaked. "That isn't my real name. I lied to you before."

A faint frown appeared between Mrs. Lambert's brows. "Never mind. We'll worry about that later. Let me look at you. Poor lamb, you're dreadfully cut and bruised! And there are splinters that ought to come out. Perhaps you should see a doctor. Dr. Knowles will be here this mo—"

"I need to see Muffet," Maud broke in. "Our hired girl. The deaf woman," she added, wanting to stop Mrs. Lambert before she said anything else that was nice.

Mrs. Lambert brightened. "Then you're Maud! Oh, now I see! Anna wrote your name—she even drew me a picture—but of course I didn't know—"

"Who's Anna?" asked Rory.

"Anna. The Hawthornes' deaf servant," explained Mrs. Lambert. "They call her Muffet, but she wrote down that her name was Anna. She's been greatly distressed—she thinks the child died in the fire." She held out her hands to Rory. "Thank you for bringing Maud here. You will excuse us, won't you? I must take her to Anna at once."

Maud didn't hear Rory's answer. Mrs. Lambert had captured her hand and was whisking her back through the lobby, up the grand staircase. Heads turned and voices murmured, but Mrs. Lambert paid no attention. Maud had to trot to keep up with her.

"Anna suffered a bad fracture," Mrs. Lambert said in a low voice. "The doctor said both bones in her right leg must have been broken at one time and never set properly—perhaps never set at all. When she tried to go back into the building last night, one of the firemen seized her. She struggled with him on the stairs, and the bone just snapped. The pain must have been dreadful—she fainted—so you must be very careful not to jolt her."

They had come to a pair of double doors. Mrs. Lambert turned the key in the lock and led Maud inside.

Maud had a brief impression of a vestibule, smaller than the great lobby downstairs but decorated in the same style. There were painted cupids on the ceiling and columned archways leading to different rooms. Mrs. Lambert led her into a room that overlooked the ocean.

Muffet lay asleep, covered with a sheet. Her eyes were deeply shadowed, the eyelids reddened from weeping. Maud could see that her right leg was encased in some contraption that kept it immobile. She felt suddenly frightened. She didn't want Muffet to look like that—so shrunken and sad, with that cruel-looking thing on her leg.

Mrs. Lambert took Muffet's hand. She rubbed Muffet's palm between her fingers and thumb. "Anna," she said urgently. "It's good news. Wake up."

Muffet blinked. Her eyes went past Mrs. Lambert to Maud. Her sleep-stiffened face underwent a change: every feature lifted and blossomed with joy. She held out her arms, whimpering like a wounded dog.

Maud forgot about not jolting the bed. She ran into Muffet's arms and Muffet caught her. The hired woman emitted a squeal of anguish but didn't let go. She dragged Maud into her lap, squeezing so hard that Maud cried out with pain as well as happiness.

Maud shut her eyes and burrowed into Muffet's nightgown. She gave herself up to the comfort of being rocked and held. Tears stole out from under her eyelids, but she wasn't ashamed. Muffet wouldn't laugh at her. Maud nestled closer, drawing in the warm kitchen smell that was distinctly Muffet's. She wanted to stay there forever.

But she did have to breathe. Reluctantly she lifted her face. Muffet was beaming. Mrs. Lambert had stepped away and stood in the door frame, watching them with misty eyes.

Muffet stuck out her hand imperiously. It was Mrs. Lambert who read her intention and stepped forward to give Muffet pencil and paper. Maud watched as the hired woman scrawled MAUD IN FIRE.

Maud nodded vehemently. She took the tablet and drew the steps. She drew herself climbing them, with wavy lines to indicate smoke. She wrote MAUD GO SEE ~~MU~~ ANNA IN FIRE. "I tried to find you," she said earnestly, hoping that Muffet would be able to read the truth in her eyes. "When the fire came, I tried to find you, but you weren't in the house."

Muffet fingered Maud's torn dress. She sniffed loudly. *You smell of smoke.* She examined Maud critically, running her fingers over every scraped patch of skin, every scab and splinter. Maud waited for the diagnosis. When Muffet finished, she nodded, and though the nod was grim, Maud relaxed. *It's not so bad. You'll live.*

The hired woman took up her pencil. She sketched two small pictures: one of Maud in a bathtub, and the other of Maud sitting before a plate, spoon in hand. She wrote, MAUD GO IN BATHTUB. MAUD EAT.—and passed the tablet to Mrs. Lambert.

Mrs. Lambert laughed. "Very well, Anna. I'll

manage it. You sleep." She pillowed her head on her arms, raising her eyebrows to emphasize the command. She reached for Maud's hand. "Come. I'll look after you. She really must sleep. The doctor gave her a sleeping draft last night, but she was so distraught, it did very little good. We didn't understand." A faint line appeared between her brows. "None of us understood why she was so upset. Of course, the others didn't know you were in the house."

They had come back to the vestibule. Maud pulled her hand out of Mrs. Lambert's. She glanced at the other archways. Any minute now, Hyacinth and Judith might appear and swoop down on her like a pair of harpies. She cleared her throat. "They knew I was in the house."

Mrs. Lambert shook her head. "No. They couldn't have. Why, I was there when the fireman asked. He asked if there was anyone in the house, and Hyacinth—" Her voice trailed off. Maud saw the dawning horror in her face.

"Hyacinth knew," Maud said in a muffled voice. "She left me there."

"Left you—? That's impossible! No one would— Where were you?"

"In the map cupboard. That's what we call the place inside the mantel—the fireplace in the parlor's hollow. I was hiding." Maud averted her eyes. "Mrs. Lambert," she confessed, "I was Caroline."

"Caroline?" The whisper hung in the air like a ghost. Mrs. Lambert touched her fingers to her lips. Her face was white.

Maud swallowed. For the past six months it had been drummed into her that any indiscretion on her part would result in Mrs. Lambert's understanding the plot against her. The minute Mrs. Lambert knew of Maud's existence, she would spring to the conclusion that it was Maud who was impersonating her dead child. But Mrs. Lambert had suspected nothing. Maud was going to have to explain the whole thing. In the midst of remorse and fear, Maud felt a pang of regret for what she was about to forfeit: the hot bath, the good food, and Mrs. Lambert's coddling.

"Rory says I have to tell you the truth. Mrs. Lambert, I was Caroline in the séances. Hyacinth taught me how to be her."

"You?" Mrs. Lambert stared as if Maud were the most appalling creature she had ever seen. "Then—it wasn't true? Caroline never spoke to me? It was all a lie?" Her whole body swayed and sagged, as if she were a marionette and her strings had been cut. She fell to her knees. "Oh, dear God!"

"I'm sorry," Maud said inadequately. "I wish I

hadn't." She wanted to put her arms around the grieving woman, but she didn't dare. "Mrs. Lambert, I'm really, really sorry. I've never been so sorry in my life. Please don't—" She looked at the ceiling, desperate to find words that would make things better. The painted cupids went on scattering rose petals. "Mrs. Lambert," she went on awkwardly, "you shouldn't have offered all that money to see your daughter after she was dead. Someone was bound to try to trick you—" Her voice died away. Whatever the right thing to say was, it wasn't that.

"Are you saying this is my fault?" Mrs. Lambert glared through her tears. "Are you saying it's my fault that people like you prey upon me—offer me comfort and then snatch it away? Oh, God!" She covered her face and curled forward, weeping.

Maud hunkered down beside her. She was reminded of the evening on the shore, when they knelt together to make the sand crocodile. With all her heart, she wished she had told the truth then. She spoke again, without thinking. "Mrs. Lambert, what did you say that day?"

Mrs. Lambert uncovered her face. "That day?"

"The day Caroline drowned."

Mrs. Lambert swallowed. To Maud's surprise, she answered, speaking in a hoarse and hurried whisper, as if this were her only chance to be rid of the thing that haunted her. "That morning, I—I wanted to pack. We were about to go home. It was the fifteenth—the seventeenth was Caroline's birthday. I had a surprise party planned for her, but there was still so much to do."

Maud waited.

Mrs. Lambert wiped the tears from her face. "I wanted Caroline—to help me pack—just her little things—but she wanted to go to the ocean one last time. And she wanted to ride the merry-go-round. She wouldn't help and she teased me so. I have—a dreadful temper. People don't expect it, because I'm patient—most of the time. But that day I lost my temper and I told her to *go*. I emptied my purse and let the coins fall to the floor and told her to take them. I told her"—her voice sank—"that I would be better off without her. I only meant the packing!" Her eyes were dazed with pain. "I meant I would be better off *packing*!"

Some instinct told Maud to answer matter-of-factly. "She prob'ly knew that," she commented. After a moment, she ventured, "She prob'ly knew she was making you mad, too. When I make people mad, I always know."

"Oh, she knew." Mrs. Lambert's mouth twisted.

"She knew. I made her promise she wouldn't go into the water—only to the carousel—but when she was at the door, she taunted me. She tossed my purse into the air and caught it and said, 'For once, I'm going to ride as long as I want! And you can't stop me!' And I said, 'I don't want to stop you. It's worth the money to get rid of you. Go!'"

She put her hands back over her face.

Maud said cautiously. "Is that all?"

Mrs. Lambert gave a hysterical little laugh. "Yes, that's all. I told my child I would be better off without her. I told her I wanted to be rid of her—and she granted my wish. She drowned. Isn't that enough?"

Maud hesitated. "Mrs. Lambert, I really am sorry." She twisted her fingers. "I know you feel bad, but why do you keep *doing* this?"

"Doing what?"

"This." Maud waved her hands back and forth, as if to indicate Mrs. Lambert's weeping, her abject position on the carpet. "I don't know what you call it, but you're making yourself feel worse. I don't think Caroline would like it."

At the sound of her daughter's name, Mrs. Lambert went rigid. She drew herself up, resuming her height, her status as an adult, her position in the world. "What do you know about Caroline?"

Maud quailed. All at once she saw what Caroline had been up against. Mrs. Lambert was sweet and generous and slow to anger, but once roused, she was iron and ice. Maud mirrored the woman's actions. She got to her feet and braced herself.

"I know a lot about Caroline. Hyacinth made me learn about her. She made me memorize a whole list about Caroline—and I pretended to be her—and I dreamed about her almost every night. That's how I knew she walked on the jetty." She broke off, confused. Had she dreamed that Caroline fell from the jetty? Or was it she who fell? Fragments of her dreams surfaced and scattered like sea foam on the shore. It was no longer clear what she had dreamed and what she had imagined.

"I believed that," Mrs. Lambert said in a low voice. "It helped me to believe that. I wanted to think her death was an accident—that she didn't kill herself because of what I said."

"Her death *was* an accident," Maud shot back. "Caroline wasn't the sort of silly fool who'd kill herself because her mother was mad at her. She wouldn't! Even if she felt bad when she left you, she'd have cheered up when she rode the merry-go-round. You *can't* be unhappy on the merry-go-round."

A flicker of surprise passed over Mrs. Lambert's

face. Maud had raised an argument that had not occurred to her. Sensing her advantage, Maud pressed on. "Anyway, she told me she didn't die on purpose."

It was a mistake. "She told you?" Mrs. Lambert flung back. "Are you trying to make me think you're a medium after all? That it wasn't all a fraud—that you weren't trying to cheat me out of my money?"

"No. I—" Maud paused a minute. "We—" She tried to find some justification for what she had done. "It's the family business," she stammered. "That's what Hyacinth taught me. There's a mortgage on the house in Hawthorne Grove, which means we might lose it—even Aunt Victoria wanted the money for the mortgage, though she didn't like lying. That's why she left." She realized she was straying from the point. "The things I did during the séances—like giving you that shell—and playing the glockenspiel—Hyacinth and Aunt Judith taught me them. But I did dream about Caroline. I guess because she was a little girl too. And the dreams *seemed* real—except her hair was brown. In the dreams, she didn't have golden hair."

"Caroline didn't have golden hair," Mrs. Lambert said dismissively.

"Yes, she did," contradicted Maud. "She had golden curls. I had to wear a wig when I was her."

"Don't tell me what color my daughter's hair was! Her hair was brown." Mrs. Lambert touched her own flaxen hair. "Caroline took after her father."

Maud stood stock still. Once again, Hyacinth had made a mistake. She had heard about Caroline's beautiful curls and assumed that the child inherited her mother's coloring. Maud's mouth fell open. If the Caroline in her dreams had brown hair, then she was the real Caroline. "Mrs. Lambert!" she cried out. "Mrs. Lambert, listen to me! I have to tell you—"

The corridor doors opened. Hyacinth stood before them.

She had been out walking. She wore Mrs. Lambert's narrow skirt and a shirtwaist of starched linen. Both showed signs of hasty alterations, but Hyacinth wore them serenely, without a hint of self-consciousness. She also wore Mrs. Lambert's hat— and she wore it at the exact angle that the milliner had envisioned. It was very flattering.

Maud fixed her eyes on Hyacinth's face. She expected the woman to reveal some sign of emotion: fear, anger, relief. But Hyacinth betrayed no hint of feeling. Her face was like the face of an elegant doll. Her eyes were bright and still.

Neither Maud nor Mrs. Lambert moved. "You

have a little caller, I see." Hyacinth nodded in Maud's direction. "Will you introduce me?"

Maud could not speak. She turned to see if Mrs. Lambert was deceived.

Mrs. Lambert appeared as composed as Hyacinth. "There's no need. I believe you know Maud well."

Hyacinth tilted her head to one side. "I don't know what the child has been telling you, but I've never seen her before in my life."

The words broke the spell that held Maud captive. Her skull contracted; her ears pounded. "You do so know me!" she shrilled. "You're a liar! You're a liar and a cheat and you don't love anyone!"

She leaped forward. Hyacinth recoiled, but Maud was upon her, clawing at her clothes, hauling and striking. She snapped her jaws together and kicked out savagely. Her bare toes throbbed with pain—she had hurt Hyacinth. She shrieked again, a berserker cry of triumph. She kicked—raised a hand to strike—and felt a stinging slap. Hyacinth was up against the doors and fighting back. She twisted a handful of Maud's hair—Maud gasped with pain. All at once, Maud felt an arm around her chest and another around her waist. Mrs. Lambert seized her, lifting her into the air.

"Enough!" Mrs. Lambert's tone of voice was one

that Maud had never heard. She half carried, half dragged Maud to the nearest chair and flung her into it.

Maud subsided, breathing hard. She looked around the room, trying to catch up on what had just happened. Hyacinth's sleeve was torn and there were three scratches on her cheek. Maud had drawn blood. Mrs. Lambert's face was scarlet with effort and temper. She pointed to a half table beside the wall, on which stood a marble clock.

"Miss Hawthorne, it is ten past eight. I will give you two minutes to leave this hotel. After that, I will call the management and have you thrown out. If you resist, I will call the police."

Hyacinth staggered and caught hold of the back of a chair. She jerked her head toward Maud. "Are you quite sure you believe her? You see what she is."

"I see what you've made of her." Mrs. Lambert lifted one hand, drawing Hyacinth's attention to the clock. "Your time grows short, Miss Hawthorne. Let me repeat myself. I want you out of this room. Dr. Knowles says your sister and your servant have serious injuries. Because of that, I will suffer them — and the child — to remain here, at my expense, until they can walk. You, however, will go. Immediately." Her tone made it clear she would brook no denial. For the first time, Maud understood that Mrs. Lambert was a woman who was accustomed to being obeyed. "As soon as your sister is fit to travel, I will send her to join you. After that, both of you will keep your distance. If you don't, I will take you to court. Do you understand?"

Hyacinth was trembling. She began to say something and changed her mind.

"Do not count upon my silence." Mrs. Lambert's voice held a deadly quiet. "I have no intention of keeping this to myself. I am not ashamed of what I wanted, and I am quite willing to expose you."

Hyacinth's eyes met Maud's. She hissed a single word: "Traitor!" Then she spun on her heel and went out. She left the doors ajar; Mrs. Lambert flew to the doors and locked them. Her face was contorted with disgust.

Maud cowered in the armchair. She flattened herself against the cushions, wondering what was going to become of her. She knew that it was the worst possible moment to ask for anything, but she sensed that there would be no other time. "Mrs. Lambert, Muffet's innocent."

Mrs. Lambert did not even look at her. She swept past Maud as if she had not spoken.

CHAPTER TWENTY-SEVEN

The days Maud spent at the Hotel Elysium were among the most miserable she had ever known. In the midst of luxury, she was plagued by guilt, grief, and dread. She was also bored. Both Judith and Muffet slept for hours during the day, and Mrs. Lambert shunned her. She had no books. She spent two days stitching together her ruined dress so that she could escape outside, only to find it was no use. Cape Calypso had lost its power to charm her. The boardwalk smells that had teased her appetite struck her as faintly nauseous; the crowds of well-dressed tourists made her feel shabby and forlorn. When she tried to make a sand castle, she thought of the crocodile she had made with Mrs. Lambert. She abandoned the castle to the waves.

The hotel seemed charged with silence. Judith was low spirited, suffering, the doctor said, from shock and burns. When Maud spoke to her, she answered in monosyllables. Maud realized that she had become something far worse than a secret child: she had become a child who was ignored.

She was desperately lonely. She spent hours sitting beside Muffet while she slept, and she tried to make friends with the hotel servants. From eavesdropping, she learned that Victoria's cottage had been condemned. It had not been insured, and there was no money to fix it. Mrs. Lambert hired a team of salvage men to pack up objects that could still be used. The men brought four trunks of smoky-smelling goods to Judith's room in the Hotel Elysium.

Maud rummaged through the trunks. She found Muffet's photograph album, her own parasol, and a tangle of garments from the laundry basket. Most of Judith's dresses had burned. Maud's clothes had survived, though they were streaked and dingy with smoke. There were no books in the trunks—Maud supposed the books, like the kitchen utensils, had been left behind in the boarded-up house.

She found nothing that belonged to Hyacinth. Hyacinth's room was at the back of the house; there should have been clothes from her wardrobe and trinkets from her dressing table. Maud could only conclude that Hyacinth had gone through the house before the salvage corps. She could picture Hyacinth stealing up the back stairs, savoring the danger; she imagined her sifting through knickknacks and mementos, filling a shawl with brooches and bracelets and rings. She had been very thorough. There was not a single piece of jewelry in any of the trunks. Even Maud's rosary had been taken away.

On the fifth morning after the fire, Judith shook Maud awake and told her to dress for a journey by train. Her manner was hurried and secretive. Maud gathered that she meant to leave without speaking to Mrs. Lambert.

Maud began to put on her clothes. Half asleep though she was, she was tempted to wake Muffet to say good-bye. She considered arguing with Judith or refusing to budge, but she lacked the heart. She knew she would not win, and she was tired of everyone being angry with her. In a stupor of obedience, she brushed her hair and buttoned her boots. Judith nodded approval and took her hand.

Maud didn't ask where they were going. Nor did she beg for mercy. She knew that a woman who had left her in a burning house would not scruple to take her back to the Barbary Asylum.

The walk to the train was a long one. The distance was not great—Maud could have walked it in fifteen minutes—but Judith limped painfully. It was the first day she had left her bed, and she grimaced every time her petticoats rasped against her burned leg. After a dozen steps, she pulled her veil over her face. Maud thought of offering her arm, as Lord Fauntleroy offered his to his gouty grandfather. Then she thought better of it. She knew that Judith hated herself for crying and would rather be left alone.

It was not until the train left the station that Judith spoke. She took out her handkerchief and wiped her cheeks. "Maud," she said in an undertone, "do you think you could creep down and unbutton my boot? It's very tight."

Maud slid down to the floor. She crawled under Judith's skirt, which smelled like charcoal, unbuttoned the boot, slid her hand up to Judith's garter, and released the stocking. Judith flinched at her touch.

Maud slithered back into her seat. "I don't think anyone saw."

"Thank you," whispered Judith.

Maud nodded. She was grateful even for ordinary courtesy.

"Maud," ventured Judith some minutes later, "I have something to say to you. You know I'm taking you back to the Asylum, don't you?"

Maud's last hope died. "Yes."

"It seems cruel to you, I suppose."

Maud set her teeth and turned her head away.

Judith sighed deeply. In the past week, she had aged ten years. Her cheekbones looked sharper and her neck more wrinkled. Even her voice had lost its rasp; it was dull and weary. "Victoria was right all along. She said we had no business bringing a child into our world. The night of the fire—"

The words hung in the air. Judith couldn't seem to finish the sentence. Maud wasn't going to help her.

"Do you hate me?" Judith asked. She sounded as though she really wanted to know, as if Maud had the right to say yes.

Maud swallowed. "I don't know. I hate Hyacinth."

"You should."

Maud fixed her eyes on the hot green world outside the window. The train was passing a cornfield that seemed to go on for miles: tall green cornstalks, hung with tassels. Maud could smell them. As if it were a thing of years gone by, she remembered how sweet the corn tasted, served with butter and salt. A week ago, she shucked corn with Muffet on the back porch. She remembered the sound it made when she ripped back the outer leaves and the way the sheathings turned from dull green to moonlit white. She liked to break a few kernels off with her thumb and eat them raw.

She was lost in the memory of shucking corn when Judith spoke again. "Maud, I am deeply ashamed."

Maud raised her eyes, startled.

"I never wanted you." Judith spoke the words dispassionately; she wasn't trying to be unkind. "When Hyacinth first thought of adopting a child, I thought it was a mistake. I knew it would be a bother and an expense. But I meant to do my duty by you. I wanted you to have a decent home. I told myself that it might be wrong to teach a child the things we taught you, but you would have clothes and books—" She shook her head. "That's all nonsense. It was horribly wrong. Our home was never decent."

Maud began, "It was better than—" but Judith cut her off.

"It wasn't," she said flatly. "If the Barbary Asylum was on fire, someone would try to get the children out."

Maud bent her head and crossed her arms over her chest. She wished Judith would shut up about the fire. It seemed to her that being left inside the burning parlor was proof of the thing she feared most: she was simply less valuable than other children. There was nothing Judith could say that would make her feel better. Unfortunately, Judith seemed to feel she owed Maud an explanation. She went on doggedly.

"When the lamp fell," she continued, "I saw the fire catch my skirt. The flames fastened onto it like teeth." She shuddered. "Eleanor Lambert grabbed the tablecloth and tried to smother them, but the tablecloth caught fire, too. Hyacinth was screaming. I thought I was about to die. That was all I could think of—the fact that I was going to die."

Maud's mind went back to her own journey, up the attic stairs.

"Afterward, once we were outside, I felt the—the burning. The pain. The doctor says it could have been much worse. The skin will heal in time but—" Judith stopped. "I didn't think of anything but myself.

That's God's own truth, Maud. I forgot all about you. I don't know whether that makes it better or worse."

Maud didn't know either.

"Then the firemen came, and one of them asked if there was anyone else inside the house, and Hyacinth said 'No one.' That's when I remembered you, and I fainted. I woke up in Mrs. Lambert's carriage. Hyacinth was with me. She told me she was sure you would get out—that she would go behind the house and search for you." Judith shook her head again. "I'm sorry, Maud. I don't expect you to forgive me."

Maud dug her fists into her armpits. She felt she was expected to say something, but she didn't know what it should be. She was grateful to Judith for trying to apologize, and she knew it would be generous to say she forgave her. Lord Fauntleroy would probably forgive her. The trouble was that she couldn't say the words. Even though she understood what Judith was saying, the words wouldn't come.

She sat without speaking while the train covered several more miles. Then she twisted to look into Judith's face. "If only you wouldn't take me back to the Asylum," she begged, "if I could just stay with you and Aunt Victoria. Couldn't I? Hyacinth's gone away. Can't I stay with you?"

Judith left no room for argument. "No."

"Why not?" Maud's voice rose to a wail. A man across the aisle turned to frown at them.

"Oh, Maud, there are so many reasons! For one thing, there's Hyacinth. The house in Hawthorne Grove is hers—you know that—and she'll never forgive you for telling—"

"I'll never forgive her," Maud said fiercely.

Judith shrugged. "Why should you? I wouldn't. But you wouldn't be safe under the same roof. She'd hurt you. She already has."

Maud unclenched her fists and laid her hands in her lap. She knew that Judith was right. She wondered if Hyacinth had gone back to Hawthorne Grove. Somehow she didn't think so. Hyacinth had been so excited about the rich ladies in Philadelphia. Probably she was with them.

"I guess you can't pay the mortgage now. Will you—are you and Aunt Victoria going to have anywhere to live?"

Judith's mouth worked. "We have a little money," Judith said shortly. "Mrs. Lambert spoke to me last night. She—she offered us a small allowance."

An allowance was money. "Why?"

"She said," Judith reported, "that you told her

about the mortgage. She said she understood we were desperate for money." The rasp was back in her voice. "She said she was willing to provide us with the means to live respectably, as long as we stop having séances. If we continue as spiritualists, the allowance will be taken away. Otherwise she'll give us enough to live."

"But that's nice," Maud said. "Don't you think that's nice of her?"

"Nice!" hissed Judith. "It's easy for her to be nice, with her money! *Noblesse oblige,* that's how she thinks of it!"

"What's no-bless bleege?"

"Noblesse oblige," repeated Judith bitterly. "It's French. It means that Mrs. Lambert thinks she has to behave better than other people, because she has so much money."

Maud didn't know what was wrong with that, but she didn't say so. She could see that Judith's pride was in shreds. Judith had been born wealthy and re-spectable, a Hawthorne of Hawthorne Grove. Now she was forced to accept charity.

"What about Muffet?"

"Mrs. Lambert's looking after Muffet. I suppose it's just as well. Victoria and I can't afford a servant who doesn't do any work."

"Muffet works," Maud began indignantly, but Judith squelched her.

"With a fractured leg?"

"I forgot," said Maud. She leaned back against the cushions and stared out the window once again. She felt a little better. After all, she had managed to convince Mrs. Lambert that Muffet was innocent. It was the only thing in the world she had done right. She had betrayed first Mrs. Lambert, and then Hyacinth, whom she had loved best of all—but she had been faithful to Muffet. Mrs. Lambert, Maud trusted, would take care of Muffet until she was back on her feet. *Noblesse oblige,* thought Maud, and she thanked her stars that Mrs. Lambert was nice.

The smell of the Barbary Asylum had not changed. In the past, Maud had not been aware of it; she had lived in the stench as a fish lives in water, without knowing it. Now she wrinkled her nose. Cabbage and bland boiled dinners, sour milk, mice, dirty diapers, mildew, wool uniforms that were never washed, sweaty little girls who washed far too seldom. Maud knew that in no time at all the smell would be part of her.

The Asylum's ugliness was unchanged. The linoleum was still cracked; the rooms were still painted in flaking mustard, olive green, and a color that was referred to as "cream" but more closely resembled bile. The vivid chromos of biblical subjects were as flyspecked as before. The embroidered "Suffer the Little Children" was perhaps a little dustier. As for Miss Kitteridge, her mouth, always small, seemed to have grown smaller. The Superintendent's lips were thinner and meaner than ever. It was a mouth that might have been designed for the sole purpose of whining.

Miss Kitteridge complained that it was a great disappointment to see Maud again. The Asylum was so overcrowded that any addition to the population was a burden, and, of course, Maud Flynn had never been what she might call an asset to the community. That was what the Superintendent said, but her lips twitched as if she were struggling to hold back a smile. That tiny half smile made Maud feel sick; she knew that Miss Kitteridge was savoring her disgrace.

"I believe I warned you," Miss Kitteridge reminded Judith. "I told you the child was saucy and deceitful—"

Judith's eyes strayed to the clock. "Miss Kitteridge—"

"Maud Flynn was the very last child I would have

chosen for such a select home," lamented Miss Kitteridge. "I said so at the time. It would have been better for everyone—"

Judith interrupted a second time. "Please be quiet."

Judith was being rude toward Miss Kitteridge. Immensely cheered, Maud raised her head.

"The trouble with Maud Flynn," announced Judith, "was not that she was deceitful, but that she was not deceitful enough. When all is said and done, she is fundamentally honest—and she has a heart. I am returning her, not because she failed us, but because we failed her."

Maud's hand stole into Judith's. Miss Kitteridge's face was a study. She was both enraged and baffled. Unable to think of a telling response, she sniffed. "I'm afraid I don't quite understand you, Miss Hawthorne."

"I suppose not," Judith replied. "It doesn't seem to me that your intelligence is of a high order."

Maud could have kissed her. But the time for parting had come; already Judith was letting go of her hand. "Good-bye, Maud Flynn," Judith said formally. "You deserved better."

Maud put one leg behind the other and curtsied with all the dignity she could muster. "Thank you," she said. She realized that she was going to be able to get through the interview with her dignity intact. She kept her head up as Judith turned away. The old woman moved slowly, favoring her burned foot. Like Maud, she was holding on to her dignity.

Maud didn't cry. She didn't even blink.

Miss Kitteridge stood up. "Maud Flynn, you are to go to Ward Three and change into uniform. Put your dress in the clean laundry bin."

Maud gave a single, staccato nod. "Yes, Miss Kitteridge."

"Are you going to leave the room without thanking me?" demanded Miss Kitteridge. "Once again, your care is in our hands. Once again, this institution is bound to provide you with everything you need, from the food you eat to the clothes on your back."

Maud had an inspiration. She lowered her lashes and tilted her head a little to one side. "Yes," she murmured, in Hyacinth's most maddening tones, "but such *frightful* clothes."

PART THREE

FULL
CIRCLE

Fall 1909

On the morning of the first day of October, Maud was picking through the potato bin, assisted by her former enemy, Polly Andrews.

It was a disagreeable task. By autumn, the bin was almost empty, and the remaining potatoes were sprouting and rotten. The reek of decay was powerful enough to make the children gag; Maud's fingers were clamped firmly over her nostrils. Polly prodded a shriveled potato, agitating a swarm of tiny flies. She whimpered with dismay. "Oh, Maud, this is awful! I do so hate bugs!"

"I hate Miss Kitteridge," said Maud, going to the heart of the matter.

Polly looked horror-stricken. She glanced over her shoulder, as if expecting Miss Kitteridge to materialize beside the potato bin. "Do help, Maud. I can't fill the basket by myself."

Maud took hold of a potato that squished between her fingers. She dropped it and wiped the ooze on her skirt. "This is horrible," she announced. "I'm not going to do it."

She sat down on the cellar steps. Polly regarded her with resentment, admiration, and fear. "You'll be punished."

"I'm always being punished," retorted Maud.

It was true. Maud's return to the Barbary Asylum had not been peaceful. The battle between herself and Miss Kitteridge had become a war. Maud had discovered that Hyacinth's airs and graces had a powerful effect on Miss Kitteridge's nerves. In the past weeks, Maud had spent whole nights in the outhouse. She had been assigned the dirtiest tasks the Asylum had to offer; she had been deprived of meals, spanked, slapped, scolded, shaken, pinched, whined at, and sent to Coventry. Often she wondered where it would end. She knew that in provoking Miss Kitteridge she was flirting with doom, but she kept on with it. There was something about hating Miss Kitteridge that made her feel she was getting back at a world that had wronged her.

Besides, she had a reputation to uphold. Maud had become the official black sheep of the Barbary Asylum, a position that gave her some status in life. The disgrace of being sent back was so dire that the other girls regarded her with a mixture of pity and awe. Maud took advantage of both. She dropped mysterious hints about her life with the Hawthorne sisters, managing to suggest that she had lived a life of terrible wickedness and luxury. The girls at the Barbary Asylum were fascinated. They became so interested in spiritualism that Maud was sorely tempted to hold a séance or two. Even without confederates, she reckoned she could hoodwink them; they were so naïve and so hungry for a little excitement.

Nevertheless, she held back. The memory of Mrs. Lambert's stricken face was fresh in her mind. Maud kept to the truth on one point at least: the séances in which she had taken part were all shams.

There were other truths that she kept to herself. She didn't talk about Muffet, not wanting to share her, and she held her tongue about her dreams of

Caroline Lambert. She made much of the fire that had destroyed Victoria's mansion—Maud had re-modeled the cottage so that it closely resembled the Hotel Elysium—but she never told anyone that her guardians had abandoned her the night the house burned. Instead she embellished the glories of her brief adoption; she regaled hungry girls with descriptions of Muffet's Floating Island pudding and shabby girls with accounts of the dresses she used to wear.

It was the tales of finery that had ensnared Polly Andrews. Maud had come to the conclusion that Polly wasn't such a bad little thing; she simply lacked the gumption to misbehave. Even now, the younger girl went on trying to fill the potato basket, while Maud sat on the steps and watched.

"You might as well stop," Maud advised her. "Just about every potato in that bin is rotten."

Polly gave up. She sat on the step next to Maud. "Maud," she said wistfully, "is it true that when you were adopted you wore velvet dresses every day?"

"No," Maud said, with gentle condescension, "not velvet. Not in the summer. Mind you, if I'd'a stayed, I'd have had 'em. But silk's what you wear in the summer. Tussore silk and marquisette."

"And satin?" breathed Polly.

"Satin *is* silk," Maud informed her. "Silk's the kind of thread, and satin's the way they weave it."

Polly looked a little lost. "You had lace dresses, though, didn't you?"

"Don't say *dint*," Maud counseled her. "*Did-ent*. It's more refined. I had five or six lace dresses—I forget exactly how many—and not that tatty stuff Miss Kitteridge wears, either. Valenciennes." Maud caressed the word with Hyacinth's best French accent. "Valenciennes lace, that's the kind I had." She closed her eyes, as if envisioning a storehouse of lacy gowns. Polly sighed with envy.

A door slammed. There was the sound of approaching footsteps. Maud and Polly leaped to their feet and made a great show of sorting through the potato bin.

A tall girl in brown gingham came down the stairs. "Maud Flynn, you're wanted in Miss Kitteridge's office."

"Oh," said Polly, in terror.

Maud wiped her hands on her skirt. "Don't worry," she told Polly. "She can't kill me. I won't tell her you didn't do any work, either."

Polly looked indignant. "I like that! You're the one who didn't work, Maud Flynn!"

"That's what I said," Maud said. She made a hideous face at the potato bin. Polly giggled and copied it, sticking out her tongue. There was no doubt about it. Maud was a bad influence on Polly.

"Hurry up," snapped the older girl.

Maud followed the girl up the stairs, mentally preparing for battle. The door of Miss Kitteridge's office was shut. Maud hesitated, squared her shoulders, and turned the knob.

Miss Kitteridge was not in the room. A woman in a light wool suit stood with her back to the door. Maud looked past her to a short, square figure in a plum-colored jacket and a hat lavishly trimmed with artificial cherries. Maud gasped with joy and cried out. "Muffet!"

She leaped forward. Muffet shoved a crutch under her arm, pivoted in her chair, and got to her feet. Maud knocked over the crutch and hugged her with all her strength.

When she looked up, she saw Muffet grinning. The hired woman took her arms away from Maud and began to gesticulate, her fingers moving rapidly. Maud turned to look behind her and saw that the second woman was Mrs. Lambert.

Mrs. Lambert had changed. She was no longer in

half-mourning, and her hat was pinned on properly. Moreover, she no longer looked at Maud with accusing eyes. There was laughter in her face as she answered Muffet's flying fingers with gestures of her own.

"What's that?" Maud asked, watching Muffet's hands. "What's she doing?"

"She's talking," Mrs. Lambert answered. "She says you've lost weight and your hair wants washing. She's not happy about it."

Maud turned to Muffet for confirmation. The hired woman plucked at Maud's brown gingham and made a face. Maud couldn't read what she said with her fingers, but she gathered that Muffet didn't think much of the uniform.

"There's a language for deaf people," Mrs. Lambert explained. "More and more people are learning to use it. I hired a tutor—he's teaching both of us. He says Anna's the quickest student he's ever had."

Maud could well believe it. She bestowed a glowing smile on Muffet. Muffet pointed toward the floor. *Pick up my crutch. You knocked it over.*

Maud stooped to obey. Muffet sat back down, holding the crutch in the crook of her elbow as if it were a scepter.

"Her leg is healing," Mrs. Lambert said. "Properly, this time."

Maud feasted her eyes on Muffet. Someone had persuaded her to lengthen her skirts so that the tops of her boots didn't show. Her clothes fitted as if they had been made by a good dressmaker. If it weren't for all the cherries on her hat, she would have looked quite stylish. "You've taken good care of her."

"I love Anna," Mrs. Lambert said simply. "She takes care of me, too. She's teaching me to draw."

For some reason, the simple statement brought a lump to Maud's throat. Muffet lifted her hands and signed again.

"She says I ought to tell you," Mrs. Lambert said to Maud, "that you are to come home with us."

Maud raised a startled face. "Why?" She remembered her wretched stay at the Hotel Elysium and stammered, "Where?"

"Home," repeated Mrs. Lambert. She added apologetically, "I have several houses. There's one in Boston and another in Washington. I thought Washington would be best for the present, as Anna is going to attend school there."

"What will Miss Kitteridge say?" For the first time, it struck Maud as odd that Miss Kitteridge was not present. "Where's Miss Kitteridge?"

"I told her we wished to speak privately," Mrs. Lambert said composedly. "I have offered—and she has accepted—a large donation for the Asylum. I don't wish to sound arrogant, but Miss Kitteridge will say whatever I want her to say."

Maud cupped her fingers around her thumbs and hid her hands behind her back. She knew she ought to feel elated. "But—that day at the Hotel Elysium—"

"I was very angry with you. Yes." Mrs. Lambert swept aside the papers on Miss Kitteridge's desk and sat down on it. "As I told you, I have something of a temper."

Maud nodded fervently.

"There was so much I didn't understand that day. When you talked to me, Maud, you spoke of the 'family business' and referred to Judith and Victoria as your aunts. That's one of the reasons I offered them an allowance—I thought they had a child to provide for. I told Judith that some of the money I gave her should be used to send you to school."

Maud's mouth opened in a silent O.

Mrs. Lambert answered her unspoken question. "Judith never told me she planned to bring you back here. We spoke very briefly. She was mortified when I offered her money—I admit I didn't offer it very graciously. The next morning she took you away. I thought you'd gone back to Hawthorne Grove. I had no idea you were an orphan."

Maud looked back at Muffet. The hired woman was following the conversation intently. From time to time, Mrs. Lambert accompanied her speech with a gesture or spelled out a word. Muffet caught Maud's eye and nodded meaningfully.

"After you were gone, Anna asked for you, and I had to tell her you weren't there. I was sure she'd fracture her leg again, trying to get up so that she could hunt for you. She was furious when I kept pushing her back into bed. We had a dreadful quarrel without speaking a word."

Maud could imagine. "I've fought with her like that."

"Then Rory Hugelick came to see me. That day when he brought you to the hotel, I forgot all about him—I left him in the lobby. But he came back. He wanted to make sure you'd told me the truth."

"I did," Maud insisted, aggrieved. "After the fire, everything I told you was true. Even about Caroline."

At the sound of her daughter's name, Mrs. Lambert's face softened. "I know that now. Since that night, I've had my own dreams of Caroline. I believe what you told me that morning."

Maud shivered. So Caroline had left Maud's dreams to inhabit her mother's.

Muffet interrupted with one of her odd noises. The short, square fingers moved restlessly. Mrs. Lambert exclaimed, "Oh, dear, Anna says I'm taking too long with this! After I spoke to Rory, I began to worry about you. It seemed to me that the Hawthorne sisters were wholly unfit to raise a child—but there didn't seem to be any way I could interfere. I left Cape Calypso and went back to Boston. It wasn't until Victoria Hawthorne came to see me—"

"Aunt Victoria came to see you?"

Mrs. Lambert smiled at Maud's wonderment. "All the way to Boston. I own I was surprised to see her. I never expected to speak to any of the Hawthorne sisters again. At first, I refused to see her. But she persisted. She wouldn't go away until I listened. At last, I agreed—and she told me the whole story." Mrs. Lambert paused and corrected herself. "*Your* whole story, Maud. She made me see how much you longed for a home—and how Hyacinth took advantage of your longing. Then she told me you'd been sent back here." Mrs. Lambert's eyes swept the office, condemning the scuffed linoleum and Miss Kitteridge's taste in art. "I thought it was the cruelest thing I ever heard. That was when I thought of adopting you."

Adopting you. The words rang in Maud's ears. She tried to imagine living with Mrs. Lambert. Her imagination hung fire. All she could think of was the surprisingly neutral fact that Mrs. Lambert was rich. She supposed that Mrs. Lambert would buy her lovely clothes and new books and pretty things. The prospect gave her little pleasure. It reminded her of Hyacinth. She must be wary of anything that reminded her of Hyacinth.

Mrs. Lambert seemed to have fallen back into her former shyness. She removed one glove and drew it through her fingers. She went on, "At first I thought I was foolish to consider such a thing. I told myself it wouldn't work. But I couldn't forget you. I wanted you."

Maud opened her mouth. Her chin was trembling, and she couldn't think of anything to say. An image flashed before her mind's eye: Muffet and Mrs. Lambert and herself, strolling down the boardwalk in broad daylight, with the wind blowing and the seagulls wheeling overhead.

"That night on the shore, when we made the crocodile—do you remember that night, Maud?"

Maud nodded.

"I think I wanted you then." Mrs. Lambert's voice

was tender. "It felt so sweet to be with a little girl again." She slid off the desk and stepped forward, laying her palm against Maud's cheek. Once again, Maud was reminded of Hyacinth. She laced her fingers together behind her back, as if she could hold on to her heart by keeping her fingers locked.

"What is it, Maud? Don't you want to come with me?"

Maud tried to find her tongue. "I won't be Caroline." She was surprised by how loud and rude her voice sounded. "I haven't got curly hair and I'd never pick up a snake."

Mrs. Lambert smiled. "Maud," she said gently, "I've thought this over. I don't want to go through the rest of my life without loving anyone. I know you won't be Caroline, but I believe I will love Maud. I want you to come and live with me."

Maud's teeth were chattering. She wondered what would happen if Mrs. Lambert found out she couldn't love Maud, after all. She didn't know if she could survive the heartbreak of being sent back again.

"You don't believe me." Mrs. Lambert spoke lightly, calmly. "You don't trust me. I understand that. If you like, I'll keep telling you I want you till you get used to the idea. I'll tell you tomorrow. Or, if you don't believe me tomorrow, I'll tell you the next day. Only, it's *nasty* here, Maud, and persuading you would be ever so much easier if we were in the same house. Why don't you come home with me now?"

Muffet raised her hands. An aggrieved noise burst from her, and the darting movement of her fingers expressed indignation and impatience.

"Anna says you want to come," Mrs. Lambert translated. "She says you want to come very badly, and she wants to know why you haven't said yes yet."

Maud turned back to look at Muffet, whose eyes were fierce and shining. *You come home with us.* Maud read the command and went limp with relief. Why, she would be with Muffet! Muffet loved her, even if she wasn't good. Muffet could be trusted, no matter what.

Maud gulped, "Yes," and burst into tears.

Her response brought about a small stampede. The two women surged forward to comfort her. Muffet got there first; her crutch clattered against the linoleum as she squeezed Maud in a bear hug and thumped her on the back. As soon as Muffet let go, Mrs. Lambert whisked her around, stroking her dirty hair and murmuring babyish endearments that Maud ought to have hated, but didn't. Once Mrs.

Lambert released her, Muffet reclaimed her, sweeping her up so that her toes left the floor. When Maud regained her footing, her face was shiny with tears and flushed with emotion.

"I want to," she assured the two women. She wiped her eyes on the back of her wrists, sniffed twice, and drew herself erect. "Let's go home."

THE END